Arrow in the
By
Pril Gurney

A tale of love and betrayal, this is the story of the life of Tomas, son of a great gladiator in ancient Rome. Although born a slave, his father wins the family's freedom and the Emperor sends them to Provence in Gaul. Tomas does not want to leave his little friend Cleolia and they run away only to be caught by a wicked youth who assaults the little girl. They are separated but Tomas never forgets her and he faces many dangers including, fire, floods and even commits murder in an effort to win her physically as well as emotionally.

Cover illustration by Patricia Icke
© Priscilla Gurney 2014

Prologue

The tall, bronzed man stood erect and unmoving on the rocky outcrop. He wore a plain skirt of rounded leather strips. His chest was bare to the hot sun and he carried a sword at his side. He looked out with a strong pride and deep moving passion for the scene before him. Into the distance rolled the massive hills, layer upon layer like giant cardboard cut-outs slotted into a base of thick undergrowth. Deep in the valley the wild busy rushing of a swollen stream came to him on the still air. No birds moved, nor animals stirred as the trees sweated into the perfect blue sky. The sun touched his greying blonde hair and it shone with a pureness of burnished gold. His sandaled feet seemed rooted like the trees to the rock and beside him like a midday shadow stood a child. The child's eyes took in not only the scene but kept wandering back to his father's solemn face. He shifted his young feet to mirror his father's. His eyes shone with the same pride, but his was in his breast like a sharp pain of love. They stood together with reflected strength and passion – man and boy – father and son…

Chapter 1

Tomas ran along the cobbles, weaving in and out as he dodged the passersby. His broad chest and narrow waist belied his nine years and gave him the air of a miniature adult. His bare back was dark as a raven and his blonde hair was bleached white by the sun. His wide blue eyes, a rarity among his fellow Romans, shone with an exquisite delight for he was on his way to the Coliseum.

Tomas was the only son of Argoutus, the great gladiator, and he was on his way to see his father fight. Argoutus had been born a slave and he had worked in the house of Marius, a Roman Senator, for ten years before Tomas was born. Later his master had noticed his broad rippling muscles and sent him to gladiator school to learn the skills of combat. When he had left he had gone straight to the amphitheatre where each afternoon the gladiators fought each other and the wild beasts to death. Argoutus had survived. Many had not, but Argoutus had not only the strength but the intelligence to outwit all comers. He was now famous across the Roman Empire and fought only at Caesar's command.

The first time Tomas had been allowed to watch his father he had been only five years old. His uncle had held him high on his shoulders while the child screamed and shouted with the crowd as Argoutus faced a lion. Across the sandy ring the beast had wandered, at first almost pathetic as it faced the light and breezes of the open air after the stifling heat of the enclosure below. It roared like a lost child trying to show anger, though its anger was long spent. Then hunger rose in its throat like bile and it looked around. It saw Argoutus standing silent and still. The crowd fell silent also as they waited with baited breath to see who would make the first move. Tomas was suddenly afraid but with the fear rose exhilaration in his heart. The mix of emotion made him grasp his uncle's shoulders with his knees so that the man whispered gruffly for him to take care. Tomas did not notice but watched spellbound as his father took a step towards the animal. It saw him. For a second it pawed the ground and then it saw the man's brown skin and, as the breeze blew across at him, he smelt the sweat of his fear. The whole arena seemed to hold its breath. A rivulet of perspiration ran slowly down Tomas' back but he did not feel it. The scene before him froze like a huge bright oil painting. Then a lone voice from the crowd shouted "Get him!" and the crowd erupted into screams and whistles which shattered the silence as if it had never been. The lion seemed to hesitate and then it turned, saliva dripping from the corners of its gaping mouth as it faced the man. Still Argoutus stood straight and still. His sword hung loosely from his hand, his eyes holding lightly to the beast's approach. Across the great space the animal moved, at first slowly and then faster until it paused a few feet from the gladiator. It threw back its head and roared. From the rising tiers of seats the crowd took up the roar, screaming, shouting, baying for blood. Still Argoutus was still. As the great animal paused, its wild sad eyes met the steadfast gaze of its enemy. Fear crossed the space between them like a lightning bolt. But the fear came not from the man but from the beast. Again the silence fell like a whisper from over the arena. As the lion composed itself to spring, a bird no bigger than a pebble flashed across between them. The lion's eyes rolled in distraction and Argoutus leaped the gap and plunged his sword into the shimmering mane. The lion's eyes held a wild astonishment before they clouded over and death released it from its cruel world. Tomas had dropped his head onto his uncle's dark hair and wept. Wept because his father was safe and because the beautiful beast lay crumpled and lifeless like a discarded coat.

But now on this hot sunny day only excitement filled his breast and pride for his father. Tomas wore his father's fame like a badge. When asked his name he would always reply, "I am the son of Argoutus". That was enough. Everyone in Rome knew the great gladiator who this very day was to fight not only for his glory but for his freedom. Augustus Caesar was to come and watch and if Argoutus triumphed he would grant him his freedom. Argoutus and his family would no longer be slaves but could hold their heads up as citizens of Rome. Tomas had dreamed with his father of the day when they and his mother Scribonia would be Freedmen of Rome.

Ahead of him now between the tall houses reaching to each other across the street, came the first glimpse of the massive walls of the Coliseum. Their size and power almost stopped him as they always did when they hit his young eyes. Beside him now people jostled and chattered. The midday sun poured heat and welcome shade across his path as he skirted the huge walls and began to climb the great steps. He jumped between men in long togas and other children clutching their mother's skirts. He felt alive and it felt good. He felt himself growing inches as he danced up the steps, the massive iron gates still closed against the mob.

On the gate, resplendent in military uniforms with flashing silver swords at their sides and polished breastplates, the guards stood disgruntled and hot.

Tomas pushed his way towards a tall angular guard with wicked piercing black eyes. He pulled at the man's leather skirt.

The man grunted and lowered his hard eyes but when he saw the boy they softened and a hint of smoothness touched his cruel face. Without a word he lifted the boy high over the wide bars, through a gap between them and dropped him silently on the other side. As Tomas voiced his gratitude a vague smile touched the man's lips. Then he turned his glance away and resumed his angry stare at the crowds clamouring at the gates.

Tomas dodged beneath another bar and put his foot onto a wide stone and began to climb. Like a young goat his sure feet found cracks and footholds as he climbed the sheer wall. Up and up he climbed until his breath pulled at him and he clambered over the top and rose to his feet.

Below him the great arena lay like a huge salad bowl. Deep, deep below, the sandy ellipse shone a dull yellow. Around it rose tier upon tier of stone seats divided by streaks of steps rising to high arches. The great dome was open to the clear sky but huge poles on which a canopy could be attached pointed upward high above the small boy perched on the highest rim. The arena sung with the voices of the crowd beginning to filter along the rows, colourful in their bright togas. The noise rose to Tomas in an incomprehensible wave of sound and his delight heightened. It was hot where he stood, alive and small against the giant stones beneath his feet and sweat poured, cooling his skin, as he brushed his eyes with his hand and looked around him. To his right a small archway welcomed him and he moved into its shade. He rubbed the glare from his eyes and peered down at the ring so far below him. It was empty now except for a solitary figure who appeared from a hidden door and began to rake the sand. Tomas knew he would do it again after his father had fought. The man did it every time, folding in the bloodstains, covering up all the signs of previous fights. Would he be covering his father's blood soon, the boy wondered? Would it be eliminated by a wooden rake so that it seemed it had never been? His heart lurched as he watched. He could imagine his father's life being swept away with one confident rush of the rake. Gone forever, like so many before and yet to come. Life rubbed out with one sweep of the tall bowed slave. Tomas swallowed hard and tried to push away the lump that rose in his throat. He looked away. That man's actions had destroyed his exhilaration. He needed it back.

"Argoutus will win!" The words sailed up from a stand far beneath him. A lone voice screamed above the din of conversation. The boy's eyes glanced down. He could not see who had spoken but his fears vanished and he raised his head and shouted an echo.

"Argoutus will win." A few heads turned upwards but Tomas was hidden by the arch. All the same a wave of voices floated up to him.

"Argoutus! Argoutus! Argoutus!" and he joined in with young pride and young passion.

A huge bell sounded and the crowd rose to its feet – silent voiced, now waiting. A fanfare broke into the hot air. The Emperor was coming. If Tomas turned his head and looked back the way he had come, he could see the chariot, stopped by the steps. He could see the tall man in his flashing gold/and red toga step from the seat and begin to climb towards the gate. He knew where the trumpeters were either side beneath him and as the

Emperor stepped into the arena, a wild unison cry rattled around him.

"Caesar! Caesar!" The boy was silent. Just now they had yelled for his father – now for Caesar. At the end of the event the crowd would shout for Caesar again, but would they still shout "Argoutus"? Tomas found it hard to hold onto his emotions. The swing from hope to despair hurt him. He felt that his fear was like a betrayal of his father. He sighed.

Looking down now Tomas watched as a line of gladiators entered the ring. This was a warm-up bout. The men separated into pairs and began shadow boxing with swords that never hit flesh. The roaring crowd screamed and yelled – each for his champion. Tomas strained to see Argoutus but he wasn't there. The boy was dazed, almost ashamed. Where was his father? As though in answer the great door opposite the Emperor swung open and Argoutus entered. He walked king-like across the arena. Tall, blonde, straight so that the boy could hardly breathe for pride. Argoutus stopped before his Emperor. He bowed his head. The fighting men around him stopped still and the noise of the crowd dipped to a whisper. Across the arena a white bird dipped and rose. The Emperor rose to his feet and a mute stillness fell on the vast arena. The Emperor spoke.

"Argoutus."

He spoke in a voice that ran round the side walls and climbed up to the highest point near Tomas.

"Argoutus, you are my greatest gladiator. Today you will fight your last fight." A murmur ran round the stands but Caesar held up his hand for quiet.

"Your last fight, Argoutus," he repeated. "If you win today you will carry away your freedom and that of your family, and descendents for all generations in the future." The crowd let out a wild cheer. When they were silent once more, Caesar spoke again. His voice strong, firm but slow.

"And ... if ... you ... lose ......" He paused and the arena held its breath. "Then you will have a hero's burial as you fly to the breast of God ....." Again a roar of approval came from the spectators.

"My people," Caesar's voice echoed up to the boy. "With whom shall Argoutus fight?"

A shout in unison travelled up into the heated waiting sky.

"Ovilium. Ovilium." The Emperor nodded and smiled.

Argoutus lifted his head and smiled back. He mouthed a word but the noise of the crowd was all that reached young Tomas. The Emperor turned and spoke to a guard who clicked his heels before he turned and went out. One by one the other gladiators moved away until they formed a huge circle round Argoutus, who now stood centre stage.

Tomas breathed hard as he saw the proud figure of his father. He saw him tall and erect with the sun gleaming on his breastplate and sword. He looked at the hardset face and found it strange to him. To him his father's face was always gentle, even when the child was in trouble. He respected his father as a wise man and would hang his head if his father chastised him. And when he had been forgiven, which was always, he would lift his head and look into a stern face and see gentle, loving eyes. Tomas could not see those eyes now but he knew they held nothing but pride and determination.

Suddenly there was a shout from the far side of the arena. Onto the second tier came a massive giant of a man, crashing the door open as he came. He shouted,

"Ovilium! I am here."

Argoutus swung round.

The giant hesitated for a moment then threw his sword away down onto the sandy floor. He leaned back his head and let forth a great belly laugh.

"Do I fight this baby?" he roared, pointing a great fat finger at Argoutus. The crowd heaved with mirrored mirth. Ovilium took a step forward. He paused again, great lumps of fists on his hips, his legs like tree trunks wide apart. Again he laughed. Then all of a sudden he made a great jump out and above the arena. He flayed out his huge arms and at the last minute as he headed down towards the ground he thrust his great head down and rolled in a somersault across the ring, rising to his feet only inches from Argoutus. The crowd sighed and broke into wild stamping and shouting. To the boy's ears the sound carried and anger rose in his throat. A moment ago they were cheering his father and now they were crying for his blood – backing this awful massive creature whose fat curled on his belly and flowed away round the hideous swollen neck. Tears came to his eyes. He wanted to shout to everyone, "Argoutus will win," and to Caesar, "It isn't fair," and last, to his father, "My father, I love you, I came," but he knew no one could hear; that his child's voice was weak and reed-like. He pulled up his shoulders and thrust wide his legs like Ovilium and shouted up to the sky.

"If Ovilium kills my father, I will kill him, I swear it." He held his pose for a moment then let his eyes fall back to the arena.

The two men stood very still and close now – hard staring at each other – the crowd's screaming grew louder and louder and still they stayed still. Argoutus moved first as he threw away his sword like Ovilium had done. His adversary grinned a wicked, sneering grin, the corners of his mouth twitching with unconcealed contempt. Suddenly Argoutus slammed a forearm with all his force into Ovilium's chest. It seemed to bounce off like a rubber toy. Ovilium stood still, grinning. Argoutus brought up his knee relentlessly towards the man's groin – but the man twisted to one side so that Argoutus was unbalanced and his knee bounced yet again, this time into the rock hard muscles of Ovilium thigh. For a moment Argoutus was aware of the crowd. They were roaring for blood. Maybe blood was what they should have. With a supreme effort Argoutus let his fist fly into the man's face, his aim fixed on the cauliflower red nose. A pain shot through him as his fist met the hard bone of the cheek. The man flinched, but only for a second, then resumed his awful grin. Argoutus felt little anger – it was an emotion denied him. He could only pity those he killed, either animal or man, but his agile brain and trained physique had always made him unassailable. But this day his wild desire for freedom had given him a desire to kill, to hurt, to maim which he had never really felt before. It had been like doing a job of work in the same way as a surgeon cuts flesh. This new surge of anger was so alien that at first he did not recognise it. His strong desire to pummel his fists and feet relentlessly into this sneering beast, taunting him with his eyes, was overpowering, taking away with it the logical calm intellect which had given him glory before.

With a sudden breath of realisation at what he was doing, he swung on his heels and turned his back on Ovilium and began walking away. A great sigh of bewilderment rose from the crowd and a voice called, "He's afraid of you Ovilium – go get him."

The silent boy in the high tower stood mesmerised. Surely his father was not going to behave like a coward. And then – Argoutus looked up. Across the space between them travelled a wave of power rising to the boy. It was as if the man was physically growing as he and his child let their spirits meet. Tomas opened his mouth to shout but a mere whisper came.

"Father," he murmured. "Oh, Father."

Argoutus stepped away, his eyes now on his Emperor. Behind him the grotesque figure was stationary. Argoutus felt his stillness, his ears straining for any sound behind him, his eyes still fixed on Caesar. The crowd murmured to silence, waiting with a tension that seemed to fill the air with ice despite the searing sun.

"My lord" he shouted. "Do you want this man killed?"

Caesar rose to his feet.

"Do you want your freedom, Argoutus?"

But Argoutus did not answer. He knew Ovilium had moved. With deliberate slowness he moved to one side and then, speeding up like a frightened gazelle, he began to skip from one side to another and set off thus round the great arena with Ovilium panting like a shaggy bear in pursuit. The crowd began to laugh and shout once more. This time taunting Ovilium for his staggering. Argoutus was thinking hard. He didn't hear the crowd and he was only just aware of Ovilium's distance behind him. He made a full circuit of the arena, passing unseeing the tall figures of the gladiators. On, still, until he judged Ovilium was panting enough and staggering with tiredness. He knew he would stop soon and he didn't want that.

Imperceptibly he slowed down. He let Ovilium get closer – he dodged less far – he let his feet drag a little. Ovilium came nearer – Argoutis could almost feel the rancid breath on his back.

Then he suddenly swung round, threw out his left foot and felt Ovilium's foot catch on his as he fell with a mighty crash into the sand. The crowd screamed as Argoutus grabbed a fence pole between the gladiators and jumped up so that he stood high above Ovilium, looking down at the prostrate figure who wriggled about on his belly like a landed fish. He jumped high and wide, his sandaled feet aimed for the man's heaving back. With a crash that jolted his whole frame he landed and, struggling for balance, stood up tall and straight on the man's heaving body.

"Kill, kill," shouted the crowd. Argoutus side stepped onto the sand and took a sword held out to him. He pushed a foot under the body and grabbed a handful of thick dark hair. With a wild cry he forced the body over. Then he stepped casually onto the swollen belly and placed the tip of his sword at the man's neck. Ovilium's eyes were wet and his white face contorted with pain and lack of breath. An eerie groan escaped his dry lips and the crowd roared louder and louder.

"Kill, kill."

Argoutus shouted to his Emperor.

"Shall he be killed?" Exhilaration and excitement were slowly leaking from him. But even as he looked at Caesar the great Emperor rose to his feet and pointed a thumb downwards. The crowd stamped and screamed.

With a blind thoughtless mind Argoutus thrust the sword deep into the man's throat. He felt the jar as he hit and splintered bone and watched as the distorted face screamed at him. The great eyes rolled – blood poured onto the sand and trickled from the gaping mouth.

As he watched death grab the great warrior he stepped away, casting the bloody sword from him. A sickness rose in him but the roar of the crowd fought through it and he raised his eyes.

Far away – high, high up his eyes sought his son. There on the highest point he saw the tiny figure waving and jumping with delight. Across the hot distance he yelled to him.

"Freedom is yours, my son – freedom!"

He turned his eyes to Caesar – standing, now smiling at him.

All of a sudden the gladiators all crowded upon him – congratulating him, thumping him on the back. Then they raised him on their shoulders and began to carry him high above them around the arena. Excitement held him like a winch – pulling at his heart – unknowingly, he yelled and screamed to them, "I'm free! Free!"

Breathless he came before his Emperor. Calm flowed from the tall man and he stood smiling quietly at his valiant freed warrior. He raised his hand and silence fell upon the crowd.

"Well, Argoutus," he roared, "you fought well – your prize is yours – you – are – free!" The crowd began its cheering but the Emperor raised his hand once more. "What have you to say, my son?"

Argoutus took a deep breath: now tears ran down his cheeks, emotions hit him from every side, his shoulders wanted to sag as a great tiredness seemed to creep up his body but he stayed firm on the shoulders of his friends.

"My God, my Caesar," he shouted.

Again a roar came from the crowd and the gladiators dropped him to the sandy floor and he stood stiff as Caesar turned away. He watched, dazed, as the Emperor moved away. The guards saluted and followed and then Argoutus turned to his audience and began to run, shouting and waving his arms round the great arena, his heart so swollen with pride that he felt nothing else.

A man, young and strong with a plain youth's toga sprang over the fence into the ring. Then another followed and another. To Tomas, still perched high above, it looked like a stream of lava pouring over the barrier and rushing towards his father. Fear gripped him. He saw his father pause and turn – he saw the lava flow gather speed and rush towards him – now men, boys, women jostled and ran towards their hero. For a moment Argoutus paused then he turned and ran for the arena door. But he was too late – the cheering, screaming hysterical hoard fell on him like a pack of wild beasts and Tomas could see him no more.

The boy let out a sob then turned and began to make his way along the ridge. He swung his legs over and dropped to the concrete below. Then over the edge and down the long climb to the ground. His breath whistled in his throat, noises of voices on the wind came to him like a muffled roar. He registered nothing, saw nothing – his feet and hands worked automatically – his brain numbed with horror. As his feet touched the ground he was running, now sobbing, as he pushed against the mob, now pouring out of the arena, out from the stifling heat to the breeze without. He stumbled but managed to keep his feet, dodging between tall legs and sandaled feet, pushing, weaving. Suddenly he broke out into the sandy floor – the brilliant sun blinded him for a moment but he ran forward. Then he stopped. A wild mass of people shouted and pawed each other ahead of him – they screamed and lashed out – a wild mixture of limbs, heads and deafening shrieks.

Somewhere in there was his father. He opened his mouth to scream too but no sound came. He stood for a moment, paralysed – not knowing what to do. His arms were flung wide above his head and suddenly he turned his face up – he screamed, "Help me."

Tomas thought he saw a strange movement in the clear blue sky – a shadow crossed the sun and a current of despair and hopelessness seemed to caress his body. It brought him up with a start as a realization of the extent of his father's danger came to him. At the same time the child in him seemed to step aside – the tears dried on his face as he looked around for help.

A tall centurion leaned against a column, laughing and running a hand over the smooth flesh of a young woman.

Tomas ran to him, catching his arm.

"Help me," he shouted. "Help me!"

The man turned to him.

"What's the trouble boy?" he said kindly, taking in the wild terror in Tomas' eyes.

"Argoutus – those people – he will be crushed. We must save him!"

The Centurion glanced at the heaving mob. Then a flash of anger crossed his features and he turned and shouted an order to the guards idly watching from the side.

"Get these people away – Argoutus will be crushed!" he roared, at once forgetting the warm fleshed girl beside him. He strode forward as his men began dragging first one then another away from the scrum.

Tomas watched still and silent, waiting. He knew what he would see soon. He had no doubt that his father lay dead among his fans. He felt it in the air. The ugly evil mask of death was hovering over the arena like a huge raven blocking out the sun. He felt no terror now, no fear, just a great emptiness filling his heart. He watched as one by one the men and women were pulled roughly from the group and flung away. Soon there were simply four or maybe five bodies sprawled on the sand. One groaned and struggled to his feet. Another let out a cry and was silent. The centurion leaned over the long form lying in the sand, his arms outstretched and the heavy breastplate shining and glittering in the sun.

A long robed elder figure hurried past Tomas and began to lean over each prostrate figure, muttering as he went. The centurion called him and two of the guards gently lifted the still body of Argoutus and carried him away.

Still Tomas did not move. Not until he saw the last man moving through the arch. Then he ran, shouting and leaping across the arena and into the dark, cool passage beyond.

He turned left down the steep steps which led to the beasts' cages and the body room. This room held the day's carcasses – those of slave, gladiator or animal piled randomly on the stone floor. Tomas had been there before. He had slipped in one day to take a peep and for weeks later had wished he hadn't. The foul smell of freshly spilt blood, even in the comparative cool of the vault, had sickened him. But he had moved on, determined, enjoying the mixture of fear and curiosity which held him. He had slipped in the open door and taken in the scene and run away all in one terrible movement. The picture had burned itself into his head like a branding iron – nothing would move it – it stayed to creep uninvited into the happiness of a spring day and lurked in ambush for his sleep. Bloodied dismembered bodies, white and red, thrown like discarded dolls onto the pile had watched him with empty lifeless eyes, mocking his youth and vivacity. But beside the awful heap was another dreadful sight. A black bear lay disembowelled across the entrance. Its eyes seemed to Tomas in that split second to be filled with pity for him. He knew the beast was dead but it seemed to be speaking to him from its wrecked body – pitying him – there was no other word for it. The broken creature feeling for him with his life ahead of him – its terrors to come while the creature now knew no more hurt. It was the bear that haunted him – not the men – they were just bodies. The bear seemed to symbolize cruelty, innocence, despair and the unfairness of death and life. Why had it died? Because unlike the men it had no guilt. To Tomas being a slave was a thing to be ashamed of – despite the fact that he was not personally responsible. It hung on his family as a black mark – and any result of that slavedom was to be expected – any punishment acceptable even to death in the arena. But Tomas could not equate that with animals. They were forced to die in the arena – plucked from their homes, shipped in awful conditions, starved, weakened and killed – just for the pleasure of people. Tomas that day had developed a characteristic rare in Ancient Rome: he had a conscience.

Now as he rushed once more round the corner to the body room he forgot his past fears. All he wanted was to see his father's body – crushed as it would be – just to see him again and say farewell. Tomas was so sure his father's body would be there that he was horrified to find only the great carcass of Ovilium thrown on his face.

Tomas stood staring, a multitude of thoughts dancing like a ghostly bullet through his heart. Where was his father? Who'd stolen him? Why? What should he do? He swung away leaning his sweaty young body against the hard stone – tears boiled from his blue eyes, despair crushed into him and he put up his hands and sobbed. He sobbed for his father, for his freedom, for the bear, for his childhood which seemed to have been plucked from him. He sobbed like a lost soul, gasping for the air which would make the next sob. He didn't hear the footsteps approaching and the hand that fell on his shoulder made him jump. His eyes flew up, his hands flew apart and startled eyes met those of Valerius the gate guard who had helped him in.

"Tomas," he said kindly, "What's the matter? And what are you doing here?"

Tomas let his eyes fall to the ground. He kicked at a loose stone with his bare toes which peeped from his sandals. For a moment he was unable to speak. Then he said, "Argoutus is dead."

The man paused for a moment, then dropped on his haunches so that his eyes were level with Tomas'.

"Tomas," he said firmly. "Argoutus is not dead. He is injured, yes, but dead, no."

Tomas looked deep into Valerius' brown eyes. He read truth and honesty in them as well as compassion and understanding. A shaft of sunlight fell on him, casting away the shadows of evil. He lifted his eyebrows and stretched out his hands.

"Thank you," he cried.

Valerius laughed. Then he put his hands on the boy's shoulders.

"My son, your father is badly wounded. He was battered and crushed by the mob. He will recover if the Gods wish it ... but ... will you come with me? I will take you to him."

Tomas nodded silently and took Valerius' proffered hand. He felt suddenly like a child again and he was not ashamed. He needed the strong hand of his friend. The relief at hearing that his father was alive had been short lived. Now fear gripped him. He found his heart filling in his chest – fighting against him. Suppose his father were still to die or, worse still, be a permanent invalid? He knew how hard it was for a great warrior to be made to live with wounds that crippled. He had seen Julius once – a friend of his father's from the gladiator school. He had survived being gored by a lion. One hand was half gone and its limb hung useless. A vivid scar crossed the bronzed face. The eyes held pride still but into them crept a dull despair. His greatness and power were only memories now. How could Argoutus face that sort of defeat if it came?

Valerius was talking to him. Tomas pulled his mind to listen.

"Your father is very strong, Tomas. He is brave, too, beyond many men. He will fight his injuries as he fought Ovilium with intelligence and humour. He will win. He was never beaten yet! Have faith."

Tomas allowed himself to smile wanly at Valerius and his heart lifted a little.

They passed now under the wide arch where the mob had moved and began to descend the narrow staircase. Off to one side was a heavy wooden door with great iron nails forming a crude pattern on it. Valerius pushed it open.

Inside was a low, long, upholstered couch with a group of men around it. Tomas let go of Valerius' hand and ran forward. He pushed between two tall soldiers and saw his father lying on the couch. His body was covered in a shawl of deep purple with a great gold eagle embroidered upon it. His father's head lay propped on a thick velvet pillow – he was very pale. His eyes flickered open and rested on his son's clear young face. Tomas saw pain in them but also a shadow of pride. His lips moved and Tomas leaned close.

"My son," breathed Argoutus. "Did you see? Did you hear our Emperor? He has freed us. We are free." He closed his eyes for a moment.

Tomas whispered back.

"Yes, Father, I saw. I saw great Ovilium fall. I saw you standing over him. The great victor. I saw Caesar rise to you. Did he call you his greatest warrior? Did he see you were the greatest gladiator of them all? I was so proud. My heart burst with it. You, my Father, from slave to Freedman ..." Emotion stopped him and Argoutus let a smile cross his face. Again his eyes flickered.

"Go now, Tomas, go to your mother. Tell her we are free. Let her know that I am safe. Send her to me, my son."

Tomas started. His mother ... beautiful, lovely Scribonia, whose hands were soft and whose eyes shone for him and his father. He had almost forgotten her. For a moment he felt ashamed. She was back at Marius' villa waiting. She never came to see Argoutus fight. She was always too afraid. Maybe word had reached her by now and Tomas should have been the one to tell her, if Argoutus could not, that she was free and her man safe. Tomas lifted his head and laid a quick kiss on Argoutus' cheek.

"Father, I will go now." He turned to the short plump man in his white toga who stood on the other side of the couch. "Care for him. I will return with Scribonia."

The man smiled at the young child with such strength in his blue eyes.

Tomas turned and darted away out into the clear hot sun, down the great wide steps to the city streets and into his heart burst a song of joy for his family.: His loved ones were free and from this moment a new life was opening for them.

****

Scribonia stood quiet beside the great oven, her hands raw from work and constant water. She brushed back her hair from her sweating brow. The heat of the kitchen pushed at her so that it was hard to breathe. Barely thirty years old, she looked older. Her dark hair was highlighted with silver and her clear, chiselled features shone from a tired, wrinkled skin – bronzed and aged by the sun. Scribonia was always tired. She rose each day at five and worked in the villa until the long day was dimmed by the falling of night's curtain. She sighed. As with most days she longed for Argoutus to be here with her. Ever since he had become a gladiator he lived most of the time outside Rome where the great school for gladiators was situated. She had no time to visit there nor would she have been welcome. The men were thought to be weakened by sex and their ladies were kept away so that there was no temptation. Tomas was their go-between. He it was who travelled up to visit Argoutus and bring gifts of food and drink from his wife.

In fact Scribonia and Argoutus were only married recently. The day had come when Marius had told Argoutus that he might marry. Argoutus had been delighted and hurried back to Scribonia to tell her. Tomas was only six then – and could only stare in astonishment as his mother and father had cried and hugged each other and danced crazily round the room. A week later they had married and Tomas had stayed confused by all the excitement – they were his parents – they loved each other and him and he saw no difference after they were officially man and wife. Tomas was no longer a bastard but that meant nothing in the slave world where few were allowed to marry. They were encouraged to have sex because more sex meant more children who grew to be slaves. The men circulated round the women freely and very often the children and their mothers had no idea who had fathered whom. But should a master wish to honour a slave he might allow a civil marriage and this had been the case for Argoutus and Scribonia.

Marius was a good Roman. He and his wife were honest, upright citizens of Rome and Marius had risen to be an architect for the Senate of Rome. He had no children – Julia was barren. The curse of being barren meant less to her than it would a slave, but still Julia pined for a child and when Tomas was born she had held him and smiled at Scribonia with tear-filled eyes.

"He is so lovely," she had said. "You are so blessed, Scribonia." But within a few hours Scribonia had folded up in agony and the dreaded fever had gripped her. Tomas had screamed as her milk dried up and a wet nurse was found by Julia. Scribonia had tossed and turned as evil pains swept through her body and her temperature rose dangerously. Both Julia and Marius had worried for her. Argoutus was allowed to stay beside her and when at last she had risen from the fever and healing sleep had held her tortured body, it was Marius who called for wine and gave a toast to Scribonia and her child.

Now Tomas hurried once again along the cobbled way to Marius' villa. He knew his mother would be cooking. All day she cooked ready for the five o'clock feast which would last at least three hours. It meant a whole day of preparation and Scribonia was happy to do it. She enjoyed the bustle of the kitchen and she was popular with the other slaves. Over the last ten years she had developed a routine which pleased her mistress and allowed her some ease. Julia was good to her just as Marius had been good to Argoutus. In many ways, although she would never admit so to her husband, Scribonia was reasonably content with slavery. She was well fed, her child was educated and she had no responsibility except to do her work. But her heart longed for Argoutus to be a freedman. That way he would stop fighting for his life and could live with her again like a real husband. Maybe she'd be able to have another child – a girl for her companionship would be nice or another son even. She adored Tomas as most mothers do their sons and it would be hard to imagine any other child replacing him. Really she cared little for freedom but a great deal for Argoutus' safety. After Tomas and her puerperal illness had left her weak and lacking in energy, Julia had thought she might never have another child, but had nonetheless encouraged her and a bond had developed between the women. But soon Argoutus had left for the gladiator school and despite Julia's attempts to get Scribonia to sleep with another man she had refused and in the end Julia had accepted it and admired her for it. Julia was happy with Marius but had many lovers: being barren had given her more freedom than most. Marius was not faithful but loved Julia dearly. He was sad about her barrenness but although he had fathered other children he never told Julia or tried to bring them into her house. Deep seated love and respect existed between them and their home was peaceful and contented. This contentment spilled over into the lives of the slaves.

So with mixed feeling Scribonia stood by the sink as her wildly excited son rushed to her with a great pride riding on his shoulder.

"We are free, Mother!" he cried. "We are free, Father killed Ovilium and Caesar said we are free!" He grabbed his mother round the waist and squeezed her – his head against her breast. As he did so a weak sob escaped him and Scribonia pushed him away and dropped to her knees.

"What happened?" Her voice was hard and firm, fear destroying any softness. She held him at arm's length, looking deep into his eyes. "Tomas, tell me," she cried, almost shaking him. "Argoutus – what of him?"

"Mother, he's alive. He was hurt by the mob. They rushed him. He was doing his lap of honour – they got over the fence – he disappeared." Tomas put his hands over his eyes and a lone tear trickled down his cheek. "Oh, Mother, I believed him dead." His childish fear overcame him and he collapsed against his mother for comfort. Scribonia was torn. Torn between her love for Argoutus and her need to comfort her child. She surrounded Tomas with her arms and love but spoke firmly into his ear.

"Tomas. Tell me. Is Argoutus badly hurt? You know I must go to him. Tomas, please ...!"

Tomas wept silently into her warmth. For a moment he took his love of her knowing that she would soon away to her husband and for a moment he wanted to take all of her. But then he knew his duty and, sniffing, he stepped away.

"Come, Mother, I'll take you. He asked me to fetch you. I had forgotten you, Mother!"

Scribonia smiled at him. He was so honest at times to his own detriment.

"Never mind, Tomas. Argoutus never forgets me. Come now, tell me as we go..."

A young girl of about twelve came into the kitchen. Scribonia spoke to her, telling her she had to go and asking her to see to the roast lobsters sizzling in the great oven. The girl was sullen but Scribonia did not care. She knew both Marius and Julia would understand and be patient.

She pulled off her white shawl, gathered round her waist like an apron, and snatched her headscarf from a table by the door. With her arm resting on Tomas' shoulder they went out into the sunshine.

Chapter 2

During the next few weeks Argoutus grew stronger but the extent of his injuries became clearer.

His chest had been pounded, causing fractures of three ribs, and one had punctured his right lung. Breathing was painful and hard and the threat of infection real. His left hip was crushed but apart from some superficial bruising his limbs had escaped serious damage. His doctors suspected some internal injuries and kept him on a soft diet of asses' milk for several days.

After a week Argoutus was returned to his room at the Marius villa. A feast was laid on for his return and Tomas spent the day helping his mother and the other slaves prepare the mountain of food.

First there were oysters freshly seasoned with mace and mixed herbs – next prawns and tiny fish cooked in crushed olives. These were served on beds of salad with great black radishes carved like the barbarians who touched the edges of the land. The men laughed as they bit the heads off their strong tasting enemies. Wine flowed from great amphorae into tall silver tankards. Next came wild guinea fowl roasted with pistachio nuts and crushed chestnuts – their bellies filled with garlic cloves buried into soft sweet potatoes. Next to them were chicken legs like fat ballerinas dancing round the centrepiece: a huge goose. Plucked and drawn, the bird was roasted with honey and brandy substituted with great glazed cherries. Piles of vegetables: sweet garlic courgettes stuffed with apple puree, great cabbages dripping with peanut oil, quails eggs on beds of parsley and spinach. A young suckling pig with oranges and passion fruit lay on a giant silver platter, its belly stuffed with lemon and cream sauce. On small plates pieces of chicken liver and heart and pigs kidneys were pierced with long shaved sticks, with a bowl of minced shallots.

Fruits and cheeses decorated the back of the great table – great, hard, strong veined globes and oozing tiny goat's cheeses dipped in green peppers. Fruit juices and vegetables laced with wine stood in vast pots and silver jugs. Laces and linens covered the wide oak tables and the sun sparkled on great silver spoons and short broadened knives.

By five o'clock the villa began to fill with friends and relatives of both the masters and the new freed slaves. Long purple togas were thrown across satin couches and splendid ladies with braided hair lay half-supported on red and yellow pillows.

A wild trumpeting welcomed each guest and at last a cry rang out as Argoutus was brought in on a high gilt litter and placed in the centre. Scribonia had thrown off her kitchen garb and came behind her husband in a pale pink toga edged with gold. Her long black hair was braided in gold and her bare neck decorated with a necklace of rubies, lent to her by her mistress.

Marius and Julia stood back among the crowds, smiling with pride at the great feast and the love they bore their freed slaves. A tall obese fellow with a royal blue toga and gold sandals entered and the crowd were hushed for a moment as the great senator took his place beside the litter. A small black boy of no more than ten years stood on the heaving table and put a long flute to his lips, while a slave girl held a harp beneath her arm and began to play. Another black child began to strum at a lute-like instrument and the crowd became quiet as the music kissed the warm air.

Tomas stood beside his father, proud and straight. Across his back hung his youth's toga of soft green – a gold clasp placed on his breast and his tanned arms rippling with growing muscles. He watched his father's face. It was grey and drawn still – his breath shallow and his eyes dulled with laudanum and the wafts of witch hazel heavy on his breath. But he was alive – alive and free and Tomas loved him with a wild pride that brought tears to his young eyes.

****

After Argoutus had come home Tomas went back to school. Despite his change of status the family continued life much as before.

Marius was keen that Argoutus, Scribonia and Tomas continue to live in their house and Scribonia continued to work in the great kitchen by choice. Argoutus still lay weak and his recovery was slow and laboured. It seemed that after his great triumph his life held no direction anymore. His whole life was bound up with getting his freedom but he had never looked beyond it. Scribonia for herself never minded her slavery – she had no ambitions but to work for Julia of whom she was very fond. Julia encouraged her to relax more, taking a new slave into the kitchen to help, but it was hard for Scribonia to respond. She was used to work and saw little pleasure in doing nothing, as she saw this as relaxing. Of course she had a new task of helping nurse her husband and she worried a great deal about his progress, or lack of it.

As she changed his bed and took him his food she was conscious that the fire had gone from his eyes. His depression grew deeper each day and when he began to refuse food she began to be seriously worried. In the end she went to Marius.

"My Lord," she began. Marius held up a hand.

"Scribonia, now I am Marius to you."

Scribonia smiled warmly. "It is hard to remember and I feel disrespectful."

"Well, you are now a freedwoman, Scribonia, you must act as one – for Argoutus' sake if not for your own. How is he?"

"That is the reason for my coming to you," Scribonia replied, deliberately avoiding using any form of address. "I am very worried about him …"

"Continue," Marius encouraged.

"He is not recovering – in fact in his mind he is still very ill and this worsens, not improves."

"What worries him?"

"As you know, his life was entirely directed into service to you and the ultimate challenge of fighting for his freedom. Now he has it, he doesn't know what to do with it! He just lies there moping … his body is recovering but slowly. He fears a future without purpose and with weakness of body. Now he will not eat … I am afraid for him," she ended quietly.

"I understand," said Marius, "but what can be done? I had hoped he would join a legion or train as an architect, but at present he does not have the strength."

For a while both were silent. Then Scribonia asked, "Does he know that you have plans for him?"

Marius shook his head.

"What purpose is there in talking about it when he is not fit to do it?" He paused and leaned nearer to Scribonia. "We realise, I believe, that he may never be fit, do we not?"

Scribonia hung her head and her eyes filled with tears. She nodded silently.

Marius put an arm round her shoulders.

"I will talk to him. He will get through this ….."

When Marius arrived in the hall where Argoutus was lying propped up on a couch he was more anxious. Argoutus had already lost much of his weight and he looked gaunt and almost emaciated. His eyes were shut but Marius guessed that he was not asleep.

"Argoutus," he said gently.

Argoutus immediately opened his eyes. He smiled at Marius but the smile seemed belied by his dull, lifeless eyes.

"Ah, Marius, have you come to see the cripple?" His voice was low and bitter.

"No," said Marius firmly. "I came to see my friend. You know, Argoutus, I missed you a great deal when you went off to the gladiator school. I missed your conversation, my friend."

Argoutus let his eyes close once more but he said, "I do not feel like conversation."

"Argoutus." Marius' voice was clear and urgent. "You must not be depressed. All will be well. What you need is the patience which I believe you have little of. If you do not try to recover, you …… " His voiced trailed away.

"I will not recover." Argoutus finished his sentence. "Well, Marius, maybe it would be for the best. I will never fight again – I may never be fit even to march with your legions. I am not fit to be a husband now that I have Scribonia again. I am not fit to be a father. Tomas needs teaching to run and fight and be strong. I shall never be your slave again….."

"It was what you wanted – what you have always struggled for. Are you not satisfied?"

"Of course, but … well, my master ……" He paused. "My friend, I feel nothing. My future was planned in my mind. I had great ambitions, but …"

Marius cut in, "My friend, I understand. I know that now you feel you can no longer achieve these ambitions, these plans because you are weak and ill but remember, dear Argoutus, time, my great friend, will heal you. The right future will become clear, never fear. The only one who is impatient is you. You must go to the temple and pray for patience. You will be guided ..."

Argoutus remained silent. Marius sat down on the edge of the couch and took Argoutus' hand. He smiled with his eyes.

"My friend, for the last three years you have been my greatest gladiator. You have fought and vanquished many men and beasts. Every time you walked into the arena you faced an unknown challenge. Each man or beast was different – each would move or attack in a different way. Now you have found an unknown challenge in life and you want to give it up? That I do not understand. If you do not face this challenge your spirit will die just as your body would have died in the arena. Is that what you really want?"

Argoutus hung his head but remained silent.

Marius tried again.

"What of Scribonia, your wife? She has waited patiently for your return. She is totally faithful to you, she loves you deeply – would you cause her pain?"

"I would not, but ..."

"Listen to me. Scribonia has waited for five years to have you home again. She has cared for your son and never allowed her spirit to love another man. She has been every day to the temple to pray for your safety. Will you reward her by making her a widow?"

He paused. Argoutus made no reply.

"And Tomas?" continued Marius. "He is so proud of you. His whole life has been affected by your glory. He loves you desperately, Argoutus – you are his sun and his moon. He believes in you – in your power, your love is like living water to him. Would you destroy his faith?"

Argoutus opened his eyes and turned his head towards Marius. His voice was quiet.

"Marius, my Lord, my friend. I know what you are trying to do and of course you are right. I must stay alive. I must recover my broken spirit for Scribonia and for Tomas but it is so hard. My spirit is broken, Marius, broken …"

"Yes, Argoutus, I know. But please try, please fight as you have always done. I will bring the Soothsayer, Tacitus, to you. Maybe he will see into your future and help you."

****

Tacitus sat on the steps of the Temple of Iris in the Forum – his head in his hands. Business was bad. His predictions over a forthcoming disaster had not materialised and Rome lay in the sunshine, calm and peaceful. He had a long wavy white beard which he hated. It itched dreadfully in the summer heat and constantly annoyed him at meal times when, despite all his efforts, it always ended up with pieces of food lodged in it. He had to keep it, of course. Soothsayers were expected to have beards and to be old and wise – Tacitus was in fact only 38. He had come to Rome a few years back and had no luck finding a job. His idea to become a Soothsayer had yielded good profits at first. He had rubbed walnut oil into his skin and drawn lines through it to make himself look older. He had smothered his beard in lemon and chalk until it looked white and wispy. He had starved himself until he looked wizen. Then he had wandered the streets wailing and foretelling doom and disaster. He had thrown in a few good omens to encourage his richest customers and had been lucky with some of his guesses. That chap Marius thought him especially good when he had foretold a large fortune coming his way, and by chance his elderly father had died and left Marius much money.

However, things did not always go his way. A few weeks ago he had told Calpernia she was barren. Her husband had thrown her out and taken a new wife. Calpernia ended up with Silenus and had had a child almost immediately. Her first husband had not been happy and had cursed him profusely, shouting around the Forum that Tacitus was a fraud.

Steps approached him and he looked up to see Marius striding towards him.

"Tacitus, my friend," he said as he came panting up. "I have a job for you."

Tacitus put on his creaked, wavering voice.

"Marius," he stammered. "Why, why do you come here at noon – your shadow holds great horrors," and he shrank back.

Marius, however, ignored him. "Tacitus," he continued, "I want you to come to my villa. You know about Argoutus the gladiator, of course."

"Yes, yes," replied Tacitus. "Was he crushed by the crowd? I foretold it, you know," he added hurriedly, remembering to play his part.

"He was my slave, you know," Marius went on, "And so I took him in. His body heals but his mind is truly disturbed. I fear for him. If you could come and help him. Foretell a good future, you know?"

"It may, may be <u>not</u> a good future," Tacitus replied.

"Well, I know that but perhaps you could just tell him the good bits and forget the bad ….."

Tacitus screwed up his face and looked worried. He scratched his beard.

"Well – well – it, it might cost you," he said slyly.

Marius smiled. "Of course, my friend."

They haggled for a few moments and then Tacitus rose, shook Marius by the hand and followed him across the Forum. Halfway across he adjusted his step, remembering he was supposed to be old, and let Marius wait for him.

Marius chatted to him busily about Argoutus and Tacitus listened carefully, picking up all the clues in the hope that he would make the right predictions. The money was good and he needed the publicity of an accurate prediction. He was puzzled by what to do – no ideas came to him ... and Marius did not seem to have any ideas. In the end it was Argoutus himself who solved the problem.

Tacitus had gone in and moaned and groaned a bit and had taken Argoutus by the hand and wept. This was a very effective way to make himself appear genuine. He did it by placing a sharp nail inside his coat sticking out the side. He would then push his bare wrist against it, scraping the skin until it brought tears to his eyes. This he did to show his empathy with Argoutus' sorry state. He said a few chants and looked heavenwards, but he was lost for a solution.

Argoutus also followed his eyes skyward. At last he spoke.

"Tacitus, I feel so trapped. Trapped by my body. Until now it served me well. Now it holds my spirit like a jailer. I want to get away."

Tacitus smiled. He had the answer. He turned to Marius and put on his most effective and ghastly voice.

"I see travel – I see a far place." He paused. "I see water – blue, clear water – strange foreign skies, mountains, rivers, a young man and a beautiful girl." He hesitated. Argoutus leaned up on the couch and stared at him.

"Go on, go on," he urged.

"A new city will rise beneath you," went on Tacitus, warming to his subject, "And a great man will rise from your loins." He always found it a good idea to predict wonderful futures for children because it took so long to come true, or rather not to come true, that he felt fairly safe.

Argoutus allowed a smile to cross his face. "My Tomas," he said proudly, "He will be great, I know it!"

"It may not be Tomas," Tacitus interrupted quickly. "There will be others. Now you are home with your lady wife."

Argoutus let the smile die and a scowl crossed his face.

"What good am I to her?" he cried. "My penis does not rise anymore!"

"It will," shouted Tacitus, "It will. Time will bring fire back to your loins. I see it – I know it – believe me."

Relief showed in Argoutus' face.

Tacitus was beginning to enjoy himself – this was going fine. He hoped Argoutus would recommend him to others, and Marius too.

"Turn your couch to the east. Take your lady one month from today and love and caress her. Do not penetrate her, however, much as your desire requires it. Deny yourself this pleasure. Do this nightly until the moon is full. On this night allow yourself full penetration to full conclusion. If she is satisfied too, then a child will result. Remember."

"Supposing it doesn't work? For Tomas we waited many months."

Tacitus threw back his head and distorted his face to one of bland horror. He screamed so that both Argoutus and Marius shrank back at the sound.

"No, no," he screamed, "Do not doubt me – I am Tacitus the Soothsayer, what I say is <u>true</u>, believe me, <u>true</u>. He sank down onto the floor, feigning a swoon.

Argoutus leaned forward anxiously and Marius went to Tacitus' side. With an expression of concern Marius touched the prostrate figure.

"Tacitus," he said, "Tacitus, are you all right?"

Tacitus shivered and groaned. Then his eyes opened and he rolled them a bit before letting them settle on Marius.

Weakly, he said, "He doubted me. It is like a burning sword into my head."

"Of course he does not doubt you." Marius spoke as if to a child.

Argoutus called from his couch.

"I do believe you, Tacitus. I never meant to question you."

For a few moments Tacitus allowed Marius to fuss over him. Then he rose slowly to his feet and asked for a glass of wine. He drank it in silence then, ignoring both men, he walked from the room and out into the sunshine once more. Although he moved slowly and dragged his feet, his heart was light. He was pleased with his performance and the bag of coins in his pocket gave him a great feeling. It had been a good morning after all.

Back at the villa Marius sat beside Argoutus, who now lay back exhausted.

"You see, Argoutus, there is a future for you!" But Marius looked anxious.

"Is he genuine, Marius? Somehow he seems shallow and his chanting and voice changes. Sometimes I wondered …"

"I believe in him," said Marius slowly, "But I am worried about what he said. If you are to travel and see a new city rise, that means I shall lose you."

Argoutus sighed. Then he said, "Of course I would return. He did not mention my death – maybe I would return …"

Marius looked at him. He saw a change in the face. Argoutus looked better even than one hour ago. Tacitus had worked the magic Marius had hoped for. Scribonia would be pleased but he was unhappy about the future now. How could Argoutus travel and where would he go? He knew Julia would be very sad to lose Scribonia and indeed Tomas. Yet despite Argoutus' anxieties about Tacitus he clearly wanted to believe him. He was now talking of life and not death.

Marius said, "Maybe your travel will not be far – maybe within a reasonable distance of Rome."

"No," replied Argoutus, "He said a far country – foreign soil – he spoke of water – across water."

There was silence. Marius watched Argoutus lie back. A peace seemed to have entered the gaunt face. Marius rose.

"I will leave you, let you rest. We will talk more later. If you are to travel you will need all your strength."

As Marius left the room he glanced back and saw that Argoutus was already asleep. He hurried across the hall and went down to the kitchen. Scribonia was there, scrubbing the oak table, her long arms rippling with muscles – her face set with effort. Marius laughed.

"You will never be a freedwoman, Scribonia … look at you. You work harder than a dozen slaves."

Scribonia returned his smile. "I am content to work – it is my life. I cannot sit about, I should die of boredom."

"Well," Marius perched on the edge of the table, "You will be pleased with my news."

Scribonia stood quietly, listening.

"Your Argoutus," he said, "I believe he will be well now. I got Tacitus the Soothsayer to visit him. He foretold a good future and a long life."

Scribonia looked pleased. "Tell me what he said."

Marius hesitated. "No, Scribonia. I think I should let Argoutus tell you. At present he is resting but later when he wakes he will tell you all …"

Scribonia put a hand out and touched Marius' shoulder.

"Thank you, Marius, you are a good friend. Without you I don't know what we should do."

Marius smiled but in his heart he felt sorry. He might have helped cheer up Argoutus and Scribonia but it seemed he was to lose them in the process. Well – it was the wish of the gods – there was nothing he could do.

As he turned to leave the kitchen there was a commotion at the other door and Tomas rushed in, his hair blowing in the breeze and his face full of excitement. He ran to Scribonia.

"Mother," he cried, clutching her hand. "See what I have." He held up a wooden wax book. "See," he shouted, "All my spelling is correct – Argoutus will be pleased … I will go and show him."

Scribonia smiled. "Good, Tomas. But leave your father for a while. He is resting."

The delight left Tomas' face. He turned his eyes to Marius. "My father is not well, Sir. He does not want to get better. Why is he like that?"

"Tomas, today the Soothsayer came to see Argoutus and told him many things which are to happen. It has helped him. I think he will get better now!"

"What did he predict?" asked Tomas anxiously.

"He said that the son of Argoutus will be a great man."

"I," remarked Tomas, "I am to be great."

"Well, maybe, but Argoutus may have other sons!"

Tomas turned to his mother. Suddenly his face scowled and his eyes flashed.

"Mother," he cried, "You would not have another son, you must not. I am your son. I, Tomas, Julius, Argoutus, I am the son of Argoutus and the son of Scribonia. I do not want a brother," and he stamped his foot.

Both Scribonia and Marius stared at the boy in disbelief. Neither had seen Tomas in a rage such as this before.

" ... But Tomas," began Scribonia.

"Listen, Mother," interrupted the boy. "You will not have another child. You must promise me. I will be enough for you. I will be the great man."

"Tomas! Tomas!" Marius tried to take the boy by the shoulder but he swung away and stood scowling at Marius.

"And you, my Lord! You do not have any part of this. It is not your affair. It concerns only me and my parents. You may leave us!"

Scribonia gasped. "Tomas. You must not speak to Marius like that."

Tomas swung round. "I am not a slave now. I am a Freedman. Marius is my equal."

"No, Tomas," shouted his mother with a horrified look on her face. "Marius is not your equal and never will be if you persist like this. You are only a child. No child is equal to a man. Now apologise to Marius immediately."

"And you," said Tomas, "Are just a woman and women can never be equal to me so please be quiet …"

For a moment the silence hung between them all like a cold blanket. Both Marius and Scribonia stood stunned from shock and the colour rose on Tomas' face. He looked from one to the other. Then as suddenly as the anger had arrived, Tomas' shoulders sank, his eyes fell and his lip began to quiver. Two large tears rolled down his cheeks and fell to the marble floor. Scribonia held out her arms.

"Tomas," she said firmly, "Come here!"

Tomas took a step towards her and then rushed into her outstretched arms and collapsed against her in a convulsion of sobbing. Scribonia held him tight and patted the golden curls. For a while the room was filled with the heartrending sobs of the child but as they subsided Scribonia held the boy away and dropped on her knees looking into the tear-streaked face.

"Now, Tomas," she said gently but firmly. "Please apologise to Marius …"

"But Mother," stammered Tomas.

"Apologise," repeated Scribonia fiercely. "I do not care why you were rude or why you weep – apologise this moment."

Tomas turned with head hung.

"Marius, my Lord," he said, his breath rasping from his sobs. "I am sorry .."

Marius looked crossly at the boy. "You may well be sorry, young man. You were very rude not only to your mother but also to me. Your father will be very angry …"

"Please, Sir, please. Do not tell Argoutus."

"Of course I shall tell him. And he will devise a punishment worthy of your wrongdoing. When you are punished I may forgive you but your mother must forgive you too. Will you not ask her for forgiveness?"

"Will you forgive me, Mother?" asked Tomas quietly, tears again wetting his crumpled face.

"Tomas," said his mother, "You have been a wicked rude child and when you have taken your punishment I may forgive you too. Now wait here and when your father wakes I will fetch you and you can tell him what you have done." She stood up. "Come, Marius, let us leave this rude boy to think about his behaviour and ponder his wickedness."

Marius turned and went from the room and Scribonia followed.

Tomas looked after them sadly. He was so confused. He had rushed happily to school that day – excited by the work which he loved because he was a quick learner and enjoyed reading and writing. The other less successful pupils had teased him in the past and called him a 'swot' but because his father was a famous gladiator he had been generally popular. They never picked fights with Tomas just in case his father's physical prowess had been passed down to his son.

But this day he had been moved from his familiar place amongst his friends at the back of the room and placed in the front row. The children of freedmen always sat in the front while the slaves sat at the back. The children of born Roman citizens were usually tutored at home so Tomas had become one of the five elite ones and the master, Parthenius, a Greek scholar, had suddenly realised that he had to promote Tomas now he had become the son of a freedman. He had announced the fact with great pride because Tomas was one of his best pupils and he was anxious to teach him more than he was expected to teach the slaves.

"Now, Tomas," he had said when he had placed the boy right in front of him. "You are now a special pupil and must work hard. No longer are you a slave. Now you are a citizen of Rome and the door of great opportunity is open to you. You are the equal of any man – the slaves are no longer your equals, nor the girls – they are now beneath you. You may hold up your head in pride over any man. Only emperors and consuls and prefects hold power above you, my son. There is but a thin barrier of time between you and greatness. This child," he said, turning to his class, "Has the fortune of Minerva upon him. Born to slavery, he has, by the great physical strength of his father, risen to the exalted state of a citizen of our Imperial Empire – the Great Empire of Rome and of our divine Emperor Augustus. He walks from now on with the pride of Rome upon his shoulders. Take heed of this boy. One day you will have cause to say 'this man, Tomas Julius Argoutus, was my classmate, I knew him.' Mark well what I say."

The other children had stayed silent then but when class was dismissed Tomas had been held back by Parthenius. The master had given Tomas extra words to spell and allowed him to carry home his work to show Scribonia and Argoutus how well he had done.

Tomas had jumped out of the school door like a gazelle, clutching his tablet, and seen young Laetus, his greatest friend, standing by the steps.

"Laetus," he called, "See what I've done. Look, all my words were right."

Laetus turned to Tomas with a surly glare. "So ...?" he asked, "Why do you speak to me, Tomas

Julius Argoutus? I am a slave while you, you are a great man of Rome."

Tomas looked shocked. "But Laetus we are friends, you and I. I still want to play with you."

"Do you indeed?" Laetus turned away. "Well, I am not worthy of you," and he began to run away calling, "Freedman, freedman," over his shoulder.

Tomas stood still watching Laetus disappear round the corner. He looked down at his work thoughtfully. "I suppose," he said to himself, "Laetus is right. I am to be a great man. I should not have slaves for friends anymore …which is a pity," he added out loud, "because I do like Laetus but I must make sacrifices if I am to become an important citizen of Rome." And he moved off towards home, his spirits rising with pride as he went.

Now he stood dejectedly in the kitchen puzzling over the day. One minute he had been hailed by Parthenius as all men's equal – then shunned by his friend Laetus, then when he had behaved as an equal of Marius and the superior of Scribonia, a mere woman, he was to be punished! He did not understand. But as he contemplated what was now to come, he hoped sincerely that his father would.

It was a full hour before Scribonia returned to find her wayward child. Her heart was heavy, as like any true mother she had been moved by the sobbing of her child and had wanted only to love him and comfort him, but he had to be taught a lesson and lessons were often so hard.

She found Tomas seated by the kitchen table. Annia, the new slave girl, was busy at the sink and there was an enormous pile of fresh vegetables beside it. She had her back to Tomas.

"Annia," said Scribonia, ignoring her son, "Will you take Julia a glass of wine? She is in the Atrium."

She turned to Tomas who had risen and was standing by the table, his eyes downcast.

"Now Tomas." She stood over him, looking down.

Tomas raised his eyes. His voice trembled a little.

"Mother, I do not understand. I was at school and Parthenius told me I was everyman's equal and that I would be a great man. Then I came home and Marius told me I was to be a great man … and then he told us you might have another child and he might be greater and … and …"

"Tomas," said Scribonia gently. "I understand – it is hard to change from being a slave to being a freedman, but …," she paused to put her hands on Tomas' shoulders "but," she repeated, her eyes hard into Tomas' clear blue ones, "you must never, never be rude to anyone, whether they are a slave or woman or freedman or child. No one. Do you understand that?"

Tomas nodded. "But," he began, but Scribonia went on.

"And you are just a child so everyone who is older than you must be respected and I mean anyone. There is never any excuse for speaking to anyone as you did. Do you understand?"

Tomas nodded again.

"Now. What did you want to say?"

"Well. When I was a slave, people were often rude to me. That man, Maximus, who visited us with messages from my father, he was always rude. He called me a weakling and a scruff and told his daughter, Tullia, never to speak to me. He is a great man, a consul, but he is very rude, even to you."

"Tomas. He may be an important man but he is not a great man. Real great men are good and kind. True greatness does not come from pride but from humility. And now …," Scribonia took Tomas by the hand. "Come and see Argoutus and tell him of your rudeness so that you may be punished."

Tomas followed Scribonia through the Atrium where they found Argoutus propped up on his cushions looking much better.

"My son," he called, "Come and talk to your father. Tell me how your day has been."

Tomas, with head bowed, walked towards Argoutus slowly.

"My father, I am sorry to say that I have not been a good child today. I have come to admit my misdemeanour and receive punishment."

Argoutus' expression changed and his eyes clouded over with concern.

"What have you done, my son? I was feeling better today and my son comes in to spoil my mood. I hope you will not make me ill again."

"My Lord," began Tomas, tears of contrition escaping his eyes and rolling down his face. "I .. I was rude to Marius and to my mother."

"You were rude!" Argoutus cried.

"Yes, Sir," replied Tomas. "I treated Marius as my equal and Scribonia as beneath me. I meant no harm Sir. I was confused …"

"I do not want to listen to your excuses," interrupted Argoutus. "Have you apologised?"

"Yes, Sir," repeated Tomas. "I will take whatever punishment my father feels is right."

"Well, my child," roared Argoutus, "Stand tall and look me in the eye. Dry your tears and prepare to take your punishment like a man."

Tomas sniffed, passed his hand across his face and looked steadfastly at his father.

"I am prepared, Father," he said as firmly as he could.

Suddenly Argoutus lay back and a ghost-like whiteness crept across his face. He gasped for breath and Scribonia rushed to his side. Turning to Tomas she cried, "Go and get the physician, quickly."

Tomas rushed from the room. He almost collided with Julia who had just stepped out from her room. She grabbed at Tomas and caught him.

"Where are you running so fast? You should walk in the house, you …"

"Madam," spluttered Tomas, "I go for the physician – my father …"

Julia let go instantly and called after Tomas' fleeing figure, "Run, boy, run," as she hurried back to the Atrium.

Tomas sped out through the front door, down the steps into the square, his head spinning with panic. For a few moments he hesitated. The physician lived a good half mile away by the theatre. The quickest way was via the dingy back alleys but Tomas had a fear of those. The buildings were old and some seemed to lean towards him and he always felt he needed to hold them apart physically with outstretched hands. The sun reached this street at midday because the buildings were only two storeys high and the Emperor had insisted that all Roman citizens should see sunlight whenever it was possible. But now the red streaks of the dying autumn sun were too low to penetrate and Tomas feared the poor and desolate places hidden behind the facades. Sometimes through an open door he had seen strange rag-covered old women whispering like creaking rusty chains and laughing with broken old voices which had mocked his clear, pure youth.

His hesitation was just an instant but as he dived to his right into the shadowy alley he let his mind unfurl its fear and his feet seemed heavy with reluctance.

The two fears in his head – his father and the alleys – jostled and crushed about inside like fighting cocks, each pushing and squawking at the other. But Tomas was a child of duty and the love he bore his father pushed him onward, faster and faster.

The first alley was clear: no one moved, not even a breeze and by the time he reached the next his confidence was growing. But as he turned into the narrow via he saw a cat moving lackadaisically across in front of him. Cats did not frighten Tomas, but this one stopped right in the middle of the cobbles and turned its green speckled eyes towards his approaching figure.

"Get away," shouted Tomas as he neared it. "Out of my way!"

The animal paused and then made to move aside, but at the last moment it seemed to freeze and turned once more towards him. Too late Tomas knew that he must collide with it – and he made a wild leap over it, feeling the hot, rasping breath hiss out as he caught his sandals on its head and crushed onto the hard stones.

The cat spat at him and moved off. Tomas lay where he had fallen, shocked and still. His mind plunged into realisation suddenly and he struggled to his feet. He must go on – he must get the physician.

Mechanically his feet moved into gear and he began to run again. However, an old man had come out into the street ahead of him and held up his hands to stop him.

He was an old, gnarled creature with a bowed back, and the shadows of the lantern he held cast weird shadows across his face. Tomas shuddered to a halt in front of him and looked up at him with wide startled eyes.

"What's the hurry, son?" crackled the old man's voice. "I never see folks along here. Why don't you stop for a bit and ..."

"Please, Sir," stammered Tomas, "I have to go in a hurry." He tried to dodge past but the old man grabbed his arm.

"And where are you going in such a hurry?"

"Sir ... Argoutus is bad – I go for the physician."

With a speed which amazed Tomas the old man released him and pushed him away.

"Go, boy, run ...," he shouted. "Be quick."

Tomas set off again. How good it was to have such a famous father. And how his heart burst with worry lest he had caused his father's relapse.

He darted round another corner and saw ahead the Via Cardo. He burst from the dim alley into a wide marketplace where groups of men were packing up the day's stalls and sweeping the litter from the streets.

Tomas dodged between them and dived for the big wooden door. The great iron knocker took all his strength to lift but he let it crash down with a great hollow bang.

For what seemed ages there was silence but then Tomas heard the shuffle of sandaled feet and the door opened slowly. A tall slave dressed in a simple skirt and bare to the waist looked out.

"Yes?" he said, unsmiling. His eyes scanned Tomas' slender form. "What've you done? Go home to your mother. The physician isn't interested in kids' grazed knees ..."

"No, no," cried Tomas as he saw the man make to close the door. "It's not for me! It is my father, Argoutus! He is taken bad ..."

For once the name did not evoke a response. The man hesitated then said, "I'll ask but he don't like to be disturbed before his meal." He turned away and Tomas stood waiting. As he did so he became aware for the first time of pain in his legs and elbow. He inspected the damage. A large chunk of flesh had been gouged from his right knee and a stream of blood still trickled from the wound. Pale bruises deepened on his shins and an ugly graze adorned his ankle. He turned his arm to look at the elbow and gasped with pain. There was no blood on it but the pain was excruciating and he winced and bit his lip. So anxious was he to summon help for Argoutus that he had not felt anything until that moment.

The door flew open and Herodes stood there, his face screwed up with concern. Behind him another tall, dark slave carried a leather case.

"Come, boy," he said, "Let's go," and he moved past Tomas and onto the street.

He set off and Tomas turned to follow. His knees felt like fire and his elbow throbbed but he limped after Herodes bravely, struggling to keep up.

Herodes strode off and shouted something over his shoulder at Tomas.

"Pardon, Sir?" called Tomas.

Herodes looked back and took in the sight of the pathetic child – bloodstained and limping with his left arm held at a strange angle. He stopped.

"Whatever have you done?" he asked kindly.

"I fell, Sir," said Tomas, coming closer, "But I'm fine, Sir. It is Argoutus who needs you."

Herodes moved towards him. He gently took hold of Tomas' arm and the boy let out a muffled scream. Herodes turned at once to his slave. He took the case off him and called to him as he moved away.

"Bring the child, Helvius – carry him. He is hurt. Be careful of his arm: I fear it is broken. I will see you later, Tomas ...," and he hurried off.

Helvius gathered Tomas into his arms and lifted him. The pain seemed to be growing and Tomas' head had begun to spin. He closed his eyes against it and groaned inwardly. Each movement sent strong rivulets of pain through his body and beads of perspiration trickled down his face. He felt waves of sickness travelling up his body as blackness descended. The next thing he knew was a wet cloth on his forehead and the soft scent of his mother's nearness. He opened his eyes and as his vision cleared he heard Scribonia's voice.

"Tomas, are you awake?"

The pain returned and Tomas closed his eyes again, but spoke shakily. "Is Argoutus safe, Mother?"

"Yes, Tomas," she replied gently. "He is better now. Herodes is with him and will come to you in a moment. Now lie still and try to take a drink of water." She held a glass up to his lips and he sipped it gratefully.

After a few minutes the door opened and a smiling Herodes walked in. He walked to the couch. Scribonia rose.

"He is awake now, Herodes, but his pain is great."

"This will help," said Herodes, crossing to Tomas with a glass vial in his hand. "Drink this, child, and then I will set your arm."

The bitter liquid flowed down Tomas' body and a gentle drowsiness crept over him. He felt pain as Herodes strapped his arm but it was dulled and soon he slept.

When he woke he could feel stiffness in his legs and arm but there was only a dull ache in his elbow which did not seem as bad as the sting of his grazed legs. Scribonia was still beside him but Herodes had gone.

"Well, my son. How do you feel?"

"Much better, Mother," he said simply. He turned an anxious face towards her.

"Argoutus is well now?" he asked.

"Yes, my son. It was only a passing sickness – he sleeps now."

"Oh, Mother," cried Tomas, "It was my fault. I could have killed him."

"No, no," smiled Scribonia, "You were not to blame. He had been up too long. Herodes said he was overtired. Now do not worry. He will be fine tomorrow."

"Then I must go to him," said Tomas firmly. "I have not yet had my punishment."

Scribonia leaned over and laid a soft kiss on his forehead.

"My love," she whispered, "I am sure you have had punishment enough. I know you did not mean to be rude – you were confused. Is your lesson learnt?"

"Oh yes, Mother," said Tomas humbly, "I shall never be rude to anyone again."

Scribonia smiled to herself. "I think that is a rash promise, Tomas, but I believe you will try at least. Now go to sleep. I will send someone to sleep beside you so that you will not be alone. If you need anything, send for me."

Scribonia rose and blew Tomas a kiss as she left the room.

The sun had set and a clear blue light of approaching night hung around the room as Tomas stared into the half-light. He heard footsteps soft and gentle like a bird's wing and he turned his face to the door.

Through the gap stepped a young girl. Her black hair gleamed with the soft light from the atrium behind her. She seemed to Tomas at that moment to glide towards him. Her face, half hidden by the shadows, seemed like a beautiful marble statue –

pale and still. From it great deep brown eyes seemed to sparkle and gleam. Gentle ruby lips moved from pure transparent skin. She was very young – maybe only his age – and when she spoke her voice seemed to caress the air around him.

"I am Cleolia – your slave." She sank like an autumn leaf to the floor beside his couch. "Whatever you need I will provide – never fear, my Master, I will not leave you, however dark the night or rough your sleep. Be calm, I have come only to serve you."

Tomas gazed dumbstruck at the beautiful child. His head was light with the sleeping draught and as he floated off to sleep the vision of her rose in his mind like a portrait to be stamped upon it forever. Her gentle words sang in his brain like a lullaby and his heart beat faster. Cleolia knelt by the couch, her wide innocent eyes steadfastly held to her young master. As the minutes drifted into hours her head bowed and her eyes flickered. Laying a gentle hand on the boy's, she floated off into sleep and in her dreams she felt strength and power emanating from the young boy. Between the children a drifting bond joined up and in the quiet hours of the long night their lives became inexplicably, but indestructibly, entwined.

Chapter 3

As the summer skies grew cloud laden with approaching winter, the family of Argoutus, Scribonia and Tomas made plans to leave Rome.

Argoutus had grown stronger but the sounds of the arena drifted into his room and made him restless. Marius saw this and came to him one day with news.

"Argoutus, my friend," he said solemnly. "There is a legion going to Gaul. Seven mighty ships will sail to the harbour of Forum Julii. There they will disperse to build a new city up from the port. I want you to go with them. The sea trip and the new land will help heal your body and mind and give you strength to take up your life again. Here you are Argoutus the great gladiator – there you will be what you wish. I will pay for your trip and Scribonia and Tomas can travel with you. There Tomas will continue his education and Scribonia will care for you. I am offering you a new start, my friend."

Argoutus and Scribonia had talked long into the night, but by the small hours they had made up their minds. A new life in a new country as Freedmen appealed to them and it was an opportunity they might not get again. The days following Tacitus' visit had been easier for them both. Scribonia was happy to see Argoutus less tense and when the suggestion of travel had arisen it was clear that the gods intended it. Scribonia was sad to leave the home she had known all her life but she saw how difficult life was now for Tomas at school. When he had returned, Laetus still ignored him and the other free boys and girls seemed reluctant to accept him. As the son of a great gladiator and a slave like them

Tomas had been very popular and his young mind found the changes in attitude around him hard to understand and even harder to accept.

By the end of the summer term Tomas had recovered but only went back to school for a few days before the summer break, and for the first time in his life the new autumn term had found Tomas reluctant and anxious about his return.

His arm had healed well and the scars on his knees faded quickly in the hot sun. It had been a magic summer for Tomas with his new playmate and friend Cleolia. At first, the relationship between them had been strained by Tomas' desire to be a friend and Cleolia's convictions that she was his slave. Gradually she had learnt to relax and one day she had agreed to go swimming with him in the clear, cool lake about two miles from the centre of Rome. They had set off at dawn carrying a water bottle and a basket of fruit and meat. Cleolia had insisted on wearing her rough servile sarong while Tomas, stripped to the waist, wore only a split leather skirt over cotton briefs.

They had hurried along the Via Cardo to the great city wall and passing out of the West Gate had followed the road to …………. After travelling along the busy road they had left it and began to climb the lower slopes of a hillside. Here trees gave some shade but still beads of perspiration decorated their young bodies, and when they came under the first tree Tomas flopped down and pulled Cleolia down beside him.

"Let's rest a little," he said, smiling at her. She smiled back and sat looking at him with her pure, steadfast gaze.

"Why do you stare at me?" asked Tomas.

"You stare at me!" she retorted happily.

"Do I?"

"Yes, an awful lot. I stare because you do so. Why do you stare?"

Tomas lay back in the brown, dry grass. He watched her, sitting over him, her dark eyes flashing with happiness.

"I cannot believe you are real."

Cleolia put out her hand and touched Tomas' cheek. "See, I'm real," she laughed.

Tomas shook his head and the sun glinted through the trees and sent a shiver of gold across his curls.

"No – I mean … well, you're mine – my slave and I never expected to have a slave of my own, and I like you as well."

Cleolia laughed again. "There is no law against liking your slaves. I won't vanish because you like me. I like you too."

"Will you always be my slave, Cleolia?" he asked seriously.

"I suppose so. Although when you get older you'll have hundreds of slaves and I'll just be one of your old ones. You'll probably sell me off then …"

"No, I shan't do that, and you're not old. You are the same age as me, aren't you?"

Cleolia jumped to her feet. "I shan't tell you how old I am. Ladies keep that a secret."

"You're not a lady, you're a child like me."

Cleolia grew quiet. "When I am a lady I want to wear beautiful clothes and braid my hair with flowers." She leaned down and gathered a handful of tiny buttercups.

"Do it now," said Tomas.

"Do what?"

"Braid your hair with those tiny flowers. They match your hair."

"My hair isn't yellow, it's black."

"I know, but I mean they suit it. Go on, show me how you'll be when you're a lady."

Cleolia dropped to her knees and, gathering her long hair, she began to plait it. But when she let go to pick up the flowers her thick tresses burst apart again.

"I can't," she said sadly. "I need a slave."

Tomas scrambled up from the ground.

"I'll be your slave," he said.

"Boys don't braid hair, silly," she scoffed, but when her eyes met Tomas' she saw a sadness of rejection pass over them.

"Well, all right then."

Ever since that night when he had first set eyes on her Tomas had wanted to touch her dark hair. Now that he had permission he felt suddenly shy, but he knelt behind her and looked at the long tresses. The deep colours within them seemed to Tomas like the sparkle of jewels and he stayed still, gazing at the smooth, silky sheen that cascaded down her back.

Cleolia shook her head. "Go on then," she said impatiently. "You'll never make a slave if you take so long."

"It looks like charcoal with jewels in it," murmured Tomas, still spellbound.

"Oh come on, Tomas, or I'll change my mind."

Tomas stretched out his hand and took hold of the dark mane. It was so soft and yet so heavy it made his breath start, but he gamely tried to plait it although he had no idea how it should be done.

Cleolia put a hand up to her head to help.

"You first make it into three, Tomas," she said impatiently, "Then twist one bit into another like this … that's it. Now when you get to the end turn it up and fix it with the comb."

Tomas tried his hardest but the hair seemed to have a life of its own. Every time he thought he had managed it and let go it all tumbled down.

Cleolia started to giggle and Tomas' frustration dissolved into laughter, and he pushed her hair to one side and scattered it about with his hands, shrieking with mirth. Cleolia tried to wriggle away, but Tomas grabbed her shoulders and she fell back against him. They rolled into the grass and wrestled like young cubs – half in fun, half seriously, until they ended up in an untidy heap. A silence fell on them – their young bodies and bare skin against each other – a magic seemed to pass between them and for once Cleolia felt it too.

Tomas found his hand was against the girl's bare shoulder and he let himself savour the softness of her skin as he caressed it.

"Your skin's very soft, isn't it?" he said, a little shakily. Cleolia stayed silent.

"You are very beautiful already – you don't have to wait until you are grown up," Tomas continued softly, letting his hand wander over her neck and shoulder.

Cleolia stirred a little. "Am I beautiful?" she asked very quietly, "Really?"

For a moment neither of them spoke. Then Cleolia moved her body so that she was looking straight into Tomas' eyes.

"I don't feel like your slave now, Tomas. I feel more … like … like a friend."

"More than a friend?" Tomas asked, returning her look.

Cleolia paused a moment. Then her face lit up with a bright smile that made Tomas catch his breath again. "I feel close to you," she went on happily, "Like your sister."

Tomas grinned back but something inside him felt a little disappointed, though he didn't know why.

****

A little later Scribonia and Argoutus had called their son to them.

"Tomas," said Argoutus, who now stood shakily, leaning on a pillar. "We have some special and exciting news."

"Yes, Father?" said Tomas, looking at his father. He was conscious of the whiteness in his skin behind high points of colour on his cheeks.

"My son. Marius has kindly, very kindly, asked if we would like to leave Rome …"

"What!" Consternation and distress flashed across Tomas' face as he glanced from one parent to the other.

"Wait, wait, my son," smiled Argoutus. "Wait until you hear what I have to say. Now, Marius is a good friend and he is anxious that I should recover fully. He has offered to send us, all three of us, to Gaul. There we can make a new start as Freedmen and we can stay as long as we wish. Rome will give me a pension and we will have a good home. There are many Romans there and Forum Julii is a big city. You will meet new friends and go to a new school."

"But … but …" Tomas' eyes were wide with anxiety, "But what about Cleolia?"

"What about Cleolia?" asked Argoutus.

"Will she come too?"

Argoutus looked solemn. "I do not feel that it is reasonable to expect Marius to pay for your little slave. After all, you are much better now and have no real need of her. You will meet new friends in Gaul – at your new school. We shall take other slaves. You will be happy."

For a second a flash of anger crossed Tomas' eyes. Then he swallowed hard and spoke firmly.

"Father, I .. I do not want to go to Gaul. I am happy here. I wish to stay in Rome. Please, Father ...!"

Argoutus limped carefully over towards the central couch and lowered himself into it. He waved his hand to call Tomas to him.

"Now, my son. You must listen clearly. I did not ask if you wished to go – I told you we are going. Your mother, you and I. You do not have a choice, my son. At the next full moon your family moves to Gaul and you are part of our family."

Tomas swallowed hard. Tears shone from his young eyes and he glanced anxiously at his mother. She smiled back.

"It will be good, Tomas, really."

Tomas looked down at his shoes. He wanted to shout and scream at them but he knew that would be wicked. He tried hard to think of something sensible to say. All he cared about was Cleolia. She was the best and dearest friend he had ever had. His mind flew to picture a great galleon taking a legion off to Gaul with his parents and him standing on the deck, watching Rome get smaller and smaller. On the quayside he saw a little girl, Cleolia, standing sadly, waving. Tears on her cheeks, waving with her tiny hands, her jet black hair shining in the sun. He saw her getting smaller and smaller, a tiny forlorn figure. And himself leaning over the rails to watch her for as long as possible, straining until she became a tiny dot and then gone forever.

His mother interrupted his thoughts, as if she had read them.

"Tomas, my son. Is it leaving Cleolia which makes you so sad?"

Tomas raised his eyes a little and nodded. He didn't trust himself to speak.

Scribonia turned to Argoutus. "Shall we tell him?" she asked gently.

"Tell me what?" asked Tomas, a grain of hope rising in his heart.

Argoutus nodded to his wife. Scribonia moved over to Tomas and knelt down in front of him.

"You will have a playmate soon, Tomas. A real brother or sister."

Tomas looked up, bewildered.

Scribonia smiled. "Yes, Tomas. I am to have a baby soon."

Tomas' mind raced. A baby! He had seen lots of babies, mostly crying. Boring little live dolls – they never spoke and it took them a long time to grow up. A strange feeling rose up in his mind – one he hadn't felt before. He felt angry and hurt but he didn't know why. All he knew was that he didn't want to have a brother or a sister: Cleolia was his sister and she was enough. Suppose it was a boy! Suppose he had a brother who would become a greater man than him. Whatever would he do? He looked up at his mother. Her face was a picture of delight. He knew he must at least try and be pleased.

"When will it come?" he asked.

"Not until the winter, Tomas. We will travel to Gaul. We will settle in and then prepare for the child. In six months he or she will arrive."

"How will it come?" he asked.

Argoutus coughed and Scribonia turned to look at him. "Scribonia, leave us. I will instruct Tomas. He is old enough to learn."

Scribonia went over and kissed her husband on the cheek. Then she turned and walked from the room.

Argoutus patted the space beside him.

"Come here, my son. Sit beside me. I will explain everything to you."

Tomas moved over and sat beside his father.

"Now Tomas," said Argoutus kindly, "Do you know anything about the birth of babies?"

"Yes, Sir. I know that if a man and a lady love each other and live together they have children. The lady grows fat and then a baby is taken out, but I do not know how, Father. Is Mother to be cut?" His big eyes were full of anxiety and horror.

"No, no, my son … But let's start at the beginning. When the man and lady live together they do something together which makes a seed grow in the lady's abdomen. That seed changed into a baby and when the time is come the baby is born. Ladies have a special place where the baby grows and a special place like a hole which gets big enough for the baby to pass through.

"What do you do to make a seed?" Tomas asked.

"Tomas, you know that you have a phallus but that girls do not. When you are older you will understand more of loving but … the man puts his penis into the special place. It is good and very pleasant for both. The seed from the father passes through and joins that of the mother. It is called sex. It is a special and beautiful gift from the gods. It is how you were made. It does not always work but if the gods wish it a child is conceived. When you become a man you will understand better because there will be a stirring in your loins and then you will want to find a young girl of your own age!" He paused. "You have seen the dogs climb upon each other. All animals do it – in fact, all creatures. It is the way of making new lives, and you have seen the cat with her kittens. Of course some animals have many children but with people it is generally only one. You have heard of Romulus and Remus who founded Rome. There were two babies from one mother, called twins because they were born of the same mother on the same day and at the same time. As you know, they were lost and found by the she-wolf who brought them up. You have seen the statue, haven't you? They are feeding from the wolf. You were fed from the milk your mother made in her breasts.

Tomas listened in silence. He did really know something of it from Laetus at school.

"When shall I become a man father?" he asked.

"When you are about thirteen years old then your voice will lower and you will grow hair on your face and body. Then you will have your pubescence ceremony and be officially a man. After that you will finish your studies and begin to work. Once you are a working man you may take a wife and begin a family of your own."

Argoutus was silent. Tomas still looked down.

"Father, may I take any woman for a wife?"

"Yes, my son, as long as she is a Roman citizen or a freedwoman."

"So I could not marry a slave."

"No, my son. But as a freedman you may take a slave for sex."

"Then she would have a child?"

"Not always – there are ways to stop it – but we will talk more of it when you are older."

"Father. I am sorry that I do not wish to leave Rome. I have never been across the sea. It is a little frightening."

"Yes, my son. I understand."

"Father," Tomas paused. "Father. May I ask you another question?"

"Of course."

"Did you and Mother want another child? Am I not a good son for you?"

Argoutus laughed. "Of course you are. But Scribonia and I wanted to increase our family. We would have had other children before but I was at gladiator school. Tomas, you do not welcome other brothers and sisters?"

Tomas' eyes flashed wide at his father. "You will have more than one?"

"I hope so, Tomas. It is good now that we are free and in a new country."

"I feel confused, Father. So much is to change." He paused. "If only ….."

"What, my son?"

"I want to be with you and Mother of course, but Marius and Julia seem to be family too … and … and there is Cleolia. She is like a sister to me. I want them all with us."

"I understand, my son. Marius and Julia are good friends and we will all miss them." Argoutus stopped for a moment and then put a hand on Tomas' arm. "Is it leaving Cleolia that causes you distress, Tomas?"

Tomas raised his eyes and looked straight into those of his father. He nodded. "I don't want to leave her. I never had a friend like her before … she is special to me and … and … when I am a man I wish to marry her."

Argoutus let a smile pass his lips, but he saw how earnest Tomas was so he looked serious again.

"One day, my son, you may change your mind. A good friend in childhood is not always a good wife when you grow up. Things do not always stay the same. That was why you asked me about slaves for marriage, I suppose. Well, in Gaul things may be different – I really should not worry about it now. Now you should think of all the good and exciting times you will have in Gaul and about all the new friends you will meet. Be happy, Tomas – all the future lies before you. There is no time for sadness and worry."

"But Father, Cleolia ..."

"Tomas, be silent," Argoutus interrupted. "Think no more of this girl. Now go and help your mother in the kitchen – she will need your help. Go, go."

"Yes, Father," said Tomas, rising from the couch. "I will go," and he walked sadly from the room.

That night when Tomas had gone to bed he lay awake worrying about Cleolia. Not only was he losing her but what would she do? She might become a slave to another boy. The thought brought tears to his eyes and he began to cry quietly in the darkness.

He did not hear the door open and Cleolia step in. Her hair was braided in a long plait and she wore a long, rough nightgown of pure linen. She tiptoed to Tomas' bed and knelt beside it. Tomas was weeping and she could hear him. She put out her hand and touched his soft curls.

"What's the matter, Tomas?" she asked softly.

Tomas jumped and turned over to see who it was. His tear-stained cheeks shone in the half light from the lanterns in the passage.

"Oh Tomas," Cleolia murmured. "Poor Tomas. What are you crying for?"

Tomas sniffed. It was sad that Cleolia had found him like that, but she had, and there was no use pretending.

"It's nothing important," he lied. Seeing her lovely face looking so anxious and concerned for him made the tears flow again.

Cleolia put her hands up to his face and wiped his cheeks with her gentle, slender fingers.

"It must be, Tomas. Are you hurt?"

Tomas shook his head.

"Well, whatever is it? Tell me, Tomas. I could help."

"Oh Cleolia … no, you cannot." Suddenly he knew he had to tell her. "It is so terrible. Cleolia, my dearest friend, I am to go away. Not just a short way but over the sea to Gaul."

"For how long?" asked Cleolia.

"Forever," cried Tomas, a sob escaping his lips. "Oh Cleolia, what shall I do? I must leave you in Rome. We will never see each other again …"

Cleolia stared at him for a moment then she rose to her feet and began to pace up and down the room. Tomas watched her miserably. Suddenly she stopped.

"Tomas," her voice was strong and firm. "Let's get this straight. Am I right in thinking that you do not want to go to Gaul because you don't want us to part forever?"

"Yes, Cleolia, you know that is the reason. If you came I should not mind, even though my mother is to have a baby. I am not pleased about that but I expect I shall get used to it. But to leave you …" he stopped. "Cleolia, you are my best and only true friend and I had decided I would marry you when we grow up."

"Marry me!" Cleolia looked amazed. "But I am just a slave."

Tomas had sat upright and was now crouched on the bed with his knees in his hands. He jumped off the bed and grabbed hold of her.

"I don't care. Most girls are stupid and silly. You are sweet and kind and beautiful, so I shall marry you."

A little sparkle of mischief crossed Cleolia's face. She pushed Tomas away.

"Suppose," she teased, "Suppose I don't want to marry you."

Tomas looked surprised and crestfallen all at the same time.

"But you must!" he cried. "I want to marry you."

"A lady has to agree," said Cleolia. "My grandmother told me."

Tomas thought for a moment. Then he said, "Are you my slave?"

"Yes."

"Must a slave obey her master?"

"Of course."

"Then I order you to obey me and marry me."

Cleolia laughed. "Actually I expect I should agree because I like being with you – you're nice, Tomas."

Tomas suddenly became serious again. "So now you know why I was crying because I am to go away to Gaul and leave you behind."

Cleolia nodded. "Yes, I see ... but crying won't help. We have to make a plan."

Tomas raised his eyebrows questioningly.

"When you grow up you could come back and get me," Cleolia suggested.

"Would you wait until then, because you might find someone else?"

"I won't, I promise."

"But, Cleolia, it would be years. I am nine next week. It will be four years before my pubescence. Then I have to finish my studies and get a job so that I can save the money to come and get you. I will be at least twenty by then. That's ... eleven years. I don't want to be away from you for eleven years ..."

Cleolia was silent for a moment. Then she cried. "I know, I've got it." She began to hop round the room with excitement.

"What?" he asked again.

Cleolia grinned and spoke very quietly.

"We'll run away."

"Run away," Tomas echoed.

"Yes…" Cleolia pulled Tomas towards the bed and sat on the edge. "Sit here." Tomas sat beside her.

"If we run away they will have to go without you. Then when they've gone we'll come back and live with Marius and Julia, just like now."

Tomas thought for a moment.

"It means I'll never see my parents again."

"No it doesn't, silly. It means that when you're grown up we can go to Gaul and see them. We might stay there then because we're grown up and can do what we like."

Tomas still looked doubtful.

"I wouldn't see them for an awful long time."

Cleolia said, "Well – it's me or them. Either you won't see me for a long time, or them. You have to choose between us …"

Tomas relaxed. "Actually, I don't really have to choose, because Mother and Father will have another child so they'll be too busy for me anyway."

"When will they?"

"In the winter. Then father told me all about making babies so that when you and I marry I'll know what to do."

Cleolia looked at him sideways.

"What do you have to do?"

Tomas looked a bit embarrassed. "I can't explain."

"Why not?"

"Because Father told me so your mother will have to tell you."

"I haven't got a mother, you know that."

"Well, your grandmother, then. That's how it works – men tell boys, ladies tell girls …"

"Well I know, actually." She bent nearer to Tomas. "I've seen the statue in the …"

"Which one?"

"The one by the door. There's a man there doing it to a lady. Tulia showed me." She hesitated, "It doesn't look very nice," she added.

"Father says it is," said Tomas, "And he should know. They made me that way."

"Is everyone made that way?" asked Cleolia.

"Yes."

"So I did have a mother once. I must have."

"I suppose so. Perhaps she's dead."

"I'll ask Grandmother," said Cleolia firmly, "And we won't think about it anymore because we've got to work out how we're going to run away."

"Well, at night is best."

"When are you supposed to be going?"

"Soon, I think."

"Well, we'll have to find out exactly. Then we'll know how long we've got to get ready."

"We'll need food and clothes, I suppose, and a tent would be good."

"Yes – because we should stay away as long as we can … just to make sure they've gone … Oh, Tomas, isn't it exciting!" and she danced round the room once more.

"Sshh," said Tomas "You will wake everyone. Go to bed now and I will see you tomorrow. I will make a list of things we need."

"I wish I could write," said Cleolia, "I am rather stupid at school."

"You don't need to be clever," said Tomas. "I shall be clever and you can be beautiful. Now off you go."

Cleolia stopped and came near him.

"You may kiss me if you like," she said, putting her face up to his. "Now we are to be married," she added.

Tomas looked at her lovely face. She had closed her eyes and her porcelain-like cheeks looked fragile, with such clear skin gently painted with pink. Her lips were pursed and they looked a little like red rosebuds. Suddenly Tomas felt shy and awkward. He reached over and dropped a casual peck on her cheek.

"Do it properly," said Cleolia, opening her eyes.

"No," said Tomas. "Not until I grow up. Little boys don't kiss on lips. It's silly. Now, Cleolia, go to bed. I order you," and he turned and walked to the bed.

Chapter 4

A few weeks later Cleolia and Tomas made their escape. It was early morning and they crept from the house and into the beginning of yet another hot August day.

Tomas went first, a strong canvas bag slung from his young shoulders carrying all their provisions. There was dried fruit, salted meat and a leather water pouch. He wore his newest loincloth and his strong sandals with a toga tied loosely about his waist. Behind him stepped Cleolia, young and fresh with ripe cherry cheeks and excitement shining from her dark eyes. She, too, wore strong leather sandals and with them a gown of pure linen, tied round her waist with a long sash she had found at the back of one of Scribonia's chests. Her heavy thick hair was pinned back to show her tiny ears encrusted with Scribonia's earrings which Tomas had given her to wear. In her hand she carried a small basket stuffed with a knife, a spoon and two wooden drinking beakers, each wrapped in clean linen napkins. She had also secreted a phial of lavender oil and a long piece of liquorice. Beneath them lay a small wood and cloth doll. With years of cuddling, playing and squeezing its features were worn thin but she could never be parted from it. In its hard, rough chest it carried the little girl's heart, all her sorrows and joys. She never went far without it and although Tomas had told her to leave it behind she knew firstly, that she could not and secondly, that he would not understand. Cleolia's mother had died giving birth to her and her father had gone away. She had loved her grandmother who had raised her, but despite this she had always felt the years between them hard to accept and the love had never been a complete one. So when life was hard or cruel, when she was tired or hungry or when she saw other children with their mothers, Cleolia had turned to her only safe companion who she felt loved her with a special love, and she would grip the doll and made it her comforter. She knew that Tomas was leaving his mother for her but she was not ready to discard the object which had calmed her distress and listened to her childish tears for so long.

"You don't need a doll now," Tomas had said. "You've got me now," and he had dismissed it with a wave of his hand. Cleolia had felt tears pricking at her eyes but she'd turned away and stayed silent. Her nameless doll would come and that was an end to it.

They passed through the great city at seven o'clock when the hills before them seemed like great purple heaps of sand and the trees breathed soft scents into the air. They followed the road towards the western gate. Leaving the straight via, they walked in silence along a dirt track which led to a farm. Their route was not aimless but sure, as Tomas had planned every detail of their escape.

After a few minutes they saw the low barns and high buildings which housed Garius' farm animals as well as himself and his wife. Every day Garius would rise early and load his cart with vegetables for the market and Tomas had watched him and seen him leave with the donkey pulling the long cart. He and Cleolia approached the first barn and could hear the noises of shovelling. They crept nearer and then sat down with their backs against the wooden walls to wait.

"Shall we have breakfast?" Cleolia whispered.

Tomas looked annoyed. "No, Cleolia. We must keep our food for later. Now, hush."

She leaned back, subdued and in silence, her basket still lightly grasped at her side. The noises in the barn continued, then after about twenty minutes silence fell and Tomas put his ear to the wall.

"He's gone," he announced. "Come on."

He got up and carefully moved round to the far side of the barn. Cleolia followed. When they reached the great door, they slipped into the dim shadowy silence of the building.

"There you are," said Tomas quietly. "He's loaded the cart and now he's gone for his breakfast. We'd better hurry and get in. He won't be long."

The long wooden cart was standing in the centre of the barn. A great orange cover was tied over it to protect the vegetables piled high inside. A rough seat was slung between the shafts, between which stood a sad eyed donkey chewing straw.

Tomas went round to the back and lifted a corner. A strong, earthy smell breathed out and made them catch their breath.

Tomas put a foot on the wheel and pulled himself up. He turned and gave Cleolia a hand up. Then he pushed a foot into the pile of sacks and pulled the little girl down after him. Even with the cover off it was dark and cramped between the sacks and Cleolia shivered with fear.

"It's very lumpy and I can't see," she whined.

"Don't complain," ordered Tomas. "We have to have a bit of discomfort – stowaways always do."

"What's a stowaway?" asked Cleolia.

"We are stowaways," Tomas answered. "We're taking a lift but the man does not know. Now be quiet and help me pull the cover over us."

When they had done so, they were plunged into complete darkness as well as the discomfort of their damp, cramped surroundings. The smell of the earth was even stronger now and Cleolia shut her eyes to drive off the sickness which rose in her throat. A sack was pushing into her back and as she wriggled away she found her face up against Tomas' shoulder. Comforted by his nearness and the feel of his warm flesh, she felt better. They huddled together in silence for what seemed like hours and then they heard footsteps, and a man's voice grumbled at the donkey.

The cart moved suddenly and Cleolia felt her foot squashed by another sack. She bit her lip and kept quiet. After all, this running away had been her idea and if it meant staying with Tomas she would have to put up with it.

Another jerk sent the two children hard against the side of the cart and Cleolia let out a squeal. The rattling of the cart over the rough ground drowned the noise but Tomas looked crossly at her. She put her mouth to where she thought his ear was and whispered.

"How long do we have to travel in here?"

Tomas whispered back. "We must stay until he reaches the outskirts of Ubis Now be silent, Cleolia."

The journey was one that neither of the children would ever forget. For over an hour they rattled and crashed about, bruised by the heavy sacks. It grew terribly hot and their limbs shrieked out to move and stretch. The dark became damp and steamy and the smell dreadfully powerful. It made Tomas nauseous but he kept his mind on other matters and tried not to give in to his churning stomach. The heat grew under the thin cover as the sun rose higher in the sky. Thirst gripped them but they could not move sufficiently to reach the water bag. At the first stop Cleolia was sure that they had reached their destination, but then they heard the voices of the city gate guards and realised they had only then reached the city boundary. Cleolia began to weep quietly but Tomas held her hand and she tried to be brave.

At last when the two felt that they must surely die of thirst and heat, the cart began to slow once more. By now Cleolia saw lights swimming before her eyes, even in the dark, and her heart was beating so fast that she thought it would burst through her chest. There seemed to be no air in the cart and she struggled to breathe. The cart stopped. The noise of its creaking and the clatter of the wheels on the cobbles of the street had been so loud that for a moment they found it hard to hear anything. Gradually sounds came to them of a market in full swing. Men and women shouted, other carts rattled past and mules and donkeys snorted. Somewhere a pig grunted and a cock crowed. They could hear Garius talking to someone and then the cart swayed suddenly as he jumped down.

For a moment Tomas was afraid. He had carefully planned how they would get into the cart at the farm but he had not thought about getting out again. If Garius threw off the cover they would be exposed and doubtless captured.

But luck was on his side. They heard Garius' voice die away as he went into a nearby tavern.

"Let's get out of here," said Tomas into Cleolia's ear. "When I push the cover up, jump out and run. Follow me. Ready?"

"Yes," whispered Cleolia, but her voice was dry and weak like her throat and no sound came out.

"Grab your basket. Don't leave anything behind. With luck no one will see us."

However when Tomas took a deep breath and threw back the cover he found himself looking straight into the eyes of an old man who was walking past. For a moment the child and the man stared at each other, both as surprised as each other, then Tomas scrambled over the edge of the cart. For a second his legs refused to work and as Cleolia joined him on the rough ground her legs buckled under her and she fell to the ground, spilling the contents of her basket across the road. Cleolia cried out and began scrambling out onto the cobbles to gather her things. Tomas started to run off but then he glanced over his shoulder and saw her.

"Leave them," he cried as he dashed back and grabbed her hand. Cleolia was just reaching for her doll when Tomas wrenched her away. A crowd had gathered and an old lady reached down and picked up the doll.

"No, no!" screamed Cleolia, both at Tomas and the old lady. She scrambled to her feet and pulled free of Tomas' hand. Moving to the woman she grabbed the doll shouting, "Give it to me. It's mine."

The woman held firm and glared at the little girl. Cleolia glared up at her. She froze. The woman's eyes were black and deep and set in an olive wrinkled skin. To Cleolia she seemed like an evil witch and without letting go of her doll she screamed and pulled harder.

"Let her have it," shouted a man in the crowd and the other people clapped and joined in.

A tall, thin man leaned over and grabbed Tomas by the arm, as Cleolia finally wrenched the doll from the woman's hand, threw it into her basket and began to run. Around her the crowd thickened and she dodged about trying to find a way through.

Tomas was struggling hard with the man and all at once he kicked at his shins. The kick found its mark and the man let go of Tomas with a scream. Tomas snatched at Cleolia and pulled her with him under the belly of the donkey and away down an alley. From the alley they sped into a quiet, wide square where a fountain bubbled and gushed. They rounded the fountain and dived through an open gate. A high villa stood in front of them and a large, fat, grey-haired woman in slave's garb was scrubbing the steps. Tomas pulled Cleolia down behind a high hedge.

When he had caught his breath he whispered angrily, "You stupid girl. You nearly got us caught." He glanced down at the doll's foot protruding from the basket. "And I thought I told you to leave that thing at home."

Cleolia swallowed. "I want a drink," was all she said. Tomas peeked out of the bushes. The slave was still busy on the steps and did not seem to have seen them.

"Stay here," he ordered and he ducked away and crawled to the villa gate. The square was still empty. He turned round and beckoned to Cleolia. She got to her feet and, holding tightly to her basket, she joined Tomas in the square. Together they hurried to the fountain where they drank eagerly and washed their faces and sweaty bodies in the cool water.

Suddenly Cleolia stopped and said, "Tomas, where's your bag?"

Tomas hid his face in the water. He straightened up at last with water dripping from his chin and hair.

"I left it in the market," he said, "Like you should have done."

"But now we haven't any food!" said Cleolia flatly.

"It was stupid to get caught just for a bit of meat. We'll have to get something here."

"We haven't any money," persisted Cleolia.

"I know that," replied Tomas, shaking himself like a wet dog. "Stop whining. I'll get some food, don't worry."

"Will you steal food, Tomas?" Her eyes were wide with horror. "That's very wicked."

Tomas leaned over and put his face near hers. "Shut up. You're just a pest. Stop nagging me. I wish I hadn't brought you."

"But Tomas, we only ran away so that we could be together."

"Yes, I know," grumbled Tomas. "I didn't realise you were going to be such a nuisance ... and as for that stupid doll ..."

"Perhaps we should go home again," said Cleolia softly. "Then you can go to Gaul and I'll stay in Rome and I won't be a nuisance to you ever again." She swung round, stamped her foot and picked up her basket. She called over her shoulder. "I think you are a horrid, spoilt boy and I shan't marry you after all. Goodbye." And she walked off towards the alley through which they had first come to the square.

Tomas hurried after her and swung her round to face him. He looked at the little girl's face. Streaks of dirt decorated her forehead, water dripped from her hair and he could see tears collecting in the corner of her eyes. Her mouth was set firm and she stared up at him. All Tomas' anger faded.

"I'm sorry, Cleolia," he said quietly.

A tear left Cleolia's face and trickled slowly down her cheek.

"Forgive me?" Tomas asked kindly.

Cleolia wiped her hand across her face and she nodded.

"Now," said Tomas, regaining his authoritative air. "Let's assess the situation."

He took Cleolia's hand and went back to the fountain where they sat down on the rough stone edge.

"We have lost our food."

"You have," interrupted Cleolia.

"OK, I have," continued Tomas. "I lost the water pouch too, which is probably the most important, although there are plenty of fountains in the towns." He paused, looking towards Cleolia's basket. "What did you bring apart from that doll?" An edge touched his voice when he said it but Cleolia ignored it.

"I've got a knife, a spoon and a cup."

"Nothing else?"

"Well, ... a piece of liquorice and a phial of lavender."

"They're not much use! No real food?"

The little girl shook her head. "I thought you'd bring food."

They were silent for a moment.

You haven't any money, I suppose?" Tomas asked.

Cleolia shook her head again.

"Then we'll just have to steal food, I suppose. It can't be wrong if we can't live any other way. Perhaps when I'm older I could repay it."

As he spoke a group of teenagers entered the square. One wore an adult toga but the others still wore the clothes of children with gold nametags round their necks. The oldest boy was perhaps fifteen and the others thirteen or fourteen. There were six of them.

They paused to glance at the two children and then the older one, who was obviously their leader, called to them.

"Who are you?"

Tomas and Cleolia remained silent. Both of them instinctively felt the malice in his voice and felt uneasy. One of the younger boys came over to them. He looked angry and Tomas stood up and moved in front of Cleolia.

"He asked you who you were," the boy snarled in a threatening tone.

"I am Tomas and this is Cleolia, my slave." Tomas could not summon up the courage to look the boy in the eye.

"Your slave, eh?" the boy sneered, pushing Tomas to one side and looking Cleolia up and down.

"She's a bit young," he remarked, poking Cleolia with a sharpened stick he had taken from his belt.

Cleolia's eyes flashed. "I'm ten!" she said, pulling herself up to her full height and glaring at the boy with indignation.

"Hey!" the boy called over his shoulder. "This kid's got spirit. Perhaps we should teach her a lesson, eh Flavius?"

Tomas felt the fear creeping up his body but he wasn't going to show it.

"Leave her alone," he shouted, making to grab the boy. The boy laughed and shook his arm free. The other boys moved towards them, making a circle round them. Cleolia still stared straight ahead but her hands were trembling.

Tomas pushed towards her and one of the boys grabbed him and thrust him against Cleolia. Tomas regained his balance and put an arm round Cleolia.

"Please leave us alone," he said as firmly as he could. He was now very afraid but determined not to show it.

"Leave us alone," mimicked the oldest boy in a whining voice. He looked round the assembled gang. "Let's have a bit of fun. It doesn't matter if they're only babies, we could show the boy what a girl slave is for," and he laughed and put his face very close to Cleolia's. "But not here. Someone might see us. We'll go up to the back of the temple."

The boys grabbed at Tomas and Cleolia who struggled and spat and kicked. However, they were no match for the strength of the group of boys and in the end they let themselves be dragged away.

Tomas kept his eyes searching for a way of escape. He had no idea what the boys intended but he knew it was not good and he knew that he was responsible for Cleolia's safety. He looked round in case there was someone for him to appeal to. They passed an old man crouched beside a doorway but although Tomas shouted, the man did not even look up.

They soon came to the great Temple of Minerva with the great goddess gazing down at them from the portico. Several people were climbing the steps.

Tomas shouted, "Help!"

The oldest boy kicked him angrily. "Shut up!" he warned.

A man climbing the steps looked over his shoulder but resumed his climb up the wide steps.

The boys dragged the children round the side of the temple where a broken gate led to a patch of waste ground at the back. A tall fig tree laden with fruit provided the only shade and the two were dragged beneath its branches which bowed down to the ground. Once beneath its shade they were well hidden from view.

The boys picked up a piece of rope which lay discarded on the bare grass and began to tie Tomas to the tree trunk, while another boy held Cleolia. Tomas wriggled and struggled and succeeded in plunging his teeth into one of his captor's arms. The boy screamed and hit Tomas hard across the face with the back of his hand. Tomas' lip started to bleed and a vivid bruise appeared on his cheek.

"Stop it!" shouted Cleolia. "Leave him alone."

The boy laughed and the one holding her said "The slave cares for her master .." and they all laughed again.

The boy finished tying up Tomas. "Are you hungry?" he asked with mock concern. "Well, have a fig or two," and he grabbed a handful and began shoving them into Tomas' mouth until he started to choke.

"That'll keep you quiet," he remarked as he turned his back on Tomas.

The boys moved away from the tree onto a small patch of grass beside a wall. One of them had Cleolia held fast in an arm lock and they gathered round her.

The eldest boy ordered: "Take her clothes off!" The boy holding her let her go and she started to run and dodge to escape them. Each time she neared one of the boys he put out a hand and ripped off a piece of clothing until she stood stripped naked with bowed head, tears of shame glistening on her cheeks. Raised by her grandmother to be modest and decorous, she had never bared her body to the opposite sex. The very horror of being naked, not only in front of these boys but even worse in front of Tomas, her master, passed through embarrassment and touched the child's mind as no less than evil. She stood frozen with shame, her tears flowing silently onto the ground.

"Make a good circle so she can't escape," ordered the boy. He stepped forward. "Look at her boys. She's a fine little one ... not a hair to be seen, all smooth," and he put out a finger to prod her. She shrank back and was pushed forward again by the boy behind her. This became a game and the boys prodded and twisted and pushed her until she fell to the ground, dizzy and sobbing.

Tomas had succeeded in spitting out most of the figs and he began to shout and struggle once again.

One of the boys turned and picked up Cleolia's loincloth, using it to gag Tomas. "Shut up kid and watch," he muttered. "You'll learn something." The boy aimed a kick at Tomas' groin. Fortunately his aim was poor and the kick missed its mark, only bruising his thigh, but Tomas knew he was outmatched and there was nothing he could do to help his little slave. He watched with rising pain. He felt helpless and ashamed that he had brought her to this thing. The bruising of the ropes on his wrists and ankles, the suffocating pull of the gag were nothing to the suffering of his heart. It rose like a great stone in his chest and he swore to himself that when he was grown he would return and kill her tormentors just as his father had slain Ovilium. And at the thought of his father the child in him broke out and he began to hear his own silent crying. "I want to go home. I want my mother and father." He tried to close his eyes against the pain but they always flew open again and he saw before him the picture burning into them of his little girl being hurt and humiliated in front of him. He saw, as if in slow motion, the tall boy tear away his tunic and reveal a swollen loincloth. He watched horrified as the boy discarded it and exposed a strong, rigid organ. He saw him step towards Cleolia. He saw him touch her soft, innocent flesh in a grotesque caress. He watched the other boys hesitate before they, too stepped nearer to watch. A little nervous laugh escaped one boy's lips.

"She's too young, Flavius," he ventured hoarsely. "Let's go." Another nodded. "Come on, Flavius. We've had our fun. She's only a baby!" Awkwardly they began to back away but the boy had taken hold of Cleolia by the hair with one hand and pulled her to her feet. With the other he thrust his phallus towards her face. "Have a taste of this," he muttered.

One of the other boys called, "No, Flavius, don't."

For a moment Flavius glanced round him at his friends.

"What's the matter? Are you afraid? Are you just a crowd of cowards? You heard the boy. She's only a slave."

Unable to tear his eyes away Tomas heard the little girl give a single animal scream and she collapsed like a rag doll in the boy's grasp.

Flavius dropped her to the ground with a disgusted snort. Then he knelt down and roughly pulled her legs apart. Tomas knew that she was unconscious and he sent a silent prayer to the gods that she had been given oblivion at least. But one of the boys had moved over and taken Flavius by the shoulder.

"She's no good, Flavius. Come on." His voice shook fearfully.

Flavius shook him off. "If you haven't the stomach for it, kid, go home," he shouted. The boys now stood around, unsure, hesitant, half excited,, half afraid.

Flavius suddenly plunged his fingers between the child's thighs. He held up his hand on which glistened a drip of blood.

The boys began to back away. The joke had suddenly gone sour and they sloped off guiltily.

Flavius called to his friends. "Look at this! Sorry kid," he shouted towards Tomas, "She isn't a virgin anymore," and he laughed a low, manic laugh.

Tomas tasted the bile which rose in his throat. He tried to swallow but began to choke. A boy close to him went near and ripped off the gag and began to untie him. As he did so, Tomas was violently sick. The boy dodged away, swearing. He glanced at Flavius for a moment and then turned and ran. The others followed.

Tomas closed his eyes.

A second later there was a piercing scream. For a moment Tomas wasn't sure if it came from him or Cleolia. His eyes flew open and it took seconds for his vision to clear. But when it did he saw Flavius clutching his groin and writhing in agony. It was he who had screamed. The man that Tomas had seen on the temple steps stood a foot or two away from him. As Flavius opened his mouth to scream again the man aimed a kick into the small of his back and let out a long curse.

He turned and met Tomas' gaze.

"I'll be with you in a minute, boy," he called and moved towards Cleolia's prostrate form.

He picked up the child's discarded stole and wrapped it round her before lifting her into his arms.

Tomas heard his soft murmurings. "Come on, little one, you're safe now." He carried her towards the fig tree and laid her down in the shade. She stirred but her eyes remained closed and her body limp as a rag doll.

The man finished untying Tomas. He was trembling and found it hard to stand. The earth beneath his feet seemed to rock like the sea and his eyes were at once clear then cloudy. He leaned against the man who dropped to his knees in front of him and looked deep into his eyes. In those eyes Tomas saw true concern and a deep peace which he did not understand, but which drew his trust completely.

"Are you all right, child?" he asked kindly. "Did they hurt you?"

Tomas shook his head.

"Can you walk?" he asked.

Tomas nodded. His voice seemed lost but his strength was returning.

A groan from behind them attracted their attention.

The man rose to his feet. He crossed to where Flavius was trying to get up. He stood over him.

"You disgusting animal!" he snarled. "I'll deal with you later." He kicked the boy over onto his face and, taking the rope with which Tomas had been bound, he tied his hands roughly behind his back. The boy struggled and let out a stream of foul language.

The man turned away.

"I'll come back and deal with that beast later," he said, calming. "Now, boy, where do you live?"

Tomas swallowed and hesitated. "Not in Ubis, Sir."

The man nodded. "OK."

Leaning over, he gathered Cleolia up into his arms and motioned to Tomas. "Come on, boy. I'll get you home and my wife will see to the little girl." And the bedraggled trio moved away, leaving Flavius cursing and squirming with his face in the grass.

Chapter 5

An hour later Tomas sat in a cool villa, clean and sweet smelling, sipping a tall glass of iced water. Opposite sat Selenius, their saviour, serious but kind.

"Tomas, my boy. You have had a terrible experience and the little girl a horror which may affect her all her life. You are too young to be away from home alone. Tell me why you came here."

"Will Cleolia recover?" asked Tomas anxiously.

"She is already much better. My wife is caring for her but she needs her own mother."

"She has not got one," said Tomas. "She is an orphan. She lived with her grandmother until she became my slave."

"Your slave? I thought she was your sister," cried Selenius.

"No," said Tomas, "I have no sister. I was ill with a broken arm and Marius gave her to me to help until I was better, but she has stayed in the house. She helps my mother but she and I … we are very close. She is more than a sister to me. I am going to marry her when we are older."

Selenius smiled to himself but continued.

"Is your father a citizen of Rome?"

"He is a Freedman."

"Tomas." Selenius leaned closer. "Tell me where you live. You must return home."

Tomas looked into the warm eyes. He knew they must return home and that he had failed his girl, and tears rose in his eyes.

"I am a Freedman of Rome," Tomas began stiffly. "My father is ….," his voice dropped to a whisper, "My father is Argoutus, the gladiator!"

Selenius' eyes flew open in surprise.

"You are the son of Argoutus?"

Tomas nodded.

"Did you run away?"

Tomas dropped his head and a tear fell onto his knee, but he nodded.

"Why?" Selenius was astonished. "Why did you run from Argoutus? He is a great and worthy man."

"Oh Sir," said Tomas, raising his head and meeting the older man's gaze, "I did not run from my father. He is the best father in the world!"

"Then why?"

"Sir, my father is not well."

"Selenius nodded. "I have heard," he said gently.

"And we are to go to Gaul for his health and my mother is to have another child ..." Now that Tomas had started, the words tripped off his tongue in a rush. "And they will not take Cleolia and we cannot be parted. As I told you, we are betrothed, Sir. I cannot leave her in Rome so we ran away. Then when my mother and father have gone we can return to Rome and live with Marius and Julia as we do now, but ..."

"Tomas, you have suffered an ordeal and Cleolia more so at the hands of that wicked Flavius. Do you understand how seriously he has hurt Cleolia?"

"I think so," Tomas whispered.

"You must take her home, Tomas. You know that, don't you?"

"Yes, Sir," murmured Tomas. "I have been a wicked fool. I have not cared for Cleolia as I should have."

"Tomas, do not be too hard on yourself. You did not, could not, have known that this would happen. "You are only a child."

"I am ten, Sir. When I am grown I shall return here and slay Flavius." Tomas had drawn himself up to his full height and Selenius felt pity and affection for the proud young boy. He hid a smile.

"However, Tomas," Selenius was serious again. "It was wrong to run away. Think of Argoutus and your mother. They will be distraught with worry. Did you seriously expect that they would go to Gaul without you? Can you imagine the agony they will be experiencing, believing their only son is lost?"

Tomas sniffed. "Yes, I do now," he said quietly. "They will be very angry. My father will beat me for sure." There was silence for a moment and then Tomas looked up at Selenius. "And I will deserve it," he added.

"That, Tomas, is for your father to decide. Now I shall send word to Argoutus that you are safe and when Cleolia is fit to travel you must return home."

Again there was silence for a while. Then Tomas asked, "Sir, why did Flavius do those things to Cleolia? And how was it you came to help?"

Selenius ignored the first question but he smiled gravely. "I saw and heard you call as I went into the temple but I did not realise what was happening. I began my prayers and suddenly I heard a voice in my head saying, "Those children are in danger," and I remembered the look upon your face. I thought my mind was playing tricks but I found myself worrying so I came out to look for you. Minerva is good to you, Tomas. If I had not come ….," his voice trailed away.

"Would he have killed her?" asked Tomas, his voice shaking.

"I suspect that he did not intend to kill either of you. But if he had continued in his evil way he could have killed Cleolia. We must hope that she is not badly scarred."

"Scarred?"

"Not a physical scar but a mental scar. An experience like that could affect her all her life."

Tomas looked puzzled. "I do not understand what he was trying to do. He shouted that she was not a virgin anymore. I thought virgins were unmarried ladies …."

"Tomas, when you are older you will understand. You may ask Argoutus but it is not my place to tell you."

Suddenly Tomas put his head into his hands and shuddered. When he looked up there were tears coursing down his cheeks.

"Oh, Sir," he cried, "I was so afraid!"

"Tomas, my boy," said Selenius kindly. "It has been terrible for you as well as Cleolia. Try not to think about it. You are safe now."

He put an arm round Tomas' shoulders.

"May I see her?" Tomas asked.

"Perhaps later. My wife is with her. Come with me and we will send word to Argoutus. Then we shall see how your little girl is, and Tomas, we must prepare a sacrifice for Minerva. We must thank her. She sent me to help you."

****

The journey home to Rome was very different from the one when they had travelled in the vegetable cart. Then Tomas had a heart filled with hope and an excitement bred of adventure. Now his heart was heavy with fear and despair. He was ready to accept his father's wrath and the inevitable caning did not seem as hard to bear as the pain he felt for Cleolia.

Selenius was a wealthy man and a fine carriage with grand horses awaited them. Tomas had been taken to see Cleolia but she had turned her face away from him. She was pale and her skin seemed to have lost its soft hue. When he spoke to her she had tensed up and whimpered like a wounded dog. Tomas was hurt and distressed and Selenius had hurried him away and told him to be patient. Cleolia, he had said, would recover but she was not yet able to talk to him. Now he watched as Selenius' wife lifted Cleolia into the carriage and settled with the child cradled on her knee. The little girl appeared to be asleep but Tomas could sense that she was only pretending. Why would she not look at him? He had not been the one to hurt her, but maybe she blamed him for taking her to that place and not being able to save her. He climbed into the carriage and sat beside Selenius, and looked out of the window sadly. Why was it so hard to live an easy life? Why did grown ups always win? He could feel Cleolia across the carriage on the lady's knee. He thought about the day when he had tried to braid her hair. How she had skipped around the room like a young fawn with delight in her eyes. Now she seemed like a marble statue, tight and silent. The magic which had risen from her was gone. Had he done that? Had he killed the wild spirit he loved?

Tomas looked away again. Tears pricked at the back of his eyes and he fought hard to prevent them escaping. Beside him Selenius put out a hand and touched his knee gently. Tomas turned to him and he gave him a kindly smile and squeezed his knee. It will be all right, his eyes said. Tomas was grateful and tried to smile back, but sadness enveloped him and he turned away again.

The journey continued in silence. Cleolia did not move at all and the lady just held her close.

After what seemed like an age the carriage was rumbling through the familiar streets of Rome, up past the Forum until they pulled up before the tall villa where Marius and the family lived.

Tomas saw his mother's anxious face at a window. Then she disappeared as she ran to the door to greet them.

Selenius opened the carriage door as Scribonia appeared on the steps. Tomas climbed out and hesitatingly let his gaze rise to meet his mother's eyes. But as he did so he found himself rushing forward into her embrace. Scribonia hugged him to her and he collapsed against her in a heap of weeping. When at last he drew back he saw that she was crying too.

She bent down so that their faces were close.

"Tomas, how could you hurt us so?" she said sadly.

Tomas swallowed hard and said, "Mother, I'm sorry. I know now how wrong I was to run away. Oh, Mother, it was terrible, I was so afraid."

"It's all right now, my son," said Scribonia through her tears. "We must thank the gods that you are safe." She rose and, keeping her hand on her son's shoulder, she turned to Selenius standing patiently by.

"Thank you, Sir, thank you so much for delivering my son to me. I am eternally grateful."

She then turned her gaze to the lady holding the motionless figure of Cleolia in her arms.

"Please bring the child in," and she led the group up the steps and through into the Atrium.

By the central fountain sat Argoutus, supported by cushions on a couch. His face was still white and drawn but his eyes were bright. To one side sat a wizened old lady who rose as the group entered. She ran to Cleolia and took her from the lady. Cleolia cried out and clung to her as the old lady's tears dropped onto her face. Although Tomas had never seen her before he guessed it was Cleolia's grandmother. A tall, strong slave girl standing in the shadows came forward and led the old lady from the room. Tomas watched them go, his eyes still bright with tears.

"Is she going home?" he asked his mother softly.

"For now, Tomas," Scribonia answered.

Tomas tore his eyes away from his mother and turned his attention to his father. He took a deep breath and wiped the tears from his face with the back of his hand. Then he stepped forward away from his mother and walked towards his father. Stopping in front of Argoutus, he looked steadily into the eyes of the man whom he loved beyond anyone.

"My father," he began, his voice strong and loud. "I have been a wicked son to you." He paused while Argoutus met his firm gaze. "I was very wrong to run away. I did not think or realise how much worry it would cause you and my mother. I allowed Cleolia to be hurt ….," here his voice wavered a little, "And I am truly sorry. I will accept my punishment. It is well deserved."

Argoutus was silent for a moment, cursing his new weakness which made emotion hard to control. A lump rose in his throat at the sight of his young son, so beautiful in his youth, and pride for this child seared his heart.

"My son," Argoutus found his voice. "I do understand that you did not mean to cause your mother and I distress and worry. I understand that you have realised your wickedness in exposing the young girl Cleolia to such danger. You could both have been killed. You owe your life to Selenius here. But whatever you have suffered it does not excuse punishment and as a true Roman and father I have a duty to punish you."

Tomas dropped his gaze.

"And so," continued Argoutus, "I have decided on that punishment. I am not strong enough to beat you myself but I have asked Marius to do it for me. It will be done now while Selenius and his wife are here to witness your humiliation. And you will swear never to see Cleolia again."

Marius, who had been standing unseen in a shadowy corner, stepped forward. He carefully removed the rope from his waist and approached Tomas, who stood still with bowed head.

Marius put a hand on Tomas' shoulder. "Remove your clothing," he ordered firmly and clearly.

Tomas looked up. "All of it?" he asked quietly, his eyes big.

"All of it," said Marius loudly.

Tomas discarded his tunic, then his shoes and stood in only his loincloth.

"Remove your loincloth!" ordered Marius, "And hurry. You are keeping us waiting."

Tomas opened his mouth to protest but then thought better of it. As his hands released his loincloth a gentle blush of embarrassment travelled up his face. He hung his head. To be seen naked was a dire punishment in itself and his heart beat fast with humiliation.

Marius turned to Argoutus. "How many strokes?"

"Six," he replied. "If he needs more I shall tell you."

Marius led Tomas to a low table and made him lean over it. Then Marius raised the rope and brought it down on the child's clear flesh. Gritting his teeth against the pain, he had raised his eyes to show his bravery, but as the rope found its mark he shut them hard to hold back the tears.

Chapter 6

The tall, bronzed youth rolled off the girl's naked form and flopped over onto his back. For a moment he stared skywards, his gaze cloudy with spent energy. Then his eyes closed and a long anguished sigh escaped his lips.

The girl rolled away from him and jumped to her feet, shaking her long hair where it stuck to her shining breasts. She ran a hand through it and pieces of grass and dust fell to the ground. She began to brush other bits from her body and then she leant over and picked up her gown from the ground.

"What's the sigh for, Tomas?" she asked. Tomas ignored her. She moved across and flicked him with the corner of his gown.

"Tell me."

Tomas only responded by pushing the gown away. He grunted.

She leaned closer, putting her face close to his. "Why?" she persisted.

Suddenly Tomas was on his feet. With a flash of fury in his eyes, he grabbed the girl by the shoulders and shook her so that fear crept into her eyes. His face a few inches from her face, he shouted.

"I sigh because you are an awful lover. You do nothing for me, nothing!" He pushed her away viciously so that she fell heavily with a cry.

Tomas turned away from her, grabbed his loincloth and shirt from the ground and stamped away across the dry stubble of the field. He did not look back. The frown on his face deepened as he walked and suddenly tears pricked his eyes. It was not the girl's fault. He knew it but it was easier to blame her. She meant nothing to him. She was just a convenient sex partner. Over the past few years there had been many but always he was dissatisfied, unfulfilled.

Now twenty, Tomas had grown into a tall, bronzed youth with bleached blond curls. He had completed his education in Gaul and had now started to work the ground which Argoutus had been given by the Emperor. For about half his life he had lived in Gaul and the land and the people had become his land and his people. He had never returned to Rome and as time passed he had lost interest in going back. Except … in his mind he knew the only thing that pulled his heart towards Rome, that same thing which even now was the cause of his present distress: Cleolia. He had struggled so hard to forget. Sometimes he thought he had succeeded but every time he lay with a girl the childish face and tear-stained cheeks haunted him with such force that the act was never finished, never completed. He had tried to block out the pain and the memory by going from one girl to another. He never had trouble finding willing partners. They were all eager to please the strong youth with the look of a Greek god. Some no doubt fell in love with him but to him the sexual pursuits were all geared to physical satisfaction. His heart was never touched. When he had left Rome, he had sworn that he would never marry unless the miracle happened and Cleolia became his. He had not seen her since her grandmother had whisked her away on the day of his humiliation, and only a few weeks later the family had left for Rome without her.

He now stamped across the wide road and looked into the distance. The road stretched endlessly into the horizon, cutting a cleft between the rolling mountains. He was immediately pacified. He loved this land more than he would ever have believed. Here was clear air and a certain freshness in the sun as though it was truly new each day. The oppressive heat of Rome had not followed him north. He remembered that journey from Rome by ship. Three days of rolling sea and restless nights. His mother constantly sick and pale. Argoutus quiet and sad.

The boat had stunk, stunk of human excreta and sweat. The water was stale and warm. Many people were ill. Tomas had soon escaped up onto the deck. Here he felt released, free. He had stood on the deck watching the might of the waves. He never felt afraid. He was exhilarated by the wildness and sound of the sea. He watched the wind tearing at the sails and throwing the boat forward. When it calmed he watched the ripple of the bow wave, and wanted more than anything to dive into it. To feel the cool sweetness of the sea around him. The clear blueness swirled with darting fish and he wanted to swim with them. Just to feel that cold world full of life flickering around him. He hated to be called inside to sleep. He wanted to sleep under the clear, silver night sky where he could hear the sound of the water and see the insects dancing on the lanterns.

They had arrived after three days and clambered onto the shore. Tomas had held himself back, almost fearful of the moment when he would set foot on his new home, his new land. He had leaned down to feel it and a man had kicked him as he disembarked. The man had sworn at him but Tomas was savouring this moment and did not hear. His mother had grasped him impatiently by the hand and pulled him onto the earth which was to be his. He had stood up and looked around. He let go of his mother's hand and ran across the dockland to where a tall oak stretched its branches over the hard ground. He ran straight to its hard, firm trunk and thrust his face against its rough bark, his arms stretched round it. He had clung to it like the lost child that he felt he was and it seemed to breathe comfort from its scent and welcome him with its sturdiness. At that moment Gaul had captured him as a willing prisoner. He had fallen in love with the warmth and gentle scent of the land and knew in that instant that it was his.

His mother had pulled him roughly from the tree and shaken her head. Tomas had changed so much since the day he had returned from Ubis and stood his punishment like a man. He was a strange child these days: half child, half adult, and she found it hard to understand him. Ever since that day when he had stood naked before them all and taken his beating she had watched him with concern. He had become quiet and morose. He had cried bitterly on the day they had said goodbye to Marius and Julia. Tomas had clung to Julia and cried as if she was his mother. But Scribonia knew he was crying for Cleolia. They had not seen or heard from her or her grandmother again. It was as if she had ceased to exist. Only once Tomas had spoken to her about the child, and when she told him she knew nothing he had turned away into his own world and nothing seemed to comfort him. Now as she dragged him from the oak, she felt a sudden lifting of his spirit and he had smiled at her with his boyish smile that she had almost forgotten. His young face had taken in her own weariness and weakness and he had squeezed her hand.

"Here everything will be good," he had said, and he had strode ahead as they followed a slave to find their new home..The journey was long and arduous but they travelled on a cart pulled by two horses and stopped at every town for refreshments and rest. At last they arrived at a small town between tall hills which spiked out of the ground like giant teeth. Here they met with an old centurion who welcomed the party to his home. The emperor had made arrangements for the family to take over a strip of land to the \South of the town, Here they would have a house built and Argoutus would oversee the running of the farm which would surround it.

Tomas had stood and watched the land beating with the sun and felt the warmth like a welcome. He had touched the soft earth and ran it through his fingers. A peace had descended on him and he knew he was to be happy here.

A few weeks later Arria had been born. She was a strong, healthy child with the same blond curls as Tomas but with deep brown eyes and a sallow skin. Tomas had tried not to show his relief that the baby was a girl and instantly adored her. He had run home from school to play with her and make her toys and teach her to walk. She had then run on her fat little legs after him. She returned his love with a strong adoration and wept when he returned to school after the long summer days had vanished. Soon she had joined him at school and showed herself to be clever and quick witted. When Tomas had moved on to military college she wrote long letters to him with her round, childish hand and sent slaves to deliver them, always wrapped with parcels of home cooked goodies and sticks of liquorice she had fashioned herself from the black root.

Tomas went to visit her now, dressed once more in his loincloth and rough shirt. He greeted her with a hug as she slipped out of the house and ran to meet him. Then he swung her onto his broad shoulders and bent down as he carried her carefully into the kitchen.

His mother, with her prematurely white hair, dried her hands on her apron and smiled at her son.

"Go and wash, Tomas. The meal will be ready soon. And take Arria with you. She could do with cleaner hands."

Tomas nodded and crossed over to the archway. He called a slave to fill a tank with warm water and moved into the bathhouse. Arria sat on the stone edge and watched him bath. They were never shy of each other and she watched happily as he let the water cascade over him, washing the toil of the day and of the girl from him. As he washed his genitals he cursed her. "Whore!" he whispered, and his eyes flashed with anger.

Arria saw the anger cross his face but she dismissed it. It wasn't for her and when Tomas came dripping towards her and began to scrub her hands she saw that it was gone. In its place was the faraway look she had come to recognise.

"Do you miss Rome, Tomas?" she asked with childish innocence.

Tomas looked into her eager eyes and smiled. "Yes a little, but not so much Rome, really."

"What then?" she asked.

"Just a friend. A little girl very like you are, Arria. She was a special friend to me. I miss her sometimes."

Arria paused and then asked, "Did you love her, Tomas?"

Tomas nodded. "Yes, I loved her. But we were just children."

"She'll be grown up now."

"Yes, I suppose so." He was silent for a moment as if he had only just realised it. "She was a year older than me … ten years old. She was my slave."

"How could you have a slave when you were only ten?" blurted out Arria. "I have no slave." Her eyes flashed with indignation and Tomas smiled to himself.

"I had broken my arm getting help for Father who was very sick. It was a sort of reward, really. She nursed me and we became friends."

"Did you play together?"

"Yes, often, and had adventures." Tomas sighed, remembering the horror of that day.

"What happened to her?" Arria asked gently.

"She was hurt. It was my fault. I had to promise never to see her again. So when we left Rome she stayed behind." Tomas was trying to keep his voice light.

"Did you want to bring her?"

"Yes, very much. That's why ...," his voice trailed off and he stayed still, looking at the floor.

For a moment Arria was quiet, respecting his silence even though she did not understand the sadness it held. After a time she said softly, "It was only a child's promise, Tomas. You are both grown up now. Why not go and get her?"

"She wouldn't want me now. She must have blamed me."

"She might not if she loved you," persisted Arria. "Did she ever say she loved you?"

"Yes. We even agreed to marry one day. That was why we ran away."

"You ran away!" Arria was delightfully scandalised. She leaned closer. "Tell me about it."

"When I heard we were leaving Rome, I knew I should never be allowed to bring her so we decided to run away. But some wicked youths caught us and hurt her and I was too small and afraid to stop them."

"Did they hurt her much?" Arria persisted.

"Yes," Tomas replied shortly, "Very much. Some kind man rescued us and took us home. I was beaten and Cleolia was taken away and I swore never to see her again."

"Why?"

"Because Argoutus wanted to punish me. He was right."

Arria jumped down from the wall and sat in front of him, her eyes filled with the dreamy romance of childhood.

"Maybe she's waiting for you, Tomas." She put her hand out and touched his cheek. "You will never be happy without her. Even I know that and I am only nine!" Her young eyes sparkled. "You must go, Tomas."

"And if she does not want me?"

"Then you can come home again on your own."

A voice called, breaking the moment. Tomas rose and gathered the child to him.

"Come on, little one. It's time to eat." And he carried her off into the Atrium.

Chapter 7

That night Tomas lay in bed staring at the coloured splashes of the ceiling. Little patterns of marble seemed to laugh at him in the stillness and he closed his eyes.

Should he go, he wondered? Should he break the oath and go? Would Cleolia want him? He knew if he never went he would never know. Could he find her? This jolted his mind. Suppose he travelled all that way to Rome and she had gone. Maybe she was far away by now. Just because she was a slave did not mean she could not have travelled. Whoever owned her could have taken her anywhere. She might have been sold on. But if he never went he'd never know if she cared for him still. Perhaps I am her nightmare, he thought. She might hate him for what had happened to her. He had not seen her again after that terrible night. All he could see was her pale body being touched by that awful boy. He could still hear the screams and then the awful silence, broken only by the boy's wicked laugh. Now he was grown up he knew better what had happened. Hatred for Flavius rose in him. He had sworn to revenge her and now he was miles away. He had failed Cleolia and was failing her still. But Flavius might be gone too. That was only the thought of a coward and Tomas was no coward.

The curtain over his doorway rustled and a dark, tall girl, barely fourteen, stepped into the room.

"Tomas," she called softly, "Are you awake?"

It was Cona, a young slave. She often came to him at night offering her body for his satisfaction. She asked nothing and said little. It was a duty to her like scrubbing a floor. He liked her because she never asked questions. Never queried his impotency.

Tomas glanced at her. She was naked except for a piece of lace which covered nothing. Her raw sexuality seemed to exude from her like a scent. As she approached, Tomas felt a yearning to be lost in her flesh. To forget the torment of his soul. To forget Cleolia. To be free of her. Maybe tonight it would work. Maybe tonight he would let his seed go. Maybe this was the time to rid himself of Cleolia's ghost. He rose on one elbow and cursed loud and long. The girl paused, a little afraid. Then she moved nearer to him. He grabbed her roughly and buried his face in the lace. Through it he felt her readiness, her wetness. He sniffed the crude smell of musk and found himself wonderfully aroused.

Everything left his mind. A wild fire seemed to light up his loins. He pulled Cona to him, dragging her onto the bed, lashing out with his tongue, biting, bruising, seeking out the hidden corners of her raw flesh. He ripped the fragile lace from her. He heard, felt, saw nothing except his own desire. He was unaware of her gasps, of her struggling, knew not if she was eager or afraid: cared not.

He threw her over, pinning her arms wide and plunging into her. He closed his eyes and let his passion rise. He crashed in and out of her, blindly like a drowning man. But as his climax rose, he let his eyes open and he looked into her face. Her eyes were scrunched closed, her lips bitten between her teeth, her cheeks wet with tears and her breath sucked in and out in great gulps. Terror defused her young skin, draining it of all colour. He fell away like a wounded dog, his passion lost in an instant. He rose and stamped over to the window, letting her sobs wash over him.

When he turned she was sitting on the edge of the bed. Her eyes were bright with tears and she held her arms across her breasts and shivered. The trembling began to overcome her whole body and she dropped from the bed to the floor where she lay like a discarded rag doll, racked with misery.

Tomas went over and gathered her up. He smoothed her hair and wiped her face with his hands. Then he cradled her against him and rocked her until her trembling died.

When he could speak he said simply, "God in Jupiter, I'm sorry. How could I treat you so? I am a crazed man. Forgive me Cona, forgive me. I had no right. I am mad tonight. I'm so sorry." Gradually the girl stopped her sniffling and looked up at him silently.

"Forgive me, Cona," he whispered, pleading with his eyes. "You must not come to me again. I had no right to treat you so."

The girl tried to smile. "I'm sorry, Master," she said, "I did not expect ... you made me afraid. I am your slave. It is your right."

"No," Tomas replied. "No. No one has the right. I had no right to vent my crazed mind on your sweet body. No man has the right to." And he closed his eyes to block out the vision of the girl's distress and in doing so saw once again the nightmare of Cleolia lying beneath those evil limbs in that far off square, transfixed with terror. He rose sharply and stood the girl on her feet.

"Go now," he said with what control he could muster. "Go. I will have no more need of you. You are too pure for me. There is evil in my heart. I shall go to the Temple in Glanum and pray for cleansing. Then I shall make arrangements to leave the city."

"Where will you go?" Cona asked, now recovered and composed once again.

"Where I should have gone months ago. I am going to Rome."

Chapter 8

This time Tomas set off for Rome on foot. He had no spare cash for the cost of the boat trip. He knew that his father would willingly have lent him money. He had a very generous pension from the Emperor and there was never any need for Tomas to work, but he preferred it. He enjoyed working the land and was planning to plant vines in the spring. Now there was little work that could not wait and so he had instructed several slaves to maintain the ground until his return. His mother had been unhappy when he told her he was going and had plied him with questions as to why he wanted to go. He thought that she did not really believe him when he had said he was going to see Marius and Julia. She knew there was more to it but held her silence and waved him goodbye with a smile.

Tomas took only his favourite slave, Pybus, with him. It was unwise to travel alone and Tomas needed an escort. Pybus was a young Greek with fiery eyes and an evil tongue. Despite this Tomas liked him. He was only a few months Tomas' junior and had been with the family since their arrival in Gaul. As a young boy Pybus had been surly and ill tempered but he had grown to respect the family. Tomas had taught him to read and Pybus had spent all his free time at the feet of Argoutus, listening spellbound at the old gladiator's tales of valour and battle. Because of the nearness of their ages Tomas and he had become close friends and the relationship was closer than slave and master.

Pybus had grown up calmer but his temper often got him into trouble. Tomas knew that the most important thing he needed in a companion was strength and loyalty and Pybus offered both. He also knew that Pybus did not have very good morals and when it came to disposing of Flavius he would ask no questions. When Pybus showed reluctance to go, Tomas took him aside and bargained with him.

"If you stay loyal and travel with me to Rome, I shall reward you well."

"How well?" the young man asked.

"How does your freedom sound?"

The man's face lit up. "You mean that, Tomas?"

"I mean it."

"Then I'll go for sure," laughed Pybus, gripping Tomas round the shoulders. "I am already your equal. Soon I'll be a Freedman like you and all the world will know."

"You cheeky devil," laughed Tomas.

And so it was decided, and Tomas and Pybus set off in the cool of a December morning to walk to Rome.

It would take many weeks to walk, but Tomas expected that he would soon get lifts part or all of the way. They set off with a ball of canvas as a cover and a roll of bedding. Tomas carried a purse containing a few semestras and a bar of gold secreted under his loincloth.

It was a clear, cool day but the sun shone and the two walked along the shore where the azure seas lapped in a quiet calm. Parasol pines leaned over the beach stretching out to sea, tall and wide, giving shade to the travellers.

Pybus whistled and their pace was eager and their strong legs carried them away from Home and along to where the red rocks of the Esterel jutted down to the sea. They came upon a band of Roman soldiers hauling red stones from the mountains and loading them into a cart. A mangy ox stood patiently tethered to the cart and Tomas approached the centurion sitting under the trees.

"Where are you bound?" asked Tomas.

The man looked up sullenly, then lifted his thumb to the west.

"We're off to Nikia. We'll be going soon."

"Can we ride the cart?" asked Tomas.

"You can ride the stones. It's of no account to me," and the man returned to his mood.

Tomas and Pybus sat down nearby to wait. A lift to Nikia was worth waiting for. The cart would carry them a good sixty miles nearer Rome.

It was hotter now and Pybus stretched out on the grass.

"Since I am to be your equal soon, Tomas, may I ask you a question?"

Tomas grinned. "You may ask. I may not answer but you may ask!"

There was a pause.

Why are we going to Rome?" Pybus asked eventually.

"I guessed that might be your question," Tomas replied but said no more.

"Will there be trouble?" asked Pybus.

"More than trouble," Tomas replied, "There could be murder!"

Pybus thought about this for a few moments. His eyes gleamed with eagerness. A good fight would be just up his street.

"What's it like?" Pybus asked.

"What is what like?"

"Rome, of course."

Tomas leaned back and looked up at the sparkling blue above him.

"Rome is the greatest city on earth. It is full of beautiful buildings including Caesar's great palace. A great river divides the city. There are shops and bars and temples everywhere. The great bathhouse has three baths and great furnaces heat the water for the houses. The streets are wide and full of people and carts and soldiers marching. But the greatest place is the Coliseum. As a child I used to go there after school to see my father fight. I was only nine when he was wounded but I still went on going. It is three times the size of the amphitheatre at Julii. When it is full the whole place pulsates with noise. You can go into the dungeons to see the animals. They are starved, of course, and so they howl and roar and it is very frightening for a child. But despite that I wanted to go and look and be frightened. But then when my father was hurt I went looking for him and found the place where all the dead are kept until they are buried. That frightened me in a much worse way. I just wanted to get away and I don't ever want to return." Tomas shivered at the thought.

"Then there is the circus. It is larger and finer than any other. Chariot racers come from all over the world to race and there are spectacular accidents. There is room for six chariots side by side and when they all try to cut the corner, you can imagine the chaos. I went with Father sometimes but I do prefer the Coliseum.

"And your father fought lions as well as men!" commented Pybus.

"Of course," replied Tomas. He reached over and slapped Pybus on the back. "Why do you ask about Rome? My father has told you so many tales, and you shall see it soon."

"I know, but I like to see your eyes light up when you talk of it. And I hoped you might let slip the reason for your trip ..."

Tomas smiled at him. "Maybe I will, but for now I prefer you to guess."

Pybus pulled a long grass from beside him and bit into it.

"Actually, I know!" Pybus said slyly.

"You do?" Tomas asked with a grin.

"Yes." Pybus sat up and looked down at Tomas. He tickled him with the end of the grass. "It is not the Coliseum or the circus or Rome itself which calls you back. It is something deeper, more personal. Perhaps there is someone? Maybe someone stole your girl! Now you are going back for revenge. Am I right?"

"You said that you knew."

"I suspect that I do. But ...hey Tomas, get up, the cart is ready!"

The two scrambled up with their bags and ran across to where the oxen were just moving off. They threw their things onto the stones and pulled themselves up on the cart.

The rocks were big and red and dusty but in time they managed to wedge themselves fairly comfortably between the great boulders.

"I don't expect you've ever had to ride a cart like this before?" called out Pybus over the sounds of the cart's rattling.

"There you would be wrong, my friend." Tomas spoke almost to himself. And in his mind he continued ... "With the sweetest little girl in the world, before disaster struck." And he sighed and pulled his thoughts away to watch the red hills disappearing behind them.

Chapter 9

The great house of Marius which Tomas remembered was not in fact as large as he had thought. He had left at the age of ten and now, as a grown man, he hardly recognised the tall portico. There were signs of crumbling on the pillars where the weather had washed away the paint. The door opened and on the doorstep stood a small, thin slave. He bowed.

"Yes, Sir?" he said quickly.

"Is Marius the Roman at home?" asked Tomas.

"The master is within, Sir. May I ask your business?"

"No. You may not. Come on Pybus, let's surprise them," and he pushed past and ran into the house.

Marius sat at the long table with Julia by his side and he turned round as he heard the footsteps enter the room. He stared for a moment in disbelief at Tomas and then rose and spread his arms wide as Julia pushed past him and ran into Tomas' embrace.

"Tomas, Tomas, is it you?" Marius cried. "Why, you are such a grown man I would never have known you."

"Marius, my Lord," said Tomas, breaking free of Julia. "Please forgive me for intruding so." He took Marius' hand and clasped it tightly. "It is so good to see you."

"And so good for us, Tomas. Come, come and sit down. Tell us all about what you have been doing. Is your father well? And Scribonia? You have a sister now, do you not? What is her name? Arria, was it?"

Julia butted in. "Tomas, let me look at you. My, what a handsome young man you are, to be sure." Julia looked over to where Pybus was hovering in the shadows.

"And who is this, Tomas?" she said, crossing to Pybus. Pybus bowed low.

"Madam, I am but Tomas' slave. I will go and wait outside." And he turned towards the door.

Tomas, meantime, had come over. "No, Pybus. Stay, Marius will not mind. We have travelled for a long way and we are weary. Marius, may we impose on you to let us stay the night?"

"Of course." Marius clapped his hands and a slave appeared. "Sulla, take this young man to the kitchens and fill his stomach, and bring food here for my honoured guest."

They talked long into the night, catching up on the news. The amphora of wine emptied and was filled again, and merriment and laughter filled the house. At last Julia rose unsteadily.

"Tomas, we must go to bed. The morning will soon be breaking and we must get some rest. We are not young anymore."

Tomas rose and smiled. "I apologise, my friends. The time slipped away. It was so good to be with you again."

"Go to your own room. It is as it was. Do you remember the way?"

"I have never forgotten. I could tell you every inch in detail. I had such fun there. I remember when I was hurt and stayed in my bed for days. Then I got so bored and began to count the tiles on the floor." His eyes gleamed with the memory. "There were 135. I counted them again the next day and there was one less. I hung over the edge of the bed to check beneath it and I fell out. I was hurt and I cried and then Cleolia ..." He stopped. His eyes dimmed and he swallowed hard. There was silence. Julia spoke quietly, moving nearer to him and looking up into his solemn face.

"Is that why you have come, Tomas?"

He nodded his head sadly then raised it. For a second his eyes blazed with a wildness that frightened Julia and made her gasp.

"I came to avenge Cleolia. I intend to find Flavius and kill him."

"It was a long time ago, Tomas." Marius had also risen and moved towards him, his eyes worried. "Better it is forgotten."

Tomas rounded on him. "Forgotten!" he cried. "How can it be forgotten? It has ruined my life and the girl's as well, no doubt." He could not bring himself to say her name again. "I shall see that he suffers. No one treats me or my lovely girl that way and is forgotten. Never!"

Julia spoke gently. "Tomas, this hatred is unjust. Cleolia was frightened but not hurt much. I am sure she has forgotten all about it. And how can it have ruined your life? You have just told us about your good life in Gaul. Do not let a shadow from your past tread on your future."

Tomas' rage had abated. He said sadly, "But it does. It is a nightmare which crashes into my days. It burns under my heart and flames my very soul. I must kill him. Without that there is no peace for me."

"And Cleolia? Do you come to seek her also? You swore never to see her again. Will you go against the oath you swore here in this room?"

Tomas did not answer and a deep gloom descended on the room. At last he turned and walked slowly from the room, turning at the doorway to bid his hosts goodnight.

For a few moments Marius and Julia stood still. Then Marius sighed.

"You know, I believe Tomas was more deeply affected than we realised at the time. He is desperate to release the terror of that day which still haunts him. He was right to come. Maybe he must have revenge before he can exorcise the hurt from his soul. Poor Tomas. He suffers much, it is clear. But of the girl, I am not sure. Is she still in Rome?"

"I do not know. We have heard nothing about her since her grandmother took her away. That in itself is strange. Rome does not keep secrets well. Maybe someone will know where she is." She paused. "But Marius, what will become of Tomas if he kills Flavius? The penalty for murder is death, Marius. We must stop him."

"Come, Julia," Marius answered. "We must rest. Tomas will do nothing tonight and we can talk again to him. Come along." And Marius took his wife's hand and they walked quietly from the room.

The quiet of the night descended on the house, but in the hills the light of another day crept over the earth, changing deep blue to gold. Tomas lay in his bed watching the new day creeping into his room and although he closed his eyes he did not sleep.

Chapter 10

After breakfast, at which there had been no mention of Tomas' reason for coming to Rome, he went in search of Pybus. The slaves lived in a small area behind the main house where they had two rooms which were large and airy. One was used for sleeping and the other for eating. They were seldom able to relax as, although Marius was a good master, they were kept busy from early light until the family retired. Tomas walked into the eating area to find a bleary-eyed Pybus tucking into a plate of poached fish and rice. He looked up and Tomas saw a livid red bruise above one eye.

"Pybus!" Tomas glared at him. "You have been in this house where you are a guest for one night and I see you have been fighting already! What am I to do with you?" He sat down beside the Greek who belched and grinned at him.

"It was a good fight, Tomas," he laughed. "Well worth the pain. For such pain I would travel the distance again and more. You should have seen him, Tomas. He was built like a bull with great ugly features and a long nose which I hope I have shortened a little. He could not match my agility and he will think twice before he calls me a Greek bastard again."

Tomas tried to look angry. "How dare you, Pybus? You will bring disgrace to me and then I shall not be able to call you free. Who was this giant who dared to question your birth?"

Pybus rose and took Tomas to the window. In the yard a great beast of a man stood pumping water for the baths. He looked sullenly at them and shook his fist. His nose was indeed a strange shape and bruises decorated his face. A large swelling closed one of his eyes.

Tomas hid a grin. He looked as fiercely as he could at Pybus. "Why did he call you names, Pybus? What provoked him?"

"Provoked him? Why, nothing!"

"What did you call him, Pybus?"

"I only explained that he was a large man who liked the ladies, or something like that."

"Exactly what?"

"A fucking giant!" Pybus threw back his head and laughed. "Tomas, I wished you had been there to see how his face is changed. Don't be cross. You are only jealous because I found him first." He thumped Tomas on the back and at last Tomas dropped his feigned anger and laughed too.

"Now, Pybus," said Tomas after their mirth had subsided. "We have to go to Ubis. It is a small village about two hours walk from Rome. There we have to find a man called Flavius."

"And when we find him?"

Tomas looked straight into Pybus' eyes.

"Then we kill him." While Pybus stared at Tomas in surprise, he went on. "We shall not kill him quickly with the sweep of a sword but slowly and as painfully as possible." The venom in Tomas' voice caused Pybus to stare even harder. This was not the gentle Tomas he knew. Something behind his simple words filled the Greek's heart with awe.

"Why do we kill him, Tomas?" he asked quietly.

"That is not your concern, Pybus. All you need to know is that he destroyed the most precious thing in my life and in doing so he destroyed a part of me. It happened when I was a child but it was my manhood he has threatened to destroy, and for that he will die." Tomas paused. "I realise that in asking you to accompany me I am putting you at risk.

When I have killed him I shall be a fugitive from the laws of Rome and you also. I therefore give you full permission to remain in Rome and so incur no guilt in this matter. What do you say?"

Pybus did not hesitate. "Tomas, my friend and master. I shall not only accompany you but I will enjoy helping you to kill this demon who has caused you such pain. Let us go."

"Not so fast. I must talk further with Marius. He is worried and although I did not tell him what I intend to do to Flavius he has guessed, no doubt. I want to be sure he will not betray us. Now I know that you are an ally, it may be easier. Come with me and we will talk to him."

They found Marius in the atrium. He rose as they entered. His face was serious.

"Come in, my boy, and you, Pybus. Julia has asked me to talk to you about what you intend to do. Tomas, does this man know what you have come to Rome for?"

"He knows and has agreed to help me. He is a friend as well as a slave. I have told him that I have come here to deal with Flavius. He does not need to know more."

"Last night you also made mention of Cleolia, Tomas. If you fight Flavius, as I suspect you intend, you may kill him and you will not be free to return to find her. It would be too risky. Have you thought of that?"

Tomas nodded. "I have thought of everything. When I have dealt with Flavius I shall return straight to Gaul. Then no one will know from where I came or to where I return. Except of course you and your household. Will you betray me, Marius?"

"Tomas, I cannot condone what you do. It is against the laws of the gods as well as of Rome. However, I love you as a son and I would never betray you and neither would anyone in my household. I will see to that. Although I understand your reasons I do not feel that you should do this terrible thing. If it was in my power to stop you, I would. But I believe you are not to be persuaded. I can do nothing but implore you to be careful. So you will not seek Cleolia?"

"Yes. I believe that I shall. That is the first thing for us to do."

"She may not want to see you, Tomas. Have you thought of that?"

"Marius, I have told you. For the last few months I have gone over in my mind everything about my mission. If I do not seek and find Cleolia I shall never know if she despises me or not. Or even, Marius, if she loves me or not. If she does I shall take her back with me to Gaul. But I am not stupid in my desires. I am prepared to return without her if that is her wish, but I must see her. I must know how she thinks of me. She may have forgotten me, I accept that, but I do not think so. I expect to be associated in her mind with the evil of Flavius which may have scarred her for life as …," he paused, "… as he has scarred me." There was silence in the room for a few moments, then Tomas spoke again. "And now to practicalities. Cleolia went home with her grandmother. Do you know where they lived, for that must be the first place to look?"

"She lived on the Via Sectus. But as no one seems to know her whereabouts I doubt she is still there. By now her grandmother may be dead and she may be enslaved elsewhere. She may not still be in Rome. Now that the Empire stretches across the world she could be hundreds of miles from here. Your search could take you throughout the world."

"I realise that, but I am prepared. Marius, I shall tell you no more of my plans. You must not be at risk. I must take my leave of you and your household. Sadly I may never be able to return but it has been so good to be here once more."

"I wish I could bless your departure, but I do urge you to take great care. It is a very risky thing you want to do and even if you succeed your own life could be in great danger. Will you not take heed of an old man's warning and return to Gaul?"

"Marius, you know that I cannot do that and, do not fear, Pybus is a good slave and indeed a friend. With two of us against one weak man, for that he must be to treat children as he did, there is no need to fear. I want only revenge."

Julia suddenly appeared at the arch. She hurried across to Tomas. "Tomas, my dear one, please consider what you want to do. I know that although you have not said so that you intend to kill Flavius. I beg you do not. It could end in your own death and that is not worth the satisfaction of revenge. Leave things be, Tomas, if not for Marius, for me."

"Dear Julia." Tomas took her to him. "You have been like a mother to me in the past and I would do anything for you, but this is a matter of honour and I am a Roman."

Julia wiped away a tear and smiled bravely. "I understand, Tomas. But take great care. Remember Scribonia and Argoutus. Do they know the reason for your travel here?"

"They may suspect but I have not said. Argoutus is a sick man and my mother grows older. When I return I will tell them the truth, whatever that may be. You may pray for me. That is my wish."

"Oh, Tomas, that I shall do, never fear. Now go and seek out the girl. That at least is safe, but if you find her do not let her break your heart. She may not want you."

"She has already broken my heart and I will accept her feelings. No one can ever know how she has suffered because of me. Now, dear ones, I must take my leave. We may never meet again, but I shall send word."

Tomas embraced both and Pybus shook hands with Marius and bowed low to Julia. She stared hard at him. "What happened to your face?"

"Madam, I had to explain something to Callus. He was not happy."

To their surprise Julia laughed. "It was time someone gave that beast a hiding. I suspect his face is worse than yours?"

Pybus bowed again. "Of that you can be sure, Mistress. And should he require more attention I should be happy to oblige."

"You have a cheeky one there, Tomas," she laughed. "But I trust he is a loyal slave?"

"I would trust him with my life, as indeed I may need to do," Tomas replied. "Thank you for your hospitality, my friends. Farewell," and the two passed through the door and into the street.

Chapter 11

The two made their way straight to the Via Sectus. It was a long street of high villas, divided into sections to support three or four families. Each belonged to a Freeman and his family with a group of communal slaves who lived in a type of one storey lean-to at the rear. They knocked on several doors and enquired for Cleolia but with no success. Within an hour they had reached the end of the street.

"Now what?" asked Pybus.

Tomas stood quiet, thinking. "Did anyone you spoke to admit that they knew or had heard of Cleolia?"

Pybus shook his head. Just at that moment a tall, elderly man in a smart toga, which proclaimed him to be a wealthy Roman, came out of one of the houses. A young boy slave followed him carrying a large package of rolled parchment. They watched him move away towards the centre of the city. Suddenly Tomas turned and patted Pybus on the back, his eyes shining.

"I've got it! That man made me think. He was no doubt a member of the Senate, which reminded me. At the Basilica they keep the latest census."

"Slaves as well?" asked Pybus doubtfully.

"This is Rome, Pybus. Not some potty little state. Come on," and he pushed Pybus forward and together they moved up the street again, towards the main square and the great Basilica which housed all public records and dealt with the general needs of the common people of the city.

In less than ten minutes Tomas and Pybus were climbing the great steps up to the portico of the giant building. Inside it was cool and spacious. Pybus stared round him.

The walls and floor were of Spanish marble. The tall ceiling stretched way above them. In the centre was a long staircase which led to a gallery where the walls were lined with large reels of parchment. Tomas made his way up to the gallery while Pybus followed, looking around him in wonder. A tall man in a Roman citizen's toga was seated at a desk. Tomas approached him and he looked up.

"Sir," Tomas began, "I am looking for the workplace of a slave. She has vanished since I returned to Rome after a long absence. I need to find her. She was a good slave and I would like to buy her back."

The man rose and beckoned the two forward. Then he stopped and looked at Pybus.

"This man waits outside. Slaves are not allowed in here."

Pybus opened his mouth to object but Tomas said, "Go, Pybus. Wait for me in the square." He turned his back and moved off with the man. Pybus went sullenly down the stairs and across the hall. At the main door he paused and glanced once more at the splendour that surrounded him. "One day I shall freely enter any place in the world," and a flash of anger crossed his face.

Pybus waited in the forum, standing watching the people passing by. The crowd was growing fast and he saw a tall but elderly man shuffling along, carrying a large box. As he approached the steps of the Senate he slipped and fell, the contents of the box spreading around him. Pybus went over and began to help the man pick up his belongings. The man thanked him and struggled to rise. Pybus gave him a hand up. The man looked at him.

"Slave?" he asked.

"I suppose so," Pybus replied.

"Well, thanks anyway." He paused. "Want a job?"

"No. I am in Rome with my master. We are seeking to find someone. A slave he had once and wants again."

The man looked at him hard. "It's hard to find slaves. Was it long ago?"

"Yes, years."

"Well, I might be able to help you. Where is your master?"

Pybus nodded over his shoulder. "In the Senate, looking for records."

The man shook his head. "He won't find him there."

Just then Tomas joined them.

"No luck," he said sadly. He bowed to the old man.

Pybus said, "This man claims he might be able to help us, Tomas. I explained why we were in Rome."

Tomas said eagerly, "Can you help? I should be most grateful."

"Come to my home. Your slave can carry my box," and he set off leaving Pybus scowling at him as he picked up the box. They followed in silence.

They arrived at a large but run down villa with broken shutters and decaying walls. The man opened the door and they entered. There was a shuffling and an ancient slave appeared. He seemed confused to see the visitors.

"Canus," said the man. "The men are looking for a slave they have lost some time ago. I thought you'd know if anyone did. But first, a glass of wine."

The slave disappeared and the man turned to Tomas.

"I am Julius. Please sit down." He waved to a dirty old couch. "Your slave can sit on the floor." Pybus glared at him but he did not seem to notice.

"I am Tomas, son of Argoutus. Once a great gladiator."

Julius smiled. "I know of him. I used to watch every match. A great man until ..." he stopped for a moment. "Is he alive?"

Tomas nodded. "Yes. He is in Gaul with my mother and sister. He will never be the same again but he manages."

"I'm glad. Now, explain your mission, young man."

"Well," said Tomas. "When I left Rome about ten years ago we left behind a slave girl called Cleolia. She was little more than a child. Before she came to our household she had lived with her grandmother on the Via Sectus. We have been there but no one knows anything about her."

"Is that all?"

"That is all. Except that I must also travel to Ubis for a different mission and I do not want to be away from Gaul for too long."

The old slave appeared with two cracked glasses of wine. He handed one to Tomas and the other to Julius.

Pybus snorted. "None for me?" he asked grimly.

Julius looked at him. "You are a slave!" he said, contemptuously.

Pybus rose but Tomas held out his hand. "Sit down, Pybus! I should explain that Pybus is a friend as well as a slave and after this journey I shall give him his freedom. Please regard him as such for my sake."

Julius nodded. "Very well." He motioned to the old Canus who disappeared once more and returned with another glass of wine which he handed to Pybus.

"Now, I will tell you. I was for twenty years a slave master. All the slaves were registered with me. I still have the lists although I retired about three years ago. I suggest you go to Ubis and finish your business there. After that return to Rome. I will hunt for the girl and tell you on your return what I can discover."

"I am grateful, Julius," said Tomas, rising. "Thank you for your hospitality and your help. I shall indeed return. Come, Pybus, we must travel now to Ubis." And he bade the old man farewell and walked out of the door.

Pybus followed, grumbling under his breath. "What a man! He is not to be trusted."

Chapter 12

The following morning Tomas and Pybus arrived at Ubis. Tomas had explained to Pybus that Flavius had seriously wronged him in the past which was all Pybus needed to know. They entered the town and made their way to the market square. It was always the best place to start looking for someone as there were always lots of people milling around. Tomas and Pybus separated and began by asking everyone they met if Flavius was known to them. At midday they met up in a local tavern and compared notes. There was little to compare. Tomas had met someone who had spat on the ground at the name but refused to say anymore and Pybus had got into a fight and was nursing a sore ear.

"You are not much help," complained Tomas. "You always let people upset you. Why can't you just get on with the job and forget your precious ego?"

Pybus grinned at him. "I like a good fight."

"Yes, I had noticed. Now please will you concentrate on our purpose in coming here. We need to find Flavius." Tomas had shouted out this last part and a man sitting at the next table rose and walked towards them.

"Yes," he said. "You are looking for me? How can I help you?"

Tomas stared at him in amazement, quite taken aback. The man was tall and thickset. His face was hard and a scar crossed his right cheek. Tomas would never have recognised him had he not looked into the piercing eyes and seen the evil glint that had stayed in his mind for all those years. For a moment no one spoke. Then Pybus rose slowly and deliberately from his seat. He turned a menacing glare at Flavius and said, "Come outside. We have business to settle with you."

"What business?" asked Flavius.

"Are you coming? Or shall I carry you?" Pybus continued.

Flavius turned towards the door and Tomas and Pybus followed. Outside the air was clear and still and the crowds were thinning as the market closed for the day. Tomas had regained his composure and now stepped close to Flavius. He spoke gently.

"Please come with me. I want to show you something."

Flavius turned round, but seeing the two set faces he shrugged and followed Tomas. Pybus walked close behind, watching the man's every step. Tomas took them into the little square where the fountain was still playing and from there to the small patch of garden behind the temple. The fig tree hung smaller than Tomas remembered, but little had changed. It was quiet and deserted.

The man turned. "So?"

Tomas spoke softly but with pure hatred in his voice. "Cast your mind back, Flavius. About ten years when you were a lad. You came here with a group of your friends. With you you brought a boy and girl only ten years old. Do you remember?"

"You must be mistaking me for someone else. I've never been here before."

"You lie sweetly, Flavius. You tied the boy to a tree …," he paused as a flash of memory stirred in Flavius' eyes. "And what did you do to the girl?" Tomas had moved right up to Flavius so that his face was only inches away. Pybus moved behind him. Flavius looked round and saw his escape barred.

"I … I … don't remember," he stammered. Pybus suddenly grabbed his arm and swung it up his back, causing the man to cry out. "It was only a childish game...," he screamed. "Let me go!"

"No, my friend. I have waited ten years for this and I intend to see that you suffer as she did."

Flavius struggled but Pybus kneed him in the small of the back and he let out a groan. "Please let me go," he sniffled. "It was a long time ago. I was just a kid. They got away all right so what's the big deal?"

"I am the boy," said Tomas, rising to his full height. "Then I was just a child: now I am a man and my revenge will be very sweet."

Flavius began to blubber and Tomas spat into his face. "You are no man and never will be. Especially after I have finished with you." There was such hatred in Tomas' face that even Pybus shrank back, but he didn't let go of the wriggling Flavius. He just pulled his arm tighter. Flavius collapsed onto his knees.

"Please," he wailed, "Let me go. I'll do anything ..." and he looked up at Tomas with bright fear naked in his eyes.

Tomas backed away and looked around. The place was still deserted.

"Pybus," he roared, "Bring that piece of shit here. We will tie him to the tree."

Pybus stripped off his belt and fastened it round Flavius and the tree trunk, lashing him securely to it. The two stood back. Flavius opened his mouth to yell but in a shot Tomas picked up a rag and gagged him.

Pybus said, "Shall I kill him, Tomas?"

"Oh no, Pybus. Death is too easy for him. Cleolia is still alive, God willing. This man must suffer as she and I have. We must be sure that he never repeats his crime." He spat again into the dust.

"We are going to castrate him, Tomas?" Pybus grinned. "A fitting punishment," and he laughed.

Tomas held up a constraining hand. "Since that day, Pybus, I have never been able to release my seed. Of Cleolia I know nothing. But, by God, I want him to feel that frustration I have felt and the horror he left in that little girl's eyes."

Tomas put his hand to his belt and brought out a sparkling dagger. He ran his finger across the blade and a drop of blood glistened at the tip.

Pybus clutched him. "Now Tomas," he said, "Be careful. His death could be easily attributed to robbers but they will know this deed was deliberately done. You will be sought out and punished by death, no doubt. Think, Tomas. He could die."

Tomas looked Pybus full in the face. "For myself I care nothing. But for you, my friend. If you wish you may leave. I can do this deed alone."

"No, Tomas. I will not go. But are you sure of what you intend?"

Tomas threw back his head and screamed into the air.

"I will avenge my little girl, I have sworn." He continued quietly. "Now turn your back if you are squeamish. This deed must be done."

When the two turned to Flavius they saw that he was slumped against the tree. He had fainted. "Get water, Pybus. There is a fountain back there. He will not sleep through this …"

Pybus hurried away. Tomas approached the tree. His wild mind was full of hatred as he remembered that day. He felt again his own terror and he saw again the poor little girl lying exposed on the ground. He saw Flavius take out his erection and wave it at her and his heart shivered and tears fell unchecked from his cheeks. Where was she? How would he find her? He loved her as a man in the same way he had loved her as a child and he knew he would never love again.

"Cleolia!" he cried. "I will avenge you." He looked at the man moaning and shaking slightly as he hung slumped against the tree.

Pybus returned and interrupted his thoughts. He approached and threw water into the man's face. Flavius groaned and opened his eyes. Tomas went close and with his knife he split the clothes from the man and exposed his nakedness. The man struggled and succeeded in spitting out the rag. His scream rang out but Pybus hit him across the face and clamped a hand over his mouth.

Tomas stood before him. His voice was harsh with emotion. "I will remove your penis with this knife. Then you will know the horror and the pain you have inflicted on me and Cleolia. Never will you rise again for a woman but your desires will still shriek from your scrotum and real frustration will be yours." He raised the knife and took the miserable organ in his hand. The man's horror coursed through his body and it was all Pybus could do to hold him. But at last he was still and Tomas raised the knife above his head. His eyes were blurred with tears and his hand shook.

"I will avenge her!" he cried and his hand came down, the knife glinting in the sun as it swept towards its goal.

But it fell clear to the ground and Tomas let out a groan of true despair. He held his head and roared.

"I cannot do it. Pybus, I cannot do it." He dropped to his knees and grasped the impotent knife in his hands. He stared at it for a moment and the silence was broken only by the sobs of Flavius. At last Tomas rose and turned his back.

"Come, Pybus," he said sadly. "I am no man and I cannot do it. Leave him. He is not worth the trouble." And he began to walk from the place.

Pybus let go of Flavius who slumped against his bonds and was silent. He ran after Tomas.

"Give me the knife, I will do it."

"No, Pybus. I am content. The swine will remember today just as I have remembered that day. There is no point. If I cannot do it neither shall you. Leave him." He continued to walk away.

Pybus turned and looked at the man. He walked back to the tree and undid the man's bonds. Flavius fell to the ground, still snivelling. Pybus kicked him viciously in the groin and he doubled up, shaking violently. Pybus leaned closer.

"Tomas may be prepared to leave you but I am not. Never forget that I am out there waiting for a chance to kill you. You can never sleep safe, my friend. I am still out here somewhere, waiting." He kicked Flavius again and hurried out of the square after Tomas.

Chapter 13

The two tramped silently along the road to Rome. Pybus started to whistle but Tomas gave him a dark look and he stopped.

"Why didn't you tell me about the girl?" he asked later.

For a moment Tomas was silent, then he said, "There was no need. You would have found out in the end."

"And she was the slave girl that we are seeking, of course?"

"Of course."

"Did he rape her?"

"As good as. He entered her with his fingers."

Pybus swore long and low. "You should have killed him, Tomas."

Tomas turned to him and shouted. "I know that. Do you think I do not? I was as impotent then as I was when I was ten. I let him off. I can't believe it myself. I am a coward, Pybus. A useless worm. We shall return to Gaul and I will try and forget. Not that I ever shall."

"You mean you will not look for the girl anymore?"

"What would she want with me? A stupid idiot with no spunk." He laughed a mirthless laugh. "I should have known I had none."

Pybus said, "I'll go back and kill him, Tomas."

"For what reason? He is no enemy of yours."

"Tomas, you are my friend. Isn't that enough?"

Tomas looked at him wryly. "That I know, Pybus. You don't have to prove it."

An old cart rattled past. "Are we walking all the way to Rome?" asked Pybus. He set off after the cart and jumped easily onto the back. "Come on, Tomas," he called. Tomas began to run but somehow he felt weak and his legs defied his will, and he fell behind. He stopped, and dropped his head. "I cannot even run now," he muttered to himself, standing watching the cart disappear round the corner. He sat down on the grass beside the road. Why had he come to Rome, he asked himself. He had failed to find Cleolia and failed to avenge her. Both his goals failed. He put his head in his hands and found himself weeping with self-disgust and pity. He sat there as the sun dropped behind the hills, hating himself and letting all the events of the last days drift through his mind. Later he let his body fall back and he lay looking at the stars. He cried out to the gods in the heavens, "There is no help for me. Your servant has failed. Let me die, a worthless heap of dung." And as his eyes closed he fell into a deep sleep.

    He woke with a start. He had been watching Cleolia standing weeping beside a fountain and had tried to take her in his arms but they would not move. He sat up and looked about him. The new day was creeping over the mountains, sending beams of light across the grass where he had lain. An old cork oak swayed in the gentle breeze and a bird sang a haunting melody above him. Everything seemed so quiet after the hubbub of his mind. He got to his feet and walked slowly to a stream bubbling beside the road. He took off his shoes and scooped the fresh, cold water into his mouth and splashed it over his face. He swung his head and beads of water flew from his tight curls and danced on the water. There was a flash and a bright kingfisher dived into the stream and came up with a fish in its beak. Tomas stood and let the scents of the morning wash into his soul. He turned his face into the clear blue of the sky.

"Is there still hope for me?" he called to the gods. "Did you make this new day for me?"

He splashed along the stream to where it twisted round the bend, kicking the cool water under his feet. Then he stopped. Lying in the grass beside the stream was Pybus, fast asleep. He stayed for me, thought Tomas, watching the sleeping Greek. He shook himself and pulled himself tall and straight. Then he lifted a handful of water and threw it at the sleeping Pybus. With a roar of anger Pybus was awake and on his feet, looking around him with his wild eyes. Tomas laughed. Pybus tried to keep his angry look, but his face gradually broke into a smile. Tomas went over and slapped him on the back.

"I'm glad you didn't go, my friend."

Pybus put an arm on Tomas's shoulder and grinned at him. "Better today?" he asked.

Tomas left his arm on his friend's shoulder. "I guess so. I went to hell and somehow I came back."

Pybus raised his head and looked Tomas straight in the eye. "Good," he said gently, and the two embraced. Pybus broke the moment.

"Now," he said, brushing himself down. "What now?"

Tomas grinned. "Rome, my friend. We have a lady to find."

A smile broke across Pybus' face. "Maybe two?" he asked slowly, a cheeky grin twitching at his mouth. Tomas laughed. "Well, my friend. I guess you deserve a little relaxation. Lead on!" And the two set off once more along the road to Rome.

***

They managed to get a lift and were in Rome again by midday. It was very hot and humid in Rome and they joined the crowds refreshing themselves in the fountains. Then Tomas bought lunch from a bakery and they sat beside the Tiber enjoying their meal.

"I suppose we should return to Julius and see if he has any news," said Tomas as they finished their meal.

Pybus grunted and Tomas laughed. "Come on." He rose and made off in the direction of Julius' poor villa.

They were greeted by the old slave, who explained that Julius was out. He did not seem to have any further information so they bade him farewell, explaining that they would return later.

"I told you!" said Pybus. "I expect he was inside because he had forgotten what he was going to do. I said he was not to be trusted."

"You are so easily against people, Pybus. I believe he is out. In fact, there he is now." He pointed to the old man hurrying across the street towards them. He was grinning broadly.

Tomas approached him eagerly. "Well?" he asked anxiously. "Did you have any luck?"

"Yes." The old man paused to catch his breath. "Cleolia the slave was sold to a travelling merchant when she was eleven. He is reported to be a kind man and he has taken her with him wherever he goes. At present, if reports are correct, they are away in a distant land."

Tomas' face fell. "Where? Do you know?" he asked.

"No, but I have just been to see a neighbour of the merchant who is expecting them home in a few days. Here is his address, Tomas. If you keep watch on the house, you should see her return later in the week."

"Thank you, thank you," said Tomas, patting the old man on the back and shaking his hand.

Julius looked up at him. "A slave you want to find again, you said?" he asked with a twinkle. "Would she be a beautiful girl, by any chance?"

Tomas grinned and shook his head. "I have no idea if she is beautiful now, but her heart is mine, old man. As I see you have guessed." He put a hand in his pocket and took out a gold coin. "Take this for your trouble."

The man hesitated. "Well, if you are sure. I have very little and Canus and I go hungry some days, so I am grateful." He pocketed the coin and shook Tomas' hand once more. Then he turned to Pybus and held out his hand.

"Serve your master well, boy," he said. "He is lucky to have so faithful a companion."

Pybus actually blushed and took the man's hand. "Take care," he said quietly.

They moved off and the old Julius stood waving until they were out of sight.

"Now," said Tomas, "It is your turn, my friend. Let us find some good company. We must wait for a few days and I shall show you the sights of Rome."

So saying he turned into a side road and then into a dimly lit tavern. When the drinks came, he lifted his glass. "Let us drink to a good time and a bonnie girl for you, Pybus." And the two drank deeply.

Chapter 14

Tomas woke feeling strange. He realised that the problem was not a hangover but nerves. Today Cleolia was expected back in Rome, and Tomas was very nervous. Supposing she didn't want to know him? Perhaps she had a boyfriend or was married. Slaves were often given permission to marry as the children would then be brought up to serve the same master. There was a strange, almost prudish attitude to sexual relationships amongst slaves. They rarely had sex before marriage unlike their masters and mistresses, for whom sex with anyone was a common occurrence.

Tomas got up and looked around him. They were upstairs in the tavern and beside him on another rug lay Pybus, his head cradled on the breasts of a dark haired girl with slender legs and a pert bottom. Neither was clothed. Tomas scanned the quiet room. He was relieved that there was no girl there with him. He could remember only snatches of the last evening and he was aware that he had paid for a girl. Had he made love to her? He could not clearly remember. He had no reason to think anything would have come of it. No reason to suppose that his virility had returned. She may have gone off disgusted with him. Well now he was glad. At least he was almost pure for Cleolia. At least he had never lost his seed to anyone else. He believed he would with her. Surely this ache for her would make him whole?

He kicked Pybus gently and the girl stirred and woke. She wound herself undone from Pybus and stood up, shaking her matted hair. She looked at Tomas, smiled and went from the room without a word. Tomas shook Pybus. The young man groaned and swore. He lifted his head and glared at Tomas.

"Is the sun up?" he asked angrily. "Have I to rise for you, my master?"

"Today we shall find Cleolia," Tomas said. "Get onto your feet, my friend. Soon you will no longer be my slave."

Reluctantly Pybus rose, holding his aching head. He suddenly grinned at Tomas. "I was good last night," he laughed. "Damn good. That girl really had a treat. I had her three times. I got my money's worth and she got a true Greek blasting. Where is your girl, Tomas? Has she gone too?"

Tomas nodded but said no more.

The two washed in the rough trough which ran along the side of one wall. Then they made their way back down the stairs to the tavern. There was no one in sight and the room stank of stale wine and stale bodies. They went out of the door and turned along the street. At the baker's they bought bread and cake and ate it as they wandered along. Tomas found it hard to swallow. The nervousness was clawing at his guts and he felt sick. Pybus, on the other hand, was in high spirits and ate hungrily. As they approached the street where Cleolia was reported to live, Tomas became even more agitated. Pybus glanced at him.

"What's the matter, Tomas?" he asked.

"Suppose she doesn't know me. Suppose she is married. Suppose she doesn't like the look of me." He ran a shaking hand through his blond hair.

"Tomas, Tomas. Calm yourself. If these things are true you can at least come to terms with them. Up until now you have lived with these questions. Soon you will be free of them," and he slapped Tomas on the back.

Just as they rounded the next corner they saw a group of young slaves round a fountain filling jars with cool, clear water. Tomas scanned the group and rested upon a dark haired figure with her back to him. His heart jumped a beat. Could it be Cleolia? At that moment the girl turned and looked at them. Immediately Tomas realised it was not Cleolia, but as they approached the girl smiled.

Tomas went forward to greet her.

"We are looking for a slave by the name of Cleolia," he said slowly. "We believe she works for the merchant who lives in this street."

"Cleolia?" The girl looked puzzled. "What do you want her for?"

"You know her?" shouted Tomas excitedly. "Tell me where she is. I have come a long way to find her."

The girl looked oddly at him. "You've come a long way," she repeated.

"Yes, yes." Tomas was grinning widely. "Tell me at once where she can be found, girl."

The girl dropped her eyes. "She is … well …," she hesitated. "She is …," and her voice tailed off.

Tomas grabbed the girl by the shoulders, his eyes flashing with temper now. He shook her.

"You stupid girl," he roared. "If you know her tell me where she is. Are you mad or something?"

The girl struggled free. "**I** am not mad," she screamed. "It is Cleolia who is mad." She ran away across the square followed by the other slaves.

Tomas called after them but they disappeared between the houses. Pybus caught him by the arm.

"Tomas, Tomas. We do not need them. The house of the merchant is over there. Let's go and talk to him."

Tomas turned to him. His eyes were troubled.

"Why did she say that, Pybus? She said Cleolia is mad. What does that mean?"

Pybus smiled. "Take no notice of them, Tomas. They are just gossiping women. Come, let us knock at the door."

Tomas went with Pybus to the door but his eyes were worried. They knocked and a short, rather fat, slave opened the door.

After they had enquired for the master of the house, they were led into a large airy atrium. A few minutes later a rather squat man with greasy hair and a large belly waddled in and greeted them.

They shook hands and Tomas said at once, "I am Tomas Argoutus. Please excuse us for this intrusion but we seek a slave girl by the name of Cleolia. We have heard that she is in your household."

The man looked up sharply and said gruffly, "What do you want her for?"

"I have come a long way to Rome in search of her. I want to take her to my home. I will pay well for her."

The man seemed a little put out and stared at Tomas for a moment. Then he recovered and said, "You want to buy her? You know of her?"

"I knew her many years ago, Sir. Now let me hear your price and we will make a deal."

"Many years ago," the man repeated. He seemed to be thinking. Then he said, a little warily, "You haven't seen her recently, then?"

Tomas was getting irritated but he held his temper.

"I must ask you Sir to tell me if you will sell and what is your price?"

Still the man hesitated. "You don't want to see her first? I do not know where she is today."

"Sir," said Tomas carefully. "I have come to buy this slave whatever the price. I ask you Sir, let us make a deal."

"I am not happy to lose her, Tomas Argoutus. She is a willing and hard worker." He paused and scratched his bearded chin. "I cannot part with her for less than 650 denarii"

"That is indeed a lot," said Tomas thoughtfully, "But I want her so I will offer you 600 denarii. That would seem fair."

"To replace her will cost me dear. I will accept 600 because I can see that you are an honest man."

Tomas paused again and then stretched out his hand and took the man's in his.

"You drive a good bargain, Sir, and I respect you for it. I will agree to 600." He then drew out his pouch and handed the man the money. "Will you call her so that we can make our way home?"

The man counted out the money and slipped it under his robe. Then he looked hard at Tomas.

"Why do you want this girl? It is a long way to come for a common slave."

"She is no common slave to me, Sir. I intend to return to Gaul with her and there I will make her my wife."

The man's eyebrows rose. "Make her your wife, eh? Well, Sir, I hope you know what you are doing."

"Why do you say that?" asked Tomas.

"When I tell you, you may regret your purchase. I would have told you before we exchanged money but I never realised you intended marriage. I think you may be disappointed, Tomas Argoutus. I doubt she will agree to marriage and if you force her you may find her a strange bedfellow."

Tomas felt his anger rise. "A strange bedfellow?" he roared. "How dare you say such a thing! Cleolia agreed as a child to be my wife. She is the most beautiful creature in the world and I shall be a lucky man."

As he turned away the door opened and in came a slave dragging a girl on a chain. She was unkempt and dirty. Her black hair was knotted and greasy. She was so thin that all her bones stood out and her skin hung like that of an old person. Her eyes were downcast and she let out muted cries like a wild animal in pain. She shook her head from side to side and when the slave pulled her into the room she collapsed on the floor like a discarded doll and lay still.

Tomas ran to her and stood looking down. "What is this?" he cried angrily. "This is not Cleolia. Are you trying to cheat me, Sir? Where is my girl?"

As he spoke the figure on the ground began to stir and then shakily she rose to her feet. Her sunken eyes seemed unable to focus but at last they looked into Tomas' blue ones. Her mouth whispered, "Tomas?"

Tomas saw the pale face and the haunted brown eyes. He saw the high cheekbones and the dry lips. He heard her whisper and his heart lunged in his chest. He looked deep into the girl's eyes and past them into her very soul, and what he saw their brought a great cry to his lips. He threw back his head and screamed.

"God in Jupiter! What have you done to her?" Then, as he felt her draw back, he stepped closer and in one movement he gathered her up into his arms and began to rock her as the tears coursed down his cheeks.

At last he spoke, now softly and gently. "Cleolia, my love. What have they done to you?" Again her lips moved and she said softly in a wavering tone, "Tomas, take me home."

He turned and glanced at the still figure of Pybus standing patiently.

"Kill the merchant, Pybus. Kill the evil creature who has done this to my girl. Now you are free, but do this one thing for me as a friend." And he walked from the room.

Chapter 15

Tomas rushed blindly through the streets, ignoring the stares of passersby, aware only of the pathetic creature huddled in his arms. She was so light that he almost believed that he carried only a bundle of clothes. When he glanced down her eyes were closed and despite the dirt and grime on her body she had a look of peace on her face, and Tomas loved her so hard that his chest hurt with the sorrow for her.

He reached the door of Marius and threw himself in, and rushed into the atrium where Julia sat gazing into the waters of the fountain. She jumped to her feet and ran to Tomas.

"Oh, Tomas, Tomas, what is this?" she cried, seeing the girl huddled against him.

Tomas did not reply but pushed past her and laid the girl on a couch. He kneeled beside her, stroking her hair and face and muttering words of comfort. She tried to speak to him but he gently laid a hand over her mouth.

"Stay quiet, my love," he murmured.

Julia had assessed the situation and stood behind him. She touched his shoulder.

"Tomas, let me take her and bathe her. She must eat also. Come, Tomas, let me take her."

At first he seemed not to have heard but at last he rose and stepped back. The girl rolled up like a threatened animal, shivering despite the warmth of the room. Julia came close and lifted her.

"Have no fear, Cleolia. You are safe here. I will take you and clean you, and then you must be fed. After that we will talk." The girl looked at her for a moment and then closed her eyes and lay still. Julia picked her up and walked with her from the room. In the doorway she met Marius. He looked at the girl and moved towards Tomas, who stood still and silent beside the empty couch.

"Tomas, what has happened to her? Where did you find her?"

"She was with a merchant, that is all I know. I have bought her. Pybus has killed the merchant. I know nothing more."

"Killed the merchant! But Tomas, what was the reason? Surely there is more."

Tomas began to pace around the room. "Anyone who treats my girl in such a way deserves to die." He struck his palm with the other fist. "I would have done the deed myself but I had to bring Cleolia home. I do not know anything more. Only that she is hurt and neglected. I cannot imagine what I have put her through."

"You, Tomas? What happened before is not your fault. You were a child. And what has happened since … you have been away. You cannot be responsible for her or what has happened to her. Be reasonable."

Tomas turned towards him. "Reasonable!" he shouted. "What has reason to do with this? I left her and see how she is now. Once before I let her down, now I have done it again. Whatever can I do to make things right, Marius, tell me that?"

"Tomas." Marius came close and took the young man's arm. "You do not control fate, my son. You cannot understand what the gods have in mind for any of us. Remember she is just a slave."

Tomas raised his eyes and looked full into the older man's face.

"She is not, nor ever has been 'just a slave' as you put it. She is mine, Marius, my girl. I shall take her to Gaul and make her my wife. I have been with other girls, other women have been in my bed, but

Cleolia is my fate and I love her. She possesses me. I came back to find her because I cannot live without her. I have not been alive since we parted. I have existed but not lived. I love the air and the colours and the scent of my new home but it has been a desert without her. And now …," he paused, "Now I come at last to fetch her and she is like this. There is nothing of her. She is scarcely alive, Marius. My heart is fired with anger for what I have done to her. Why did I not come before? It took a mere child to make me see that I should come at all. My head splits with the anger of it and you tell me to be reasonable!"

Marius turned round and picked up a goblet of wine.

"Here, my friend, drink this and be seated. You are overwrought. Calm yourself. Here, be seated."

Tomas sat down and took the wine. He drank deeply and then leaned back and closed his eyes. From between his closed eyelids a single tear fell onto his cheek. He suddenly leaned forward and put his head in his hands and giant sobs shook his body. Marius sat beside him and waited for the torrent to abate. At last Tomas lifted his head and turned to him.

"My apologies, Marius."

The older man patted his shoulder.

"Let us forget the past. Now that we have her here we must make plans. Is she fit to travel? You are in grave danger, Tomas. You have killed a man, or rather, Pybus has. Even if the authorities do not find you this man will have friends. They will soon find you." He paused. "And Flavius? Is he is dead too, I suppose?"

"I do not care." Tomas spoke quietly. "That merchant deserved to die. But I must leave your house. I do not want for you to suffer because of me. At dawn, if she is well enough to travel, I shall set off back home."

Marius rose. "I will go and see what should to be done to provide your travel needs. I think it would not be wise to wait at all. If you can, you should go now. I will lend you horses if the girl can ride."

"She can ride with me. She is so small, the horse will never feel her. Thank you Marius, you are a good friend."

Tomas sat quietly as he waited for Julia to return. His head spun with a myriad of thoughts. Would she be well enough to travel? How ill was she? Did she still love him? That last thought Tomas felt happier about. She had been expecting him. She had come willingly into his arms. Her torment must now end. He would take her home and Scribonia would care for her. "When she is well, I shall marry her and all this terrible mess will be forgotten," he said aloud to himself.

For some time he sat there until the door flew open and in crashed Pybus.

"I feel we should leave Rome, Tomas," he roared. "Already there are people looking for us. I saw a guard waiting at the gate. I just hid my head and walked in but I feel we could be in danger. They will have found Flavius by now and soon they will find the merchant. Where is the girl? We must go home at once."

As he spoke Marius returned.

"The horses are ready, Tomas, and I have instructed that food and water be put into panniers. Where is Cleolia? Has she not returned from Julia's ministrations?"

As he turned to go out again, Julia came in carrying the girl, who at least looked cleaner but still hid her face.

Tomas went over to her and took her from Julia. Cleolia looked up and it seemed that a smile passed her lips, but she did not speak. Tomas held her close and spoke to Julia.

"Has she eaten? Is she strong enough to travel? I fear we have not made any friends here and must go home in haste."

Julia resisted the impulse to ask the reasons. She just said, "Tomas, she has eaten, but she is very weak. She will not tell me what has happened to her. She seems as in shock as she was last time we met. But she is young and I have no doubt she will recover. As for a journey ... it could be hard for her."

For the first time Cleolia spoke.

"Take me, Tomas. I will be all right. I know you will keep me safe."

Tomas gently lowered her to her feet and although she swayed a little she seemed able to stand unaided. Tomas lead her to a couch where she sat down. He knelt beside her on the floor and looked into her eyes.

"Cleolia, I came from Gaul to find you. We must return there quickly. Pybus was instructed to kill your merchant. He has done so. We must flee the city. It is a long and dangerous journey back to Gaul. Do you feel able to come with us? I cannot leave you here, in fact, I will never leave you again – and that I swear. I should have come back years ago but we will talk of that later. At this time all I want is to get you home where my parents and Arria await us." At the sound of the last, Cleolia's eyes opened wide and a flash of fear crossed them.

"Who is Arria?" she asked tentatively and her body shook.

Tomas let out a soft laugh. "Never fear, Cleolia. Arria is my little sister. It was she who persuaded me to come and find you. She is only a child but a wise one. She knew I was unhappy without you. I did not tell her anything of you but she guessed I had left my love here in Rome. She and Argoutus and Scribonia will welcome you, I know it. And when you are well, we shall be wed as we always knew we would be." And he squeezed her hand.

Cleolia closed her eyes for a moment but smiled bravely at Tomas.

"I only want to be with you, Tomas. I will go anywhere for that."

Tomas rose. "Now all we need is to find Pybus."

"And here I am." Tomas swung round as the tall fiery young man stepped into the room. "As ever I am here at your command. Although not for too long now, I hope." He grinned his wide grin at the company. Then he stepped over and bowed to Julia and Marius.

Tomas grabbed his shoulder.

"Is the deed done, Pybus? Is the merchant dead?"

"Let us just say that he will not be bothering us again for a while. I will explain Tomas, but at this stage I feel we should leave Rome for our health at least."

Tomas nodded. "Indeed, we must go now. Pybus, Marius has kindly prepared us horses and supplies. Let us be off." He turned to Marius and Julia. "Thank you, my friends, for your care and support. I owe you greatly. One day I trust we may meet again. Perhaps you will come to Gaul one day. Argoutus and Scribonia would be so happy to see you again."

Marius slapped Tomas on the back. "Go my son and may the gods be with you. Send word when you are safe. We shall pray for you."

Julia stepped up and embraced Tomas. "My son, take care. Take care of the child also and relay my love to your parents. God speed, my son." And she wiped away a tear.

Tomas gathered Cleolia to him and the three made their way towards the back entrance where the horses stood ready. Pybus mounted and Tomas carefully lifted Cleolia onto the other horse, and then mounted behind her, his arm protectively around her waist. He took the reins with his other hand and dug his heels into the horse's flank. "Let's go," he shouted, and the little convoy moved off with Pybus leading the way.

Behind them, Julia sighed.

"I hope the gods will be kind to them," she murmured, and Marius put an arm around her waist.

"We will pray for them," he said gently. "But now we need to talk. If the guards come looking we need to have a good story ready for them. For the sake of Argoutus we must see that they are not followed."

"Why not for Tomas?" Julia asked.

"Because I feel that Tomas can look after himself." He smiled grimly and they turned back into the house.

Chapter 16

They walked the horses slowly through the streets of Rome in an effort not to draw attention to themselves, and were nearing the west gate of the city after about ten minutes. Tomas called a halt.

"We must take great care, Pybus." Tomas drew Cleolia close to him and spoke quietly into her ear. "If we are stopped I shall say that you are my wife and that we are travelling to visit relatives in Pompeii. Pybus is my slave and is with us to protect us. Unless they are looking for us there should be no trouble. Hopefully no one has connected the death of the merchant with us. If I wrap your cloak tightly around you it will appear that you are an ordinary woman. After all, if you were a slave you would not be sitting with me on a horse."

They moved on again and with some relief found themselves going through the gate with no challenge from the guards. Once free of the city they moved on more quickly and had reached a fork in the road when Tomas again halted his horse.

A lone horseman appeared, riding hard towards the city. Tomas held up a hand to stop the man.

"Where are you off to in such a hurry?" he called to the man, who had come abreast of Tomas' horse. In answer the man drew a sword.

"Let me pass. I am in a hurry to fetch the guard. Flavius has been attacked in Ubis. The Prefect has ordered me to Rome to fetch help to follow this fellow."

"Is he alone?" asked Tomas.

"As far as we know it could have been a gang. But there were two strangers in the town yesterday asking for him." He looked hard at Pybus and back to Tomas. "Have you been in the town recently?" he asked.

Tomas let out a laugh. "I have been visiting friends in Rome with my wife. Why should I visit Ubis?" The man looked hard at him but nodded and rode on, calling over his shoulder, "They were both great strong men with wild eyes and murderous hearts, so beware …"

As he disappeared into the city Pybus grinned. "I am a wild man with evil in my eyes," he laughed happily, but Tomas held up a warning hand.

"Come on," he shouted, "And take heed. That man may remember us later and wonder who we were. Let's be going."

Tomas held tight to Cleolia, wondering at her thinness. She seemed at times like a soft feather before him, and he kept glancing down at her lovely hair and dreaming of the time when he had tried to plait it as a child. So much had happened since those days of their innocence, and he longed to talk to her and find out what had happened to her.

As the day drew to its close he began to look around for a place to spend the night. They reached a small hamlet and stopped to seek lodgings. An old man directed them to a tavern where the owner offered them a room.

The room was one of several above the tavern. It was barely furnished with two beds and a worn rug on the floor. Pybus went down and fetched some bread and wine from the tavern while Tomas settled Cleolia on one of the beds.

He sat beside her with an arm around her shoulders. She did not look up but sat still and rigid in silence. He spoke softly to her.

"Cleolia, my love. I cannot wait to hear what happened to you after I left Rome."

Cleolia did not speak so he went on. "Can you tell me how you came to be with that merchant?"

Still Cleolia did not speak. Tomas put a hand to her cheek and gently turned her face towards him. Very slowly she lifted her head and he saw that she was crying. He pulled her to him and cradled her against his chest.

"Never mind," he murmured. "I am here now and I shall never leave you again. I will take you home to my family and you will be welcomed by Scribonia and Argoutus, and you will meet Arria, my little sister. There you will get well again, and then when you are well we will be married."

At this Cleolia let out a cry and pulled away from him. Looking down once more she muttered, "I cannot marry you, Tomas."

"Why ever not?" Tomas exclaimed. "I have travelled all this way to find you because I cannot live without you. Of course we will be married. We made that vow when we were children. I have never changed my mind. You have always been my girl, Cleolia. Despite all this time I still love you deeply. I do not care what has happened to you back in Rome. I need you to be my wife. I will build us a fine house and we …"

"No, Tomas, no." Cleolia swung round and at last faced him. Her cheeks were splashed with tears but her eyes shone bright and he could see some of her old spirit in them. "No, Tomas. You do not know me anymore. I have changed. I am not the child you knew. There are so many things you do not know. Do not speak of marriage."

"If you no longer love me, why did you come to me? Why are you here?" Tomas' eyes were troubled.

Cleolia put a hand on his knee. "Tomas, I did not say I did not love you, I have always, and will always, love you. I knew you would come one day and rescue me and I do want more than anything to be with you but …" Her voice faded away and tears began to flow once more. Tomas gathered her to him and kissed her forehead.

"Do not cry, my little one. You are safe now. We will talk of the future later. First we must get you home and well. Then we will talk." And he began to rock her like a child until the door opened and Pybus entered.

"Tomas," he shouted excitedly. "We are not safe here. A man came to the tavern talking of the murder of the merchant. He said that the city guard were collecting together a posse to chase the two strangers who had been seen in Ubis and who had been in Rome asking about a slave girl. We must hurry on."

Tomas rose. "I was afraid of this. Come, Cleolia, we cannot stay here."

Pybus held up his hand. "If we walk out now they will be suspicious. We must wait until everyone is asleep and just slip away. Then we will have a few hours to get ahead before they realise anything is wrong."

Tomas sat down again. "Of course you are right. Now, let's try and get a bit of sleep. You sleep first, Pybus and then I will wake you in a couple of hours. Then I'll take a turn. If we all sleep together we may not wake before the morning. Cleolia, lie down and rest. We are going to have a long night and you are tired already."

Cleolia lay back without a word and closed her eyes. She seemed quickly asleep and Tomas saw too that Pybus was the same. In a matter of minutes he was snoring away. Tomas supposed this was because they were both slaves. When you worked hard you had to learn to snatch sleep whenever it was offered. He sat beside the bed where Cleolia slept, looking at her quiet restful face. Over and over in his mind he wondered what could have happened to her and why she had so fiercely said she would not marry him. The thought came into his mind that she might be married already. After all, she did not know he was coming back even if she said she was waiting for him. And why, he wondered, had the merchant been so sure that she would not be a good bedfellow? How would he know that unless he had himself taken her? Many a master had sex with a slave. It was common practice. Perhaps he had just said that because Cleolia had not pleased him. Well it would be different with him. Cleolia said she loved him. That was enough. They would be so good together. He studied her face. She had not changed much. Her features were those of an adult now, of course, and her skin was pale and drawn so that the cheekbones stood out, but essentially it was his Cleolia. He knew that one day her eyes would sparkle for him again. He let his eyes roam down her body. She was so thin. Through her rough gown her bones stood out and the curve of her breasts were hardly visible. Tomas found himself wondering what she would be like undressed. He felt his body stir at the thought of her dark pubic hair, but even as he did so he pushed the thoughts away.

"Whatever she is like physically, I shall love and desire her," he told himself.

He sat there quietly thinking as the night deepened and the sounds of the tavern rose up to him from the room below. Many a tavern would still be serving drinks at two in the morning and Tomas wished that perhaps this one would be closing earlier. As he sat dreaming he was suddenly roused by a hammering on the door. Pybus shot awake, his hand on his sword even as Tomas rose to open the door. Cleolia sat up sleepily rubbing her eyes.

Tomas flung open the door. Outside the landlord stood with a grim smile on his lips.

"I expected you down for a drink," he said accusingly.

"Have you not enough drinkers?" asked Tomas in a matter of fact voice.

"Yes." The man eyed Cleolia sitting on the bed. Pybus had pushed back his sword and was once again on his bed. "I just thought maybe you wanted something brought up," the man continued, looking hard now at Tomas. "Maybe your lady needs nourishment."

Tomas stepped between him and the room. "There is no need to be concerned about us," he said in a quiet, friendly voice. "We have come far and are tired. We only want sleep. Thank you for your trouble. Please leave us."

The man seemed reluctant to go. "Is that your wife?" he asked, trying to step past Tomas.

Tomas suppressed his annoyance. "Yes, it is, and she and my slave are tired as I said so please leave."

Again the man hesitated. "There's strangers downstairs asking questions," he said. "Looking for two men who have hurried from Rome with blood on their hands. What should I say about you?" A lurid grin passed over his features.

"There is nothing to say," remarked Tomas with ordered casualness. "We are but travellers. We are not two murderers travelling alone. I have my wife with me. You could hardly think of us as having anything to do with murder. If I was bent on such action I should certainly not have brought my wife with me." And he smiled at the man and leant closer to him. "My wife is here to warm my bed not conspire to murder."

The man seemed unconvinced but still he moved away. "Oh well," he muttered. "All I can say is that they are interested in strangers and you are strangers, but maybe I will not disclose you presence. But to be sure …" He made to hold out his hand and looked expectantly at Tomas.

Tomas frowned at him. "I am not in the business of bribery. We have nothing to hide so get out." And he slammed the door in the man's face.

The three listened to the man's footsteps passing down the corridor and then Pybus spoke. "I feel uneasy, Tomas," he said, leaning his head in his hands. "Can we afford to wait? Maybe we should get out now."

"If the men are here we are in more danger from trying to get out, are we not?" Tomas began to pace up and down the floor.

"Is there no other way out?" Cleolia had spoken and the two men stared at her in surprise.

She rose from the bed and went to Tomas. "Don't look so astonished," she said, putting a hand on Tomas' arm. "I may be weak but my mind still works."

Tomas put an arm round her. "Sorry, my love." He looked into her eyes. "Of course you have a mind but you have hardly spoken before now."

Pybus had moved to the window. "I think she may be right. Maybe we can climb out of here and escape while the men drink. We could, of course, confront them but there are at least twenty horses out there and even I feel we might not be able to hold our own against so many."

Tomas left Cleolia and went to the door. "I will just have a look outside and see how the place is laid out."

He quietly opened the door and stepped outside. A few moments later he returned. "It is good news," he said. "At the end of this corridor is a window. From there we may be able to climb onto the next roof. It seems to be a private villa with a servants' attic. If you go first and explain that you are a slave they might help us."

Pybus hurried to the door. "Right, despite the fact that you seem to have forgotten that I am really a Freedman now, Tomas, I will do this thing for you." He slipped from the room, saying over his shoulder, "Wait here while I investigate."

Tomas went over to the window again. He looked out into the dim street lit by the torchlight of the tavern. Pybus was right, there were at least twenty horses tied up to the tavern wall. The noise from below wafted up. It seemed innocent enough but every minute Tomas expected to hear the clatter of the men ascending the stairs towards to room. He was sure the landlord had not been truly convinced. How long would it take before the posse came to check them out? As he stood there time seemed to slow and he turned anxiously towards the door of the room. Cleolia had sat down once again on the bed but she rose and crossed towards him. She slipped her hand into his and he looked down into her dear face and felt such a sweep of emotion that he suddenly found it hard to take breath.

"We will be all right, Tomas," she whispered. "I know it. The gods did not send you to me in vain."

All Tomas wanted at that moment was for the time which had been so slow now to stop altogether. He saw in Cleolia's eyes not only a great inner strength but a tenderness which stirred in him the heat of passion which he had dreamt about and knew would come to him when he saw her again. He let his heart rise a beat as he lowered his face, until he could feel her breath on his face.

"Why did I wait so long?" he murmured. "How did I come to leave you? You are my life. You are my being. I have been no more alive since we parted. All I have dreamed about, have cared for over the last ten years, has been you. I have tried to push away my love but it has always plagued my nights and my days. I have seen your face in the waters of every stream, in the movement of the grain, in the rush of every cloud. Beneath my feet has been your shadow, above my head your voice calling to me. In the night I have lain awake and longed for you, my heart has searched every corner of my mind to find you. Laughter has been swept away by my longing. Tears have clung to my eyes ready to spill with loneliness."

Tomas drew back and pulled her face against his chest. "And what did I do? Nothing. I went on from day to day denying what my heart and even my body were telling me. I was angry and bad tempered and blaming those around me for it. And all the while all I needed was to come back to Rome. What a stupid fool I have been! How crazy! And yet again I have let you down." He felt Cleolia's body shift but he continued. "I thought that vow I made in Marius' home was true and right. I believed I could not break it. That my father was right and I did not deserve to see you again. But he was wrong. I did not deserve you, that was true, but to pass from your life forever was to rid me of the sun. To plunge my life into darkness and torment. And to cloud my mind so that I did not know that I was failing you once more. Leaving you to rot at the hands of cruel masters. Leaving my love to be beaten and abused by strangers when I could have had you near me."

So wrapped was Tomas in his emotion that he did not hear the door sliding open until Pybus tapped him on the shoulder.

"Tomas, Tomas. Get off that girl and come. I have found a way out. But we must hurry."

Pybus grabbed the saddlebag from the bed and led the way out of the room. Tomas pushed Cleolia in front of him and followed behind her. They made for the window and with little trouble scrambled onto the roof of the next-door building. By a skylight a skinny tanned slave waited, and, holding out his hand to Cleolia, helped them through and into a dusty attic where seven or eight mattresses were laid out against one wall. On two were the sleeping figures of old slaves. The air was thick with dust and the smoke rising from the fires below. It made their eyes smart and their throats dry as they made their way through the long room and down the stairs into the relative luxury of the house below. There was no one around. Their guide told them that his master and mistress were out dining with friends. They went out of a back door onto the street.

Pybus said, "Wait here. I will go and get our horses."

Tomas grabbed his arm. "No, Pybus, wait." He turned to the slave who had led them out. "Are there horses here? If we take ours they will soon be sure we have gone and there may be a guard outside."

The man looked doubtful. "Well, yes there are, but if you take the horses we will be blamed. We are here to guard the house, our Master is a cruel man and …"

"You could come with us," Tomas interrupted. "I will reward you well when we are home in Gaul."

The man hesitated. "What of my son? He is here too. Will you take him also?"

"Go and get him," urged Tomas. "But be quick."

The man dived back into the house. Pybus moved across to the stables and looked inside.

"You always rush into things, Tomas," he complained. "We have no idea what his son may be like and he is after all an old man. He may only hold us up."

He emerged a moment later leading two strong and tall horses. He handed the reins to Tomas and disappeared into the stable once more, coming out a while later with two more.

"I suppose the girl will ride with you?" he said sulkily.

Before Tomas had time to reply, the slave reappeared with a bag over his shoulder followed by one of the biggest men Tomas had ever seen. He stood head and shoulders above them all and had a broad, thick chest and giant thighs. His face bore the scars of many fights and as he grinned a toothless grin at Tomas he clasped his hand with such force that Tomas nearly cried out.

"Sir," he said in a deep thick voice. "You will never regret your actions this day. My father may be old but he is strong of spirit just as I am strong of body. For us slavery is a way of life but we have a cruel master. Escape is sweet for us. If you take us we will serve you truly. There is nothing here for us and I crave adventure."

Tomas pulled away. "Well, let us waste no more time. We have a long way to go. Remember this girl, my slave and I are being hunted for deeds done for truth. Take the horses and show us the best way out of this town. Our pursuers are in the tavern. There is no time to lose."

Tomas swung up onto the largest horse and Pybus passed Cleolia up to him. In a few moments they were away, the giant man leading the group.

Chapter 16

Dawn saw the party some twenty miles from the town. Tomas reined in his horse and called a halt.

"We must rest a while. Let us go into this forest and make a camp."

The group followed as Tomas led them into the forest. After a while they came upon a clearing and Tomas pulled up. He lifted Cleolia and swung her to the ground as the rest dismounted. Tomas ached with the long ride but he could only imagine how hard such a ride must be for Cleolia in her weak state, but she seemed no weaker and sunk gratefully to the ground, smiling up at him so that his heart missed a beat.

"Stay here and rest, my little one," he whispered. "We will get something to eat." He turned to the giant slave and asked, "What food have we? We may not have much of a chance to get more so we need to ration our supplies."

The big man grinned. "You make a fire and I will get us a rabbit or two." So saying, he disappeared into the trees.

The old man was holding the horses while Pybus tied them to trees. When they had done he approached Tomas who was squatting over a pile of sticks from which came a thin wisp of smoke.

"I have got the water," he said, holding up a leather bladder, "and some wine which I took from my Master's store."

"Good." Tomas stayed watching the growing fire. "Collect a few more sticks for me and we will soon have a meal, old man."

The man rose to comply, calling over his shoulder, "My name is Chilo and my son is Ovilium."

At the sound of the man's name Tomas raised his head. Chilo had moved away and he looked at Cleolia and Pybus.

"That name reminds me of my father's last fight. It was a man named Ovilium that my father killed that day. How strange that he has the same name. He was a giant of a man too."

Pybus had taken his bag from his horse and was laying a blanket on the ground. He looked up.

"Let's hope he keeps his strength for us. We could need it. It seems clear that they have connected us to the death of the merchant. We did not find out how many there were in the band looking for us. I do not think we should stay here long, Tomas."

"I think we should get some rest now. It is safer for us to travel at night. That way few will see us. If we lie low during the day and travel at night we will still hopefully reach Gaul before them. They must rest too."

Pybus opened his mouth to speak but at that moment the big giant crashed into the clearing, carrying two bloodied rabbits by their ears. He crouched beside the fire and drew out a long handled knife from his belt. He put each of the feet on a stone and cut them off. Then he sliced each down the belly and in seconds the two were lying skinned and ready by the fire. His father had returned with sticks and tree branches and Ovilium quickly selected a couple and fashioned them into an arch. He then speared the rabbits through with a sharp stick and hung them over the fire.

Tomas grinned. "That was quick," he laughed.

Ovilium turned to him with a wicked smile which split his ugly face from ear to ear. "Not just good looking," he jested, "But clever too." Everyone laughed.

After they had eaten and drunk their fill of the wine, Ovilium sat back and said, "Well, now we have had our fill, perhaps, my Master, you would tell us why you are running from justice."

Pybus grunted. "It is no concern of yours."

Ovilium turned on him. "I spoke to your master, slave."

Pybus made to rise to his feet, an angry glare appearing on his face, but Tomas put a restraining hand on his arm.

"Hold your temper, Pybus. We shall not fight between ourselves. There are too many others to fight. Ovilium deserves our trust if we are to trust him." He turned back to Ovilium. "My friend, let me enlighten you. First, Pybus is my friend not my slave. Secondly, let it be sufficient for you to understand that we came to Rome to find Cleolia here. At the same time it was necessary to deal with <u>certain persons</u>. One in revenge for past evil and one for his part in mistreating her. Let this satisfy you for the present."

Chilo spoke. "Who is she that has caused so much trouble?"

Cleolia, who had not spoken since they arrived, said in a quiet voice, "Tomas and I were friends as children. He was taken from me and went to Gaul with his family. He came to bring me home." She smiled a weak smile at Tomas.

Tomas started to speak but a lump had risen in his throat and he coughed before he spoke. "This is true, and all you need to know. We are returning to my home near Glanum where I live with my parents and sister. We were slaves in Rome but now we are Freedmen by order of Caesar himself. Our old master found land for us and we have lived there for ten years."

Pybus still looked disgruntled and threw himself on the ground. "Well, whatever. But remember I am a Freedman also, now, and I need to sleep."

Tomas nodded. "Pybus is right. We must rest now and when dusk falls again we can move on. There are many miles to travel."

Chilo threw water on the fire and even under the canopy of trees the air was warm with the coming day. Ovilium took first watch and the others lay down. Tomas pulled Cleolia near to him and cradled her in his arms. In no time he was asleep. So the day passed, each man taking a watch, and when the dusk fell they had a meal of bread and cheese, gathered their things together and moved back towards the road.

Tomas was in the lead. He paused as they approached the road and called the group towards him.

"Remember we do not know if our pursuers have passed by or if they are still behind us. We must be very vigilant. If we see any persons on the way, we must speak only to greet them. They are looking for two men so hopefully they will not suspect us. However, amongst our followers may be someone who knows us so we must be very careful. Now let us make good time. At midnight we will stop once more to eat and rest the horses." He looked up at the clear sky. "There are no clouds so we will have plenty of moonlight to guide us."

They set off along the empty road. It was late and few people travelled at night. Tomas found himself in a dream as the sound of the horses hooves clattered through the still air. He remembered how he had felt when he had woken and found Cleolia sleeping in his arms. It was late afternoon and he had looked at her, silent and motionless beside him. Her hair, crumpled and tousled, lay in an arch around her head and on his arm. It was so black and Tomas remembered how he had tried to braid it once so long ago. He touched it now gently so as not to rouse her. Despite her ordeals it was still as thick as ever. Her ordeals, he wondered. One day he would find out all that she had gone through while he was away and he cursed himself once again for staying away so long. She was still so pale, and in the shadow of the wood he traced the curve of her brow with his finger. He felt a strong surge of love as he looked at her closed eyes and the long lashes which bordered them.

"My little girl," he murmured to himself, and she had opened her eyes and smiled at him. He pulled her closer and kissed her forehead and suddenly he wanted to cry out for the joy of having her near once again. She had moved her lips and he had leaned close to hear.

"Thank you for coming for me," she had whispered. He had thought that at that moment his heart would burst for love, then a despair had gripped his as he remembered how his actions had affected her life.

"If only I had come sooner," he whispered in reply, and he had felt tears of regret prick at his eyes. "I never dreamt you would be suffering so much. I want only to love you and care for you."

Then her large eyes had opened wider and she had clasped his hand. "I do love you, Tomas. I always have and always will. I know you love me and we are together now."

At her words he had felt the passion in his loins, and as he pulled her closer he felt guilty for it and let his head drop on her hair. "I am so sorry," he murmured. "I will make life good for you now.

Nothing will ever come between us again. When we get home I shall make you my wife and you will be a Freewoman and belong to me and my family for all our lives."

She had sighed against his chest, but when he had tilted her head up and lowered his lips to hers she had drawn away.

"Not yet, Tomas. I must have time."

He had groaned with frustrated passion but he had stayed still, holding her close until her breathing became gentle and he knew she was asleep. He had not slept but had stayed holding her tight and trying to quell the longing which was overtaking his body.

He was jolted out of his reverie by a shout from Pybus who was riding ahead. "Halt. There are lights ahead."

They reined in the horses and pulled off to the side of the road. Through the trees there could clearly be seen a group of lanterns stretching across the road some hundred metres away.

"Have they seen us, I wonder?" Tomas asked, staring into the gloom. The lights seemed motionless but in the silence they could hear voices although they were too far away to hear what was said.

Pybus turned his horse and dismounted. "Move deeper into the woods. I will go on foot and see if I can find out who they are."

Tomas nodded in the dark and pulled the others further into the woods while Pybus moved off silently. They waited what seemed a long time and then suddenly there was a slight movement in the bushes and Pybus stood once more beside Tomas' horse.

"It is a small group of soldiers. Tomas, I hate to tell you but Flavius is with them. There was talk of the merchant that I killed and somehow Flavius has contrived to lead the group hunting you. The soldiers addressed him as a senator so he has good standing in the area which also means for us that he has power. He was cursing and swearing about you. He is clearly out for revenge and will be a dangerous opponent. Finding we are wanted for the murder of the merchant has suited him. He has a good reason to seek you without explaining about the truth of what happened."

"Is there any chance we could skirt round them, Pybus? If we get ahead we will be a lot safer. They clearly know they are in front of us."

"We would need to make a big detour to do that. The forest is thick there and the road narrow. They have picked their spot well. The five of us moving through the forest would cause too much noise."

"How many of them are there?" asked Ovilium. "Could we not ambush them? If we took them unawares we might be able to win through."

"There are six soldiers and Flavius. The girl cannot fight nor the old man, so we are outnumbered by four. That is poor odds, even with surprise on our side," replied Pybus.

"I have the strength of ten men," said Ovilium gruffly.

"Strength is not the issue," said Tomas. "We have no weapons."

"There are weapons all around us," said the old man slowly. "Trees make good weapons, my son."

Tomas was silent for a moment. "If we could just distract them somehow, we might be able to slip past."

"The girl would distract them," said Ovilium.

Tomas turned on him, grabbing him by his tall shoulders. "The girl will have nothing to do with this. She is weak and has suffered quite enough. She is here under my protection. There is no chance of her being involved. Is that clear?"

Ovilium pulled away sulkily. "It was just an idea," he muttered.

"And a very bad one," retorted Tomas.

"What should I do?" asked Cleolia softly to Ovilium.

Tomas turned on her. "No, Cleolia, be silent. This is not a problem for you. We shall think of something else."

Cleolia's eyes widened. "Not a problem for me? You are all here because of me and Flavius has revenge in his heart because of me. How can it not be my problem?" She turned back to the others. "Tell me, how do I distract them?"

Pybus laughed. "You must know that, Cleolia. I am sure you know how to distract a man. Why …" His speech was cut off suddenly by a strong blow from Tomas which sent him reeling, blood pouring from his right cheek. He recovered himself and looked up at Tomas from where he had fallen. Tomas stood over him with a wild and furious glint in his eyes.

"Be silent," he roared, "Or I shall kill you."

"Tomas, Tomas." Cleolia took his arm. "Calm down. It will do no good for us to quarrel. Of course I am no fool. I can distract a man, but how does that help?" Tomas opened his mouth to protest but Cleolia put her hand to his mouth. "Sshh, Tomas, and listen to Ovilium."

Pybus had struggled to his feet and stood dabbing his cheek on his shirt. "You could pretend to be in trouble. They will all come to see what is the matter. Then the rest of us can slip past."

"And if he recognises her?" Tomas shouted.

"She was a child then. He will not know her now."

"And how will Cleolia escape?" said Tomas roughly. "Or would you have us leave her there?"

"Of course not, you idiot," said Pybus through clenched teeth. She stays with them until they sleep and then slips away to join us."

"You are more of a fool than I reckoned with, Pybus." Tomas' rage had not abated and he pushed off Cleolia's restraining arm and made to hit Pybus again. This time the Greek was ready and swung a counter punch at Tomas which hit him on the chin with enough force that he went flying and crashed into the bushes.

"Tomas, Pybus!" shouted Cleolia in a surprisingly loud voice. "Will you stop this nonsense." She made to move towards Tomas when there was a sudden shout from behind her and she spun round, coming face to face with three soldiers.

"What have we here?" said the first soldier in a slimy voice. "A sad little group fighting over a girl no doubt. Why are you here and where are you going at this time of night? Who speaks for you?"

Tomas had got to his feet and now he stepped forward, brushing the twigs and dust from his clothes.

"Hi, fellow," he said amicably. "Yes indeed, my friend would take my girl and I didn't care for that. A mere dispute among friends. What is your business, soldier?"

"I asked first," said the man. "Speak up and state your business here."

"It is quite simple," said Tomas in a conversational voice. "I am a Freedman of Rome with my Greek friend. We travel with our two slaves to visit my grandmother. We are simply travelling late because we stopped rather long at the tavern." He took hold of Cleolia and pulled her to him. "This young lady was in the tavern and I thought she would make a good travelling companion." He sneered at the man. "Thought she'd keep me warm, if you know what I mean, but Oralius here," he pointed to Pybus, "Had other ideas."

The man listened quietly. He seemed unsure. "I must take you to Flavius. He seeks two murderers who have killed a merchant. My master, Flavius, knows this man. His name is Tomas Argoutus, the son of an old but famous gladiator."

Tomas answered in a casual voice. "If you know who he is surely he will be easy to trace."

"He left Rome some years ago and went to Gaul, apparently. If we miss him on the road we will find him there."

The other soldiers were restless. One spoke.

"Marcus, what shall we do with these people? They were making so much noise arguing, they could have woken the dead. Hardly the way fugitives from law would behave. They seem to have nothing to do with your murderer."

The first soldier turned towards him. "I am not so sure. Bring them all to our Master and let him talk more with them."

Ovilium moved forward but Tomas caught his arm. He spoke with a firm, hard voice. "We have nothing to hide, so we may as well go with them. We are already late. We can stay here for the rest of the night and travel on tomorrow."

As he spoke Pybus, who had been unusually quiet, sprang forward with a shout to Ovilium. In a moment a giant tree branch crashed on the first soldier's head while Pybus dived for the legs of the second, and Tomas, recovering in an instant, punched the third with all his strength. In those seconds the three soldiers lay dead or stunned on the ground.

The sounds of the fight now brought the other soldiers rushing towards them with Flavius at the rear. Chilo suddenly grabbed Cleolia and ran with her back to where the horses were still tethered. He threw her onto Tomas' horse and undid the reins of the others. Shouting to his companions, he mounted his horse and released the others beside Tomas, Ovilium and Pybus. As the party of soldiers entered the clearing the mounted party rode straight at them, sending them diving for safety. Tomas made a lunge towards Flavius and the hoof of his foot split the man's arm and sent him reeling.

But as they made off, Flavius got to his feet, the blood pouring from the wound, and his voice carried after them.

"I'll get you, Tomas Argoutus. You will never be free of me."

Chapter 17

The girl sat on the rough wooden gate dandling her feet in the warm air. She gazed into the far distance where the river wandered its way across the valley. Suddenly she saw a pall of dust rising from the earth, way beyond the path of the river. It grew and as it reached the banks she saw it was a group of horsemen coming towards the farm.

She dropped from the gate and began to run back towards the farm house calling to her mother as she did so.

"Scribonia!" she cried, "There are horsemen coming. See! See!" She grabbed hold of the woman who had appeared at the door and pulled her onto the veranda.

"Who can it be?" she asked pulling at the woman's hand. She felt a beat of excitement bubbling into her throat although she did not know why.

Scribonia looked up shielding her eyes from the glare of the sun. And then she cried out and began to run towards the approaching figures. "It is Tomas" she cried. "It is Tomas."

Mother and daughter ran down the slope and across the field and as the horsemen neared them, Tomas dismounted and began to run towards them.

They met in a jumble of arms and hugs while the other horsemen stood waiting. At last Tomas broke loose.

"See, mother" he said disentangling himself from the other two. "See who is here." And he went and lifted Cleolia down from his horse and set her before him.

Scribonia looked long and hard at the girl who stood with downcast eyes.

"Cleolia. Is that you?" she asked taking in the tall thin girl with matted hair and bedraggled clothes.

The girl raised her eyes and returned the look and then like the breaking of a spell she ran into Scribonia's arms. "My child" murmured Scribonia. It is so good to see you and to know you are all safe." She turned to Tomas. "Who are these men?"

The old man dismounted and bowed his head. "I am Chilo" he said quietly and this is my son Ovilium."

Scribonia started and stared in puzzlement at the great man who was also dismounted. "Ovilium?" she said. You are Ovilium?"

The man bowed. Scribonia turned to Tomas. "Who is this man and why have you brought him here?"

"He helped us. Without these two we should not have managed to return." He banged Ovilium on the back. "Do not fear him, mother. He looks like a giant but he is a good man."

Scribonia took a step backwards, still staring at Ovilium, as she bit her lips between her teeth. Then she turned to the old man. "This is your son?" she asked. The old man nodded. "Are you sure?" she persisted.

Tomas interrupted. "Mother what on earth is the matter. I have told you that these men have helped us. Why are you looking this way?"

Scribonia dropped her eyes and forced a smile. "I am sorry, "she said taking Cleolia by the hand. "Come along in. You must all be in need of food and rest. Your father is resting. He cannot do much in the heat of the day."

As she led the party towards the house she stopped and turned again to Ovilium. "Ovilium," she said, "Please do not mention your name to my husband. He is a frail man and once he knew a man with your name. It was a bad meeting and I do not want him reminded. Is that clear? In fact, Pybus please take these men to the back and see to the horses. Then they can go into the kitchen and feed and rest. I think it best that Argoutus does not meet them today." And she led Tomas, Cleolia and Arria up the steps to the door.

Pybus opened his mouth to explain that he was now a freed man but then shrugged and led the others round the back of the house.

The atrium was cool and a central fountain tinkled over the stones. Tomas moved towards it with Cleolia by the hand and together they washed their faces and drank from the amphora which stood beside it.

Arria danced up and down impatiently. "Tell us all the news." She cried. "We want to know everything, don't we mother?"

Scribonia laughed. "Give them time, Arria. " she admonished. First they need food and clean clothes. I will go and organise it." And she hurried off though the far door.

"Well I cannot wait." Said Arria, sitting down beside the fountain. "So you are Cleolia," she said looking hard at the young woman. "You are here because I told Tomas to go and get you. He was really grumpy without you, you know. Weren't you Tomas?"

Tomas smiled. "Yes I was and, little sister, I am very glad you pushed me into going. We both are, aren't we Cleolia?"

Cleolia smiled. She looked around her at the fine tall pillars and the lush couches and then her eyes rested on Tomas once again. "Tomas," she began hesitantly. "I am indeed glad you came for me. But it is all so strange here. You have such a fine home."

Tomas put his arms around her. "My precious girl. Of course it must feel strange but it is now your home and soon we will marry and we shall be together forever."

The door at the end of the far wall opened and in came Argoutus leaning heavily on his stick. Tomas went towards him and embraced him. "My father. Now we are home once again and I have brought Cleolia back to be with us. All those years ago you made me swear never to see her again. I hope you will retract that and welcome her as your future daughter."

Argoutus came forward and took Cleolia by the hand. He saw her pale thin face and her sunken eyes. He saw her as a poor image of the happy pretty girl she had been and he sighed.

"My child, I feel that I have done you a great wrong. I did not see how much you two meant to each other. I had no idea how sad I had made my son and how you must have suffered all these years. Will you forgive me?" and he took Tomas by the other hand. "You have my blessing, my children. I want only for my family to be happy and I can see in your eyes Tomas that you are indeed happy. All those years ago you were but children. If now you still care for each other nothing would give me greater pleasure than to have you together. But, I think it is too early to talk of marriage. Stay here and get to know each other again and in time we shall see what the future may hold."

"Thank you, father" said Tomas "but we do not need time. I want to be married straight away. We have lost so much time….."

Argoutus turned to Cleolia. "And you, my child. You have said nothing. What do you want?"

Cleolia dropped her head. "I hope indeed that one day Tomas and I shall be married but I am no longer healthy and I need time to recover. Just now all I want is a bed."

"What a wise girl you are, "said Argoutus smiling at her. "Tomas take her to your mother and let her rest and recover. You have all your lives to lead. We will talk again when she is well. Go along..."

"Thank you, sir." Cleolia smiled back at him. "Come Tomas and show me the way." And she took his hand and led him from the room.

Chapter 18

The days passed and Cleolia grew strong and colour returned to her cheeks. She passed the days out in the fresh warm air, helping with the harvest as well as in the house with Scribonia. At night they sat around the fountain eating and talking long into the night. Arria became her close companion, talking and laughing with her in the fields and by the river where they went to watch Tomas fishing. For weeks Tomas worked hard to make up for his long absence and had little time alone with Cleolia. Whenever he sought to find her she was with Arria or Scribonia or hurried away from him talking of work to be done. Tomas began to see that she was avoiding him and at last cornered her in the woodland picking mushrooms.

"Oh Tomas," she said "I really must hurry. Your mother needs these for dinner."

But he took her arm and pulled her towards him. As he looked into her eyes he was astonished to see fear in them. "Cleolia, my love. What has happened? Why do you avoid me? Why are you afraid? You know I will never hurt you."

"Tomas, I am not afraid nor do I avoid you but your mother needs these mushrooms."

"No Cleolia. My mother can wait. I want to speak with you. I came so far to find you and now you seem distant. What is the matter?"

"You misunderstand me., Tomas. Please let me go. We will talk later. "

But Tomas gripped her arm firmly and pulled her to face him.

He looked into her eyes and took her round the shoulders. "Do you fear me, Cleolia?"

She dropped her gaze and stayed silent.

He shook her gently. "Cleolia. I met you and loved you as a child and now I am a man and there is nothing in the world I would ever do to harm you. But I cannot bear that you should fear me. What have I done?"

"You have done nothing, Tomas. Nothing."

"So what shall I do to make you happy? You have a good home here and you have grown well and more beautiful. Every day I fall more and more in love with you and yet you turn away. When we were children I told you every secret in my heart. I cannot bear that you should turn from me now. We are to be married. Do you not love me anymore?"

"Tomas I do love you. You have given me back my life and I am so happy here with your family but......"

Tomas led her to a nearby tree stump and sat her down beside him. He put his arm around her and pulled her head onto his chest. "Now little one, Tell me all. I must know what is in your heart. If you say you love me what could be wrong? "And he lifted her face towards his and kissed her gently on the mouth. In an instant she jumped away from him, and started to run away through the trees. Tomas ran after her catching her and pulling her back to face him. Gathering her close to him until she stopped struggling and he felt the shivers of her grief running through her body. "My Cleolia," he spoke gently and softly. "Talk to me or I will die of sadness. You are my life and my reason to live. Please do not run from me. Tell me what you fear. You know you can tell me anything. I love you more than my life. I would never harm you. Never."

They stood together until Cleolia lifted her face and looked into his eyes. "I cannot marry you Tomas. Please do not ask me."

"Why can you not marry me? You say you love me. You say you like it here in Gaul. I shall build us a little home and you shall have everything a wife should desire. We will be so happy……"

"Please do not ask me anymore." Cleolia pulled free of him and stood looking down at him. "You must accept what I say. I cannot marry you and that is that…..I suppose I shall have to return to Rome. I am not the girl you loved and never will be…" and she turned and ran from the clearing.

Tomas did not follow. He watched her go with a heavy heart. There was something she was not telling him and he knew that she did love him. He remembered that moment when he had found her in Rome. When she had said 'take me home' He remembered when they had slept side by side on the road to Gaul. "You do love me, Cleolia." He called out to the wind. "I will marry you, if I have to wait all my life." And he rose and trudged sadly home

*

He arrived back at the farm house and went to find his mother. She was busy shelling peas and she did not look up when he entered. "So Tomas. Are you having a good day?" she asked over her shoulder.

Tomas did not answer straight away but went and sat beside her at the long wooden table. He leant his head in his hands and sat silent for a moment. Scribonia glanced at him, then looked away and waited for him to speak.

"Cleolia says she will not marry me" he said at last.

"Will not or cannot?"

"Does it make any difference?"

"Yes, Of course it does. If she will not then it is her decision, if cannot then it suggests some outside reason..." Scribonia put a hand on his shoulder. "It makes a world of difference."

Tomas raised his eyes to hers. "I think she said cannot."

"And did you ask why?"

Tomas hesitated. "She did not give me any reason. Mother she seems afraid. How can she be afraid of me, I would never hurt her."

Scribonia looked at him seriously. "Tomas, she has had terrible experiences. Maybe it is not you she fears but what marriage will mean."

Tomas returned her gaze. "I don't understand. She loves me I know. Whatever would she fear marriage for? Years ago when we were children she promised to marry me. Why does she not want to now?"

"I said Tomas that she may fear marriage because of the physical side of it. Remember she was as good as raped as a child and heaven knows what she had had to put up with as a slave. You know that as a slave she may have been expected to sleep with her master. Don't forget that."

Tomas rose and began to pace round the kitchen. Eventually he came to a stop. "The merchant who owned her said a very strange thing. He said that if he had known I wanted her for marriage, he would have warned me against it. He said she would make a strange bed fellow. I thought he was just trying to be nasty, but maybe......" Tomas came to sit beside Scribonia once more.

"Mother can you ask her what troubles her?"

"It is not my place Tomas. You must ask her."

Tomas got up again. "I am afraid she will not be frank with me. You are a mother to her and she would be more inclined to talk to you. Mother please."

"All right, Tomas I will try but I cannot do this in a hurry. The moment must arise naturally or she will know we have been discussing her. Be patient and in the meanwhile be a friend to her. At the moment it is all she can cope with."

"She has been here now for several months. How long must I wait."

Scribonia put a hand on his shoulder. "I know it is hard, my son, but you must be patient or you may scare her away."

The following morning, Tomas again sought out Cleolia and found her with Arria in the garden picking flowers. He walked up to them and spoke to Arria.

"Sister", he said gently. "Will you take what flowers you have picked to our mother and she will find a vase for them. I need to speak to Cleolia." And he took Cleolia's hand and led her away to a quiet corner of the field and sat her down beside him on the grass.

"My love, we must talk. Yesterday you said you could not marry me and I need to know why. You must not be afraid. There is nothing you can say to me that will change my love for you. Understand that I travelled far to find you and encountered some dangers. I would do it all again just to have you here, but I am a man and you are the girl I love and if you did not love me why did you come with me?"

"I do love you Tomas." She replied softly. "all the years you were away I thought of nothing but of you. I wanted to belong to you in every way…"she paused.

"So what has changed ? You are here with me and all my family love you and want to see us married. I ache for you still and it is so hard for me when you turn away. Do you not understand?"

"Yes. I understand. I do not fear you Tomas but I fear marriage. I have a conflict in my heart every time you are close. I want something more and yet I fear what it is."

"Cleolia, my sweet, I think you should tell me more about the years we have been apart. What happened to you may well be stinging your heart and body. Will you tell me?"

The girl rose and stepped away from him. Her face was white and her eyes full of terror. She clasped her hands together and fresh tears ran from her eyes. When Tomas rose and moved near she stepped back and held up her hands. "Don't touch me please. If I am to talk of the terrors which invade my soul you must stay away from me. When I am close to you my body confuses me." She paused and then sat down on the grass and indicated that Tomas do the same. He sat down some four feet away and folded his arms.

"Whatever helps." He said although his arms and body ached to take her to him and soothe her weeping. For a long time she just stood with downcast eyes and then she raised her head and looked at Tomas through her tears.

"Tomas. When you went away my life seemed ended. I went home with my grandmother and for a long time I had terrible dreams about..." and here she faltered. "about what had happened the terrible day when we had run away. I do not need to tell you about that. You know all. But I got better and as time passed I felt that I was getting back to normal and that there was a chance that I would eventually be able to put the horrors behind me. But then my grandmother died and I found myself alone. The city guard came and took the body away and chased me away too onto the streets of Rome. I was so young and scared but I found a friendly woman who took me in and let me stay with her in her single room amid rats and squalor. It was a vile place and she had little money. She sent me out to beg or steal as she was too old and her legs were weak. So for almost a year I lived there and found enough to keep us alive but many days we went without food. Then one day I was creeping round the market looking for odd pieces of food on the pavement when a man saw me and grabbed me. Although I kicked and wriggled he was too strong and he dragged me back to his home. He was a slave to a rich merchant and he hid me in a stable out the back and came to feed me but left me tied up. I was nearly twelve years old by then and one night I woke to find blood on the straw where I lay. I was desperately afraid and thought I was going to die from some terrible disease. Even though my life was nothing I was not anxious to leave it." Now Cleolia rose and walked away a bit turning then towards Tomas again.

"I waited for my captor to return and when he did I showed him the blood hoping he would take me to a doctor but, of course, he just laughed at me. "Are you so ignorant? He asked me, that you do not recognise this blood. I will get Laura to come and see to you and he went away. After some time an old lady came into the stable. She was rough but kind and she told me about the monthly bleed but also told me that now I was of age I was in danger from the male slaves. I pleaded with her to undo my bounds and in the end she did so and I ran from the place back onto the streets of Rome. After a few hours I found my way back to the place where I had lived with the old woman and found her lying dead on the floor. I was very afraid and ran from the place as fast as I could. I went on running until I came to the outskirts of the city. I found a pile of wood and lay behind it for many hours shivering with fear. In the end hunger drove me out and I came to a small alley where there was a kindly looking man tending some flowers outside his door. I pulled my strength to me and approached him. I asked for food and he seemed friendly and took me into his house. What an ignorant fool I was. No sooner had I entered the house than he called a slave to him and ordered him to take me to the slave quarters. To cut the tale, from then I became a slave to the man but at least in the beginning I was grateful for a roof and food. I worked hard and made friends with other girls and began to grow up. Then one day I was called to my master's bedroom." Cleolia suddenly stopped and dropped to the grass in a heap. "I cannot tell you, Tomas. I cannot." And she put her head in her hands and wept.

Tomas could not bear to see her distress and rushed to her side gathering her to him and this time she did not pull away but clung to him until her sobs died down and she was left with her head on his chest. After a few moments Tomas whispered;

"My love. Be calm. You have started to tell me and that is good. It hurts me to see how unhappy you have been and what unspeakable things have been done to you. We will talk more of it all later. Now come with me and I will wash those tears away and we will live the days together. When the time is good we will talk more and I promise not to press you into marriage until you are ready however long that may be." And he kissed her forehead and together they made their way back to the house.

Entering the cool of the building, Tomas kissed Cleolia lightly on the cheek and she moved away to her room while he stood watching her. His heart was heavy with concern for her and for their future but as he turned to go and find his mother there was a commotion in the rear of the house and a slave rushed out calling for him;

"My master," cried the man bowing hurriedly before him "you are to come to the chamber of your father. He is sick and your mother sends for you."

Immediately all other thoughts sped from his mind and he ran through the house and up to his father's room. He flung open the door and brushed past his mother and sister and looked down at the pale and draw face of Argoutus. Taking in the lines of the old face drawn with pain, Tomas made to turn but his father grabbed his hand.

"Father," cried Tomas, "I must go for the physician."

"No. no my son" the old man held tightly to his hand, "It is too late. I am dying and nothing can save me. Draw near and listen to me."

"But father," Tomas tried once more to escape the thin hand grasping his arm.

"My son. Be at peace. I am happy to go. You cannot save me and run for the physician as you did so many years ago. This is my end and I want my family here with me."

Tomas sighed and knelt beside the bed. He took the old man's hand.

"My father," Tomas leaned closer, "Hear this. I understand that since that fatal day in the arena, your life has been hard and many times you have wished for the end. But your family need you. We love you and your life has never been wasted for us. Let me go for help."

"Tomas, my son. there is nothing for anyone to do now. I want you to be at peace as I am. Where is my daughter?"

"Arria is here father. And my mother."

"No son, my newest daughter, Cleolia. For that she is. You and she are blessed by the gods and I am grateful that I have seen you reunited once again. I was wrong to separate you all those years ago but I see now that you are happy and love each other and it is my dying wish that you be wed. Bring her to me so that I may bless you both...."

Tomas rose and saw Cleolia standing by the door. He beckoned her over. She came and knelt down beside the bed and Tomas did the same. The old man reached out a hand and placed it in turn on both their heads.

"Your destiny is here together. May the gods bless this union and give you children and a peaceful life together. As Scribonia and I have loved, you will love also. Go now and arrange the wedding and send my wife to me."

"I am here, Argoutus," Scribonia stepped forward and took his hand as Tomas and Cleolia left the room still hand in hand,

**

As the simple pyre floated away on the clear surface of the lake, Tomas sighed. Had they still been in Rome, his father's funeral would have been a grand affair and the streets would have been full of people bidding farewell to a hero. Here by the lake stood the little group. His mother, dry eyed and still, his sister openly weeping, the motley group of slaves heads bowed, Pybus, gazing skyward as if seeking to see the spirit of Argoutus rising up and Cleolia beside him, pale and solemn her hands clasped as if in prayer.

"He is gone now." He said quietly. "The gods have taken him to their world. He is at peace. Come let us go home. There is work to do and lives for us to live." And he led the procession back to the house.

Later he and Cleolia sat together by the fountain. His mother had retired to rest and Pybus had gone home. He sat with bowed head remembering his father. How he had run to the arena to watch him fight. How he had stumbled upon the dead beasts. How his childish mind had been seized with terror when he thought his father had died. And now many years later he was gone. Years of fighting the pain and twisting of his body. Of struggling to be brave against showing that pain. All finished now. At peace.

Even as he thought that, Cleolia took his hand and as he turned to look at her, he saw compassion and understanding in her eyes.

"It is true." She said as if she had heard him speak, "he is at peace now. It was so hard for him, Tomas. You know that."

Tomas nodded.

"So now we must live our lives as he would have wanted."

"He wanted us to marry, Cleolia!"

She dropped her eyes from his and was silent for a few moments. "Yes, he did." She said at last, "so I suppose we must." She raised tear filled eyes to him. "I will marry you Tomas. Argoutus wanted that."

"And you, Cleolia, do you want it too?"

Cleolia smiled through her tears. "I want it too, Tomas but……"

"No buts, my love. All is going to be well. Don't fear that I shall be anything but gentle and kind. I swear that I will never do anything against your will. You know that don't you?"

"I do know that Tomas and I will try and be the wife you need and deserve."

Chapter 19

On a crisp Autumn day six months after the death of his father Tomas stood looking across the fields where the horses grazed. He stood tall and proud for this day he was to marry Cleolia. Preparations had gone on for weeks and many were expected at the feast which would follow. As he had bade Cleolia goodnight, the night before, he had smiled at her and dropped a gentle kiss on her cheek.

"Are you happy, my love?" he asked as she leaned against his chest.

"I am happy, Tomas" she replied softly, "and a little afraid also."

"How can you be afraid? You are to marry me. Am I not Tomas the one you love and the one you have loved as I have loved you, since childhood? How can fear have its place in such love?"

"You know what I fear, Tomas. Surely you know even though we have never spoken of it. That day all those years ago…."she faltered and then fell silent.

"Cleolia, do not think of that. That was the act of a cruel and vicious boy. Love makes all things good. I swear upon the grave of my father so recently laid to rest, that I will in no way ever hurt you nor will I force myself on you until you are ready. I have told you that again and again. Can you doubt me?"

"I do not doubt you. But what of after the feast? I know what is expected when we go upstairs……..that we must perform the act. It is expected and your friends will wait to see the bloodied sheet. As you know that cannot happen."

"Then let them wait. I care not for convention. Please, please do not fear me or what should happen. I understand all that you have had to bear and will NEVER ask you for what you do not wish to give."

Now as he stood in the clear air, he remembered his promise and his heart was heavy. All these years he had waited and longed for the moment they would lie side by side and how he had longed to feel her body become one with his. He knew that all would be well with him then, as this young woman would cure all his ills. He would show her the beauty of sex and cast aside her fears. Yet deep down he held fear himself that he would not be able to rid her of so much agony in her soul. He knew that Scribonia had talked long into the night with her. Had she left the door open for him? Soon he would find out.

He turned away and walked slowly back to the house where there was comings and goings, the kind of bustle which preceded such a ceremony. He went to his room where Pybus sat grinning in a chair, a glass of wine in his hand.

"Well, young Tomas," he chuckled, "are you ready to give your life away to a scrap of a girl. Will you not miss the tavern girls?"

Tomas snarled at him. "Be quiet, my friend. You know nothing. Maybe you are happy with those wanton women, but I shall have Cleolia all for myself and I will have no need of anyone else."

"Maybe you think that now," Pybus returned, "but wait until she is with child or has children pulling at her skirts. Will you be faithful then?"

"Pybus," said Tomas pulling the Greek to his feet and putting his face near to his. "I swear I will never go with another woman for all our lives. I want nothing more than that which I shall have today. There is no other woman in the entire world who can measure up to her. So be silent and prepare yourself for your duties as best friend and go softly on the wine. There is a lot of drinking time ahead for us this day."

"More important for you than I. We all know what too much wine can do to a man's prowess." And he laughed and turned away.

Tomas felt his anger rise but he also turned away. Fighting would not change the man, and to be true Tomas knew that Pybus would always look for trouble. He loved a fight more than anyone and Tomas accepted that in him. In fact he accepted all Pybus's ways for he loved him as a true friend with all his faults.

But deep in his heart there still lay a niggling voice telling him that much of what Pybus said was true. Tomas straightened his back and took a deep breath. He would not think anymore but get himself ready for the most important day of his life. As he turned to his closet, he heard movement behind him and there was his mother dressed in a long pink robe with jewels at her neck and white sandals on her feet.

He went to her. "Mother," he cried, "How good you look. But try as you may you will never outshine my Cleolia."

Scribonia smiled and out her hand to his face. "My son, your girl has the body and soul of a young goddess. No one will outshine her, let alone an old lady like me." She moved away and motioned Tomas to sit beside her.

"Tomas," she began laying a hand on his arm. "I must speak with you one more time."

Tomas went to speak but she silenced him. "Listen to me, my son. Cleolia loves you and you her, there is no doubt of that, but she is still very concerned about what will happen when you are wed. And so am I. Last night I spoke to her as you asked and tried to make her understand that you will do her no harm. She knows that but still she worries. She has been deeply scared, Tomas and I fear for you also. She may not come willingly to your bed. You do realise that, my son don't you?"

"Yes, mother I do."

"And you are prepared for that? That she may never be willing? That you may never bear children? That you may have to go elsewhere for your own manly relief?"

"That, mother, I will never do. How can you think that of me?"

"Tomas I know that that is what you think now, that you will be able to calm those fears and make everything right. But I am not so sure. I know that you love her deeply but that may not be enough for you. Nature will have its way."

Tomas rose to his feet. "Mother, "he said turning to face her. "Please give me some credit for being intelligent. I know what I am taking on. I know what that devil did to my girl. And whose fault was that? Mine. I will never forgive myself that I led her into such danger."

"But you were a child, Tomas."

"Yes. I was. But nevertheless I am to blame. Not just for putting her in peril that day but for forsaking her for years after. I know that Argoutus made me swear not to see her but as I grew older I should have challenged that oath. I am sure my father would have understood when I became a man. But No. It took Arria, a child herself, to make me see what I should have seen years before. Now the gods have given me a chance to put things right and if it takes all my life, I will do that.

And now I must dress. It will soon be time. Go and see to our guests, Mother and trust me. All will be well."

Tomas took his mother's hand and helped her from the chair. Putting his hands on her shoulders, he kissed her forehead.

Scribonia smiled at him. "Well, my son, if anyone can do it, maybe you can. You are a good and honest man and you have a great treasure of love waiting for you. Go to it and may the gods aid you." And she turned form the room.

A moment later he heard horses hooves outside. Before long a slave entered. He bowed to Tomas and then said" There is a woman at the gate, master asking for you. She will not be denied but presses me to let her pass. I have not let her into the house but she asked me to tell you that she has urgently to speak with you."

"What kind of a woman is she? Did you ask her business?"

"I did, sir, but she said her words are for you alone and that you must hear her before you are wed this afternoon. She is but a gypsy woman unkempt and in rags but I found it hard to turn her away. I will now, of course, if that is your wish."

"I will come and see her." Tomas replied and walked towards the door. In the yard he found the woman sitting on the rim of the well. She rose and shuffled towards him. The slave had been right in his description of her. She stood but a few inches shorter than Tomas himself but she was bowed and her face was crumpled as if she has just been aroused form sleep. When she approached him she did not make a greeting but merely stood before him staring into his face.

The power and clarity of her deep almost black eyes seemed to bore into his mind and he recoiled from them and stepped away a bit.

"What business have you with me?" he asked.

"None of mine but only yours," she muttered. Her voice was deep as a man's and Tomas could see her craggy fingers winding themselves around each other until they fell into an aspect of prayer.

"Tell me what brings you here." Tomas said fighting a desire to flee from her harsh stare.

"It is you who brings me here, Tomas." She moved her eyes away and laughed to herself. "You who have made me travel miles to this place."

"How do you know my name?"

"For the same reason that I know everything about you."

Tomas swallowed and pulled himself upright. "No more of these riddles. State your business. I have a busy day ahead."

"Ah!" the woman chuckled, "the wedding. Well young man. You would be wise to reconsider this wedding. I have come to warn you." Her face became serious and she moved close again and held his eyes with her once more.

For a moment she paused and then she stretched out her hand and touched his arm. "Tomas. This wedding should not be. That girl has a curse upon her. She is not a suitable wife for any man. Her soul has been blackened by the act of a devil and she will bring trouble and sadness to your home. Turn back from her. Let her pass from your life or else……………" Her voice trailed away.

Tomas was silent for a moment then he turned his head away and spoke loudly and with all the dignity he could muster.

"Go from my land, woman. You and your prophecies of doom. I will wed my girl this day and nothing you can say will change that." And he made to walk away but she followed him and grabbed his arm forcing him to stop. He pulled himself free from her and then swung round to face her, his eyes now full of anger. "Get away from me." He shouted, "Leave my land and don't come back or you may the one in need of help."

The woman shouted back; "this is an evil day, my son. She is tainted by the devil. She is cursed. She will be no bedfellow for you."

"Silence woman." Tomas screamed back at her. "or I will set the dogs on you. Be gone." And he turned away and made for the house stamping his feet and cursing under his breath.

The woman stood watching him, her shoulders hunched and her piercing eyes on his back. Under her breath she muttered. "and you are cursed now by me .I give you but ten years" And she moved away across the dirt and ashes on the path and when Tomas turned as he entered the house she was gone.

He pushed past the bevy of slaves labouring in the Atrium and went to his room. He stood still before the window, his anger dying and his mind in confusion. What had this woman meant? Was his Cleolia cursed? How could his sweet girl have the devil in her? No, this woman was crazed. He would forget her words and shrug off her threats. He snorted in disgust. What did she know? His girl would wed him. That was for sure and nothing would divert him.

Pybus was at his door. "Come in, my friend. Tomas shook himself. "I must make ready.

"Who was that woman and why did she come here?" Asked the tall Greek giving ,Tomas one of his ready grins. " Friend of yours? Come to wish you well?"

"No friend but a crazy soul. Forget her, I have." And he went to the table and poured wine for them both. But in his heart fluttered the worry of her words.

Chapter 20

So the time had come. Tomas stood ready awaiting his bride. As she came to him his heart went out with love and he took her hand with reassurance that all would be well. She looked up at him silently affirming her love for him and he looked into her eyes and knew he had at last his heart's desire. The ceremony lasted a long time and it was with considerable relief that they at last took their places at the table for the feast. Before them was a mountain of delights. Fowl and meat cooked and savoured with the best herbs and spices.

As the throng took their places Tomas rose and with a hand silenced the crowd.

"My friends, my family and all those who have gathered here to wish us well, I thank you. It has been for my bride and I a long and difficult journey but at last we have been joined in love and in the sight of the Gods. Now be merry and take your fill."

"We wish you well" cried a voice from the crowd and all raised their glasses and the feast began. Tomas and Cleolia moved among their friends and all was merriment. Pybus rose from his seat between two ladies and held his glass high.

"Should not the happy pair leave us now?" he cried "Surely they have better things to do?!" and the crowd began a chant. "Away away to the bed chamber."

Tomas held on tight to Cleolia's hand and whispered. "Come my love. Let us depart and leave them to their carousing." and he led her to the stairs which led up to the bedrooms amid the call and whistles of the audience. As he closed the door to the chamber, he turned and looked into her face.

Her body beneath the bridal gowns was shaped to him like a statue of Venus. He leaned near her and said. "This day, my sweet love, you have made me the happiest man that the gods have created. That you have become my wife is a privilege I am not worthy to accept. You are the most beautiful girl in the world to me." And he took her in his arms and laid gentle kisses on her face and felt of a sudden tears on her cheeks. "What is it?" he murmured. "Why do you cry? Are you not happy to be my wife at last?"

She laid her face on his breast. "Tomas, you know that I love you. I have loved you since I was a little girl sent to care for you. But now you are a man and I fear I cannot be what you want."

"My love, There is nothing more I want of you but that you have become mine. Do not fear. I am at peace. I want only to be yours."

He felt her heart beating quickly against him and he dropped a kiss on her hair. "We are tired to night. Let us sleep close and worry not about anything else. Is that good enough for you?"

He felt her nod and she moved away from him and began to undress. He turned form her and did the same but as he looked once more at her standing naked before him he could not control his body as it rose for her. All he wanted at that moment was to take her. At last his. He tore away his eyes from her beauty and looked into her eyes where he saw only fear.

"Do not fear me." He cried. "Never fear me. What my body wants is not what I have to do to you. Go to the bed and I will sleep on the floor." But as he said it he knew it would be the hardest thing he ever did.

She looked at him, tears close to her eyes and said:

"Tomas, my lord and my husband. I understand what you need and what you should have. I am ready. Take me."

Tomas turned away. "How can I when you do not want me?"

She moved towards him her young breasts rising and falling with each breath so that the power of her sex overcame him and he gathered her to him and felt her body close and moved her face so that her lips were on his and the sweetness overpowered him and against all he tried to do he could not resist her and he took her gently and laid her on the bed until a fierce craving overtook him and he plunged into her and shutting her cries from his ears came in a glorious passion unlike all he had felt before. As he withdrew satisfied at last, he became aware of her tears on her cheeks and he felt a sadness flow over him.

He gathered her to him. "Oh God, Cleolia, I am so sorry. I was overpowered by your beauty and I could not help myself. Forgive me."

For a moment Cleolia lay crying in his arms. Then she extracted herself from him and rose from the bed. She took a cloth and wound it round her body. The tears still glistening on her cheeks, she moved towards him. Standing beside the bed, she looked down at him with eyes that seemed for the moment harsh and cruel.

"You do not care for me. Tomas Argoutus. That is clear now. I did want to please you and be as other wives but I cannot." Suddenly she averted her eyes and screamed at him. " And whose fault is that? Who was it took me to that dreadful place where that terrible man cursed me with his body? Who took me there? Tell me that."

Tomas watched in awed silence as she stamped away across the room. Her fine hair glistening in the light creeping through the window. He rose from the bed dumbstruck and defeated, his head low. "It was I. I took you there but Cleolia I was a child. We ran away because we wanted to be together. I didn't know what would happen. How could I? And believe me I have cursed that day and myself for my uselessness." He moved towards her and she shrank back against the wall.

"Get away from me." She shouted.

"Cleolia, be silent. We have guests below. What will they think to hear you screaming. Come calm yourself."

"Me. Calm myself. Were you calm when you took me against my will?"

"You came to me. I love you. You were too beautiful to resist. I have waited for years to take you. I did not mean it to be like that but I am no saint. Forgive me, please."

He took hold of her arm but she thrust him away. "Don't ever touch me again, Tomas. I will go away. I will go into the hills and find a life without beasts in it. Men who want only to abuse me. "

Suddenly Tomas felt the rage rising in him. "You will do no such thing. You are my wife and that is how it stays. Get yourself onto the bed and sleep. I will lie here on the floor. We will talk more tomorrow when maybe you will be a bit more yourself." He put out his hand and pulled her from the wall and gently but firmly laid her on the bed. He watched as the hatred in her eyes faded. She curled up like a child and began to sob. He sat on the bed his own rage gone and taking her into his arms cradled her, rocking her gently.

"Cleolia, be calm." He said in a quiet voice quivering with tenderness. "I have hurt you but \I love you and \I promise, no I swear, I will never take you again unless you want me. You are safe, really. Let the Gods do their worst if I ever do anything again to distress you." And he dropped a kiss on her hair and stayed holding her until her cries stopped and she fell asleep. Only then did he move her and rise from the bed. He dressed and quietly opened the door. The silence of the house told him that the revellers were gone. He walked quietly through the house and out into the night.

Chapter 21

As soon as he had left the house he began to run. Unseeing he ran. Through the silent town, past silent statues and along rough pathways. On and on he ran until he had left all buildings far behind him. There was no one about at that time of night. Only Ovilium clearing away the debris from the party saw his master and called out. But Tomas did not hear him. He did not see the man put down his broom and follow him into the night. Tomas turned at last into the forest. But even then he pushed his tortured body on relentlessly, unaware of the branches which clawed at him and the thorns which grabbed and sliced his arms and legs. He ran until the pain in his chest grew and he had to stop at last. He grabbed at a tree and buried his panting body against it. Soon he dropped to the ground and lay among the pine needles. It was a full five minutes before he was again breathing gently and could focus his mind.

  He could not believe what he had done. He had abused his darling girl, his sunshine and his delight. He heard again the cruel words she had spoken. He cursed loudly and long. What had he done? And why had he let his body control his mind so that he had hurt the person he loved best and for so long. He cursed his body for its insistence. Cursed himself for his weakness. But she had offered herself to him. He was only a man after all. Maybe she would forgive him. He rose from the forest floor and looked about him. The moon had been shining when he had run away but now the forest was dark and no light penetrated the trees above him. He began to walk hoping he was walking back the way he had come. Now he was anxious to go back. He did not want Cleolia to wake and find him gone. With no sex with his wife what was he to do? He dearly wanted a son. It had been a strong desire and he had hoped that Cleolia would give him one. Miserable and confused he wandered on. Although he knew the forest well at night it was a stranger to him. He had no lamp to guide him and he moved slowly with arms in front of him to stop the branches crashing into his face. After half an hour of walking he began to suspect that he was lost. The forest was not quiet around him but many sounds of animals came to him as he struggled on. Snakes scurried away from his footsteps and birds seemed to mock him from their nests in the canopy. Insects came to bite him and his mouth was dry. He knew there was a stream in the forest but would he find it? He went on slowly trying to see something which would let him know he was going the right way. He stopped now and then hoping to hear the water of the stream but there was nothing. Would he walk all night? Maybe he should stop and await the dawn.

He found a fallen tree and sat on its trunk. He closed his eyes and let his dreams encompass him. He remembered the warning of the old lady. Was she cursed? His beautiful girl. He could not believe it. He slipped from the trunk and lay down on the leaves. Against his will he fell into a deep sleep. A dream came to him. He saw once again his father amid the crowds. Saw the tortured beasts in their cages and the pile of rotting corpses. He found himself running away from the amphitheatre, felt himself falling. Saw again the house in Rome. Heard his mother singing before a roaring fire. Smelt the burning.......smelt the acrid smoke.

He woke suddenly, his senses reeling as he smelt that smoke. But now he was awake and still on the breeze came such a smell. The forest was on fire!

Tomas jumped to his feet. Ahead of him he saw the flickering of yellow and red through the trees. He turned round and saw the fire all around him licking at the trees and running along the ground, crackling the dry leaves and sending flames high into the trees which bent from the force. From its light he saw that he was in a clearing and there was a rough path to his right. He had no idea which way to go. The fire seemed to be all around him roaring like a hungry beast.. Soon he would be cornered by the fire. There must be a way through. Along the path he could see only one tree alight. Maybe he could get through. He took a deep breath and doubled over as the smoke hit his lungs and sent him into a spasm of coughing. He must get lower. On hands and knees he made for the path. Keeping his head low he began to move along the rough path. He held his breath as beside him long spirals of smoke rose into the jungle of leaves above. He knew the smoke was just as sure a killer as the flames. The noise of the fire assailed his ears and seemed to be getting louder. He managed a quick glance ahead. A tall tree was beginning to fall, crashing through the undergrowth and twisting itself across his path. He sprang back. Rising to his feet he ran back to the clearing, waving his hands in front of his face in an attempt to ward off the falling debris. He collapsed back on the trunk where he had sat before and looked around once again. There was no clear way and he had no idea where he was. He could be going deeper into the forest and further from the safety of the village. He knew he deserved to die. Was not this what he was destined for? To marry his girl and then rape her! What life was left for him anyway. As he sat waiting for the flames to devour him, a strange and different noise came to him. A crashing of undergrowth and suddenly into the clearing came a wild boar sow She seemed to stop and sniff the air and then turning to her right she made for a hole in the undergrowth. Tomas jumped to his feet. This animal had instinct far above his and maybe she knew the way to safety. But before he could move to follow her out from behind her came six little striped piglets. Falling over themselves to catch up with her, they scrambled after her retreating figure. Tomas dropped to his knees and crawled after the last piglet into the clawing, scratching branches of the low trees and plants. The sow was moving fast but the little ones could only do their best and as he followed he heard behind him the squeaking of yet another piglet. He turned and without thinking gathered it into his arms. The tiny creature wriggled and squeaked but Tomas pushed it down into his tunic and it became quiet/

"Good boy," he murmured.

Carrying the little bundle was making it harder for him to make progress as he had to hold it with one arm, but he could follow the squeals of the other piglets. He struggled on totally unaware of where he was going just trusting in the senses of the mother boar. He could feel the heat from the fire and smell the arid smoke but he felt strangely at peace. He found that his mind emptied of thoughts and all he did was move his limbs and feel the little heart beat of the piglet on his chest. He had no idea how long they made their way but all of a sudden the sow slowed and as Tomas caught up closer he saw her disappear! Where was she going? Was she going into her lair? If so there was no hope for her or him. He hurried after her and watched as the little piglets dropped out of sight as well. When he got closer he saw that she had dropped into the bed of a stream. Although it had dried up the high backs gave some protection against the fire moving towards them.

Also he was sure it would lead them out of the forest. It was going to be hard with the little piglet snuggled inside his tunic. He carefully lowered himself down the bank. By the time he was safely down, the sow was far ahead. On he went. The little piglets were far ahead of him now and he struggled to catch up. The bed of the stream was rough with stones which bit into his knees and hands as he ploughed on. Just as he rounded a corner he saw a tall tree falling across the stream. He flung himself forward to get beyond it but too late he felt the crash of the tree as it fell onto his back and sent his body floundering into a pit of darkness.

When the light came back into his eyes he found himself lying face down on the stones. He tried to move but a pain griped his back like a vice and he cried out. He lay still for a moment and then carefully raised his head. The little piglet was lying prone beside him, mangled and still. His crazy mind made the tears fill his eyes. It was dead. There was no sign of the other piglets. Maybe they had escaped but his little ....He pulled his mind away from the thought. Was he crying over a dead piglet when his life was in so much danger? He knew now he had to live. He had to make things right with Cleolia, or at least try. Again he tried to move and again the screaming pain bit into him. But as he lay there he realised that there was no weight of the tree on his back. Perhaps it had rolled off. But if it had what was the pain. He managed to turn his head enough to see above him. He glimpsed the tree. It was behind him straddling the stream like a bridge. He could see it smouldering but around it the air was clear. The fire had gone. With relief he let his head sink back to the ground. He had to move. He could not stay where he was. No one would find him. No one knew he was out in the forest. After a while no doubt, .he would be missed, but he had no idea where he was and how far he had strayed. It was light now so he must have lain there all night. He tried again to pull himself up but he had to clamp his teeth together against the pain. He managed to get onto all fours at last and stayed like that while he got his breath back. It seemed best to stay in the body of the stream and follow it. It was bound to bring him out of the forest eventually. He prayed it was not too far. All attempts at getting to his feet failed as the pain bore down on him. He would just have to crawl. Even that caused the pain to wash through him and after a couple of metres he sank back onto the ground. He felt weak and shaken. He was thirsty and even though it was summer he shivered with cold. After two more attempts to struggle on, Tomas sank finally to the ground again and knew he could go no further. In a few moments he felt the balm of sleep creep over him and he slipped into darkness once more.

The next thing he knew, there were voices coming to him in the wind. He tried to raise himself once more but he seemed paralysed and too weak. He tried to shout but his mouth was dry and his throat slaked and only a whisper came out of his mouth. With a supreme effort he clenched his teeth and managed to raise himself onto his knees despite the pain which screamed through him. He tried again to shout to no avail. His voice was small and weak and there was no chance the men would hear him. He looked round. The only way was to climb out of the bed of the stream. Could he do that? In his weak state he doubted it but he had to try. If he stayed here he would die. He must get help. The voices were still floating towards him but he knew they might easily miss him, hidden as he was by the bank of the stream. Suddenly, a voice came to him so close that he was sure the man was near him. He screamed as loud as his poor voice would let him and to his relief, the man heard him.

"Here he is." It called, "he is here." Tomas fell back to the ground. He was saved. Within minutes there were several men clambering into the bed of the stream. He heard one voice say. "Is he alive!" another man was now kneeling beside him.

The man touched his back and Tomas groaned. "He is badly burned!" the man said. "We must carry him out. But take care his back is raw." The men lifted him and as carefully as they could, carried him up out of the stream and away. As they lifted him he felt the pain career through his body and all was black once more.

Chapter 22

The next time Tomas opened his eyes, he found himself lying face down on a soft bed. He moved his head and saw her. There she was, kneeling beside him, her eyes wet with tears and her beautiful hair streaming around her face..

"Oh my love," he whispered, "Are you real or have I died and am with the gods."

Cleolia smiled at him. "Oh Tomas, you have frightened us all. We thought you had died in the fire. Your back is badly burned but the physician thinks it will heal. I want to know what happened but you must rest now" She put out her hand and stroked his blond curls. "I was so afraid. No one knew where you had gone and then we saw the fire and feared the worst. I could not bear to lose you."

"But Cleolia" he stammered, "After what I did........"

She silenced him with a light kiss on his cheek, "Let us not talk of the past. We can talk later when you are well. All your thoughts must be in getting well."

"I do not deserve your love," he muttered.

"Now Tomas," she rose up speaking determinedly, "I am going to leave you to rest." I will be back very soon." And she went from the room.

Sometime later she returned but Tomas did not hear her enter the room for he had slipped into unconsciousness and a fever ravaged through his body and he tossed and turned with wild dreams. The sweat poured from his body and Cleolia sent Arria running for the physician. When he came he nodded sadly.

"There is nothing I can do. He must fight the fever. If he wins he will get well, but if not............." He left the words hanging in the air. For three days the fever raged and Cleolia sat beside him, mopping his fevered brow with cold well water.

Tomas was dreaming. At first wild dreams. Flashes of colour, streams of clouds, darkness studded with light. Then came strange jumbled glimpses of the people he knew. His mother calling to him, His father standing in the arena holding a sword high over a vanquished lion. A wild snarling bear ready to pounce on him. He was on horseback, chasing a group of men. He was swimming against the current of the river, being swept against the rocks He was dying and then he was running barefooted on the cool grass which turned to ice while the relentless sun beat down on his head. He was a child. He saw his teacher throwing papers at him which caught in the wind and he could not catch them. He was falling, trying to run and save his father. He was lying on his couch looking at the doorway when this lovely little girl walked into the room. He called her name but she shook her head and laughed at him. He saw her perfect body standing before him begging him to take her. He was screaming "No, no, no!."

Her hand was on his arm. He could smell her scent. He tried to open his eyes but they seemed stuck closed. He heard her voice. "Tomas! Tomas!" The sound reverberated in his brain over and over. A coldness was creeping up his body, slowly pulling him back into darkness but he shouted "No, no."

And then a sweet sleep engulfed him and he drifted off into nothingness.

Cleolia was sleeping too. Her head resting on the pillow beside him. For three days she had stayed with him while his fever raged. Now he was quiet and she slept. It was daylight when Scribonia entered the room. She saw the two sleeping silently and knew that the fever had gone from her son's battered body.

Gently she roused Cleolia

"He is asleep, his fever gone. See how peacefully he sleeps. Come you need food. I will watch him."

Cleolia rubbed her eyes. "I want to be here when he wakes. All he has done is scream. He must be having violent dreams. I have tried to call him but he seems unable to wake up."

"He will soon, my child. His body needs sleep and he is peaceful now. Go. I will call you if he wakes. You will be no good to him if you are ill too. Go and bathe and eat. The danger has passed."

Reluctantly Cleolia rose. She was stiff from sitting so long and she knew Scribonia spoke the truth. She took one last look at the sleeping man on the couch and went softly from the room.

Scribonia sat by Tomas's side and stretched out and touched his hand. She was desperate to know what had happened. What had he been doing out in the forest? How had he wandered so far that he was caught by the fire? He who knew every branch and tree in that place. Had something happened between the newlyweds. Scribonia shivered. She hoped deeply that nothing had gone wrong. She knew how Cleolia had dreaded that night. Had she refused him?

She was interrupted by the giant person of Ovilium, who bowed to her as he entered. Inside she felt a coldness creep into her heart. She could not bring herself to like this giant of a man. But there was nothing in his manner or his actions to cause her distress. He had been a trusty slave. He worked hard in the fields and the house carrying things lesser men could not lift and he was always polite and willing. His father was getting older and less agile and he seemed always to show concern for him. She could not fault either of them but somewhere inside her she felt only unease in their presence. Now Ovilium stood before her looking at Tomas lying still on the couch.

"How is my master?" he asked in his deep gravelly voice.

"He is out of danger now. The fever has passed. It will be sometime before he is well. His back was badly burnt. He will be scared but that is all." She replied.

"Is there anything I can do to help?"

Scribonia stood up. "It would be good if we could lift him and take him to his own bedchamber now."

Ovilium moved to the couch and lifted Tomas with ease and moved from the room. Scribonia followed. Suddenly there was a scream from Tomas and Ovilium nearly dropped him.

"What the hell are you doing?" Tomas's voice was surprisingly strong."For the sake of the Gods put me down."

But like a shot Ovilium threw Tomas over his shoulder and carried on into the bedchamber where he dropped him a little unceremoniously onto the bed. Tomas let out a groan and lay still.

Scribonia rushed to his side. "Tomas! Tomas!" she said touching his side carefully avoiding the red scars of the burn. "Be still. You are safe now but you must rest, my son. The Gods have spared you."

"What happened?" Tomas asked "and why was I being carried?

"You are not strong enough to walk, my son. You have been below where we could look after you.

But now your fever has passed so Ovilium brought you to your bed. "

"Where is she?" Tomas asked. A soft dread filled his mind. Had she deserted him? He remembered her voice when he woke. What had she said to him?

"I sent Cleolia to rest, Tomas. She has been beside your couch for three days. She is exhausted. "

Tomas sank back onto his cushions. "Has she forgiven me?" he asked quietly.

"Has she forgiven you for what, Tomas?" Scribonia laid a hand on his arm. "Wait." She signalled to Ovilium to leave the room. When he had gone she asked once more. "What was there to forgive, Tomas?"

Tomas was about to speak when Cleolia ran into the room.

She ran to the bed and grasped Tomas's hand. "You are awake now." She cried leaning over to kiss the blond curls spread across the cushions. "How are you feeling now? Pybus is here to see you. I told him to wait. I wanted to talk with you first."

"Cleolia," Tomas began but she silenced him. "We all want to know what happened, Tomas. Why were you so far into the forest? "

"I do not remember. Only that I was walking in the forest thinking of......." he hesitated. "well just thinking and I must have wandered further than I expected. Then I saw the fire and it was all around me but a wild pig came with her piglets and I followed them to the stream. Then the tree fell and I thought I was to die. I don't remember anything else until I heard the men."

There was a loud knocking at the door. "Tomas!" called a deep voice. " Can I come in?" Cleolia laughed and rose to her feet. "OK Pybus. You may come in."

So the days passed and Tomas grew stronger. His back healed. He began to walk around and do light work around the farm. Each night he lay with Cleolia holding her close but he did not try again to have sex with her, much as he wanted to. They did not talk about what had happened on their wedding night. Cleolia said it was in the past and there it was to stay. Tomas still felt the guilt of what he had done but gradually that too faded in his mind but he knew one day they would have to discuss it again.

One morning he was in a shed sorting the animal feeds when Pybus entered.

He slapped Tomas on the shoulder. "Well, my friend," he said, "How is it to be married. No rolling in the hay with the village lasses these days. But coming home to a warm woman, that must be heaven."

Tomas threw down his rake. "That is no concern of yours," he answered crossly."What are you doing here anyway? Is there no work now you are a grand freeman?"

"Do you not want to talk to me anymore?" said Pybus putting on a sad expression. "Are you in a bad mood?"

"Pybus, you know I care for you but I do not need you making coarse remarks about me and Cleolia."

"Sorry, Tomas," Pybus tapping Tomas gently on the back. "I was trying to be your friend and to bring a little levity into our lives. You are so serious these days. What happened to you?"

"I had a serious argument with a burning tree. It is not something which will ever make me laugh"

"I know that, but you still need to get your life back. You were always such a fun person except where Cleolia was concerned and now you have her you should be full of joy!"

Tomas sat down on a pile of hay and slapped the space beside him. "Pybus, sit down and I will tell you. Lord knows I need to tell someone. This problem is eating away at me and you are right I do need to talk about it. I did a terrible thing, Pybus. I raped my new wife." He put his hands over his face. "I cannot believe that I did but I did."

Pybus was quiet for a moment. "Did she refuse you, Tomas?" He asked a few moments later.

"No, Pybus, that was the trouble. She offered herself to me. She said it was her duty. Then I went to her and ....I cannot believe this but....I took her. Not gently as I had planned but with force and afterwards she cried and told me never to do it again. So I went away and walked and that was how I ended up in the forest. I am still amazed that the fire came. It is not the season for fires. How can it have started?"

"Do you think someone set off the fire, Tomas? Do you have any enemies?"

"You are suggesting someone knew I was there and deliberately set off a fire? I saw no one as I walked along. It was late by then and the revellers had gone home."

"I know you will not like this suggestion but was Cleolia very angry with you?"

Tomas made a bitter laugh. "I may have deserved her wrath, my friend, but she would never try and kill me. She does not have a revengeful soul. I do believe she loves me. She has been very attentive while I have been ill."

"Have you spoken about your wedding night?" Pybus asked.

"I did try and ask her forgiveness but she said it is in the past and will say nothing. She says she loves me whatever happens."

"Sounds like you have nothing to fear from her and in time things may get better."

"But suppose she never agrees to sex or enjoys it, what then?"

"Do as you have always done, my friend. Find it elsewhere."

"But she is what I want. She is my wife. I want no one else. Cleolia is my life, as you well know. I cannot, do not, want to be unfaithful to her. Ever since I was a boy and she came to me, I have wanted only her. That was my downfall I suppose. I wanted her too much to behave the way I should."

"Look, my friend, you must not despair. She had a bad experience as a child and probably even more as an adult. She may have to learn to express her love in a sexual way. There is no doubt she loves you. You must be patient. She will come round. Have you talked about having children?"

"Yes we have. She has said she wants as many children as possible. She wants to make a loving home for them to give them what she did not have."

"In that case there is nothing to fear. She knows she will have to have sex with you for that." He laughed "If she wants many children she knows what that means. For goodness sake Tomas, be realistic. She loves you and wants kids. All will be well. You will just have to be very gentle with her."

"It wasn't a very good start, though was it?"

"Stop worrying. You will make yourself ill again." Pybus stood up. "Now I came here to ask you if I may borrow Ovilium. I have a great old tree by my house which I fear will fall when the wind is high. I can cut it down but Ovilium has such strength, he could help me take the wood away. You may have some if you wish, in exchange."

"Of course you may borrow him. He is a good worker. He will enjoy using his strength. I sent him to turn the earth in the lower field. He is there with his father."

"You trust him Tomas?"

"I have no reason not to. He did help us escape after all. Have you doubts?"

"Not really, but sometimes he stares at you as if he hates you."

"You are imagining things, Pybus. Go and use him."

But when Pybus had gone Tomas was thoughtful. He remembered when he had met Ovilium and how he was cheerful and seemed happy. He realised that now the man did seem a little hostile. His father was old and weak but he too did not seem as happy as he had been. Tomas decided to talk to him at the next chance he got.

Chapter 22

Cleolia was in the kitchen peeling fruit, when Scribonia walked in. She crossed to the sink and began to wash the vegetables for dinner.

"I can do that." Cleolia said, "Why do you not rest for a while?"

Scribonia smiled."I can't just sit around. I get bored and anyway I need to talk to you."

"What about?" asked the girl putting down her knife and turning to Scribonia.

"When Tomas was first awake after his fever, he asked me if you had forgiven him. I know it is not my business but I think he is worried about something and I just thought maybe you would tell me."

Cleolia laughed. "It was only a lover's tiff. It is of no importance now."She became serious. "I think Tomas is in more pain than he lets on. Even now he is in the fields working. I cannot get him to rest." She paused. "I suppose he is like his mother!" she added smiling.

"Did you know that a soothsayer came to see him just before you were married?"

"No. What did she want?"

"She came to warn Tomas not to marry you. Said you would make a poor wife.. Something like that."

"He never said anything about it to me."

"He took no notice but it has worried me."She leaned closer to Cleolia. "Is everything all right between you. Really. You know you can trust me."

"We did have some problems........on the wedding night. I love Tomas so much. You know that. I wanted to be a proper wife to him....it was hard." She paused. "I have found it hard to be the way I wanted. I thought all the demons would go when I was with Tomas. It just hasn't worked out like that. But he has been very patient since he was ill. He has made no demands on me....."

"Have you talked to him about it?"

"I told him all that has happened to me since we parted and you know about what happened when I was a child." She put her hands over her face for a moment. When she looked up at Scribonia there were tears in her eyes.

"Come here, my child" Scribonia gathered Cleolia into her arms and let her cry softly for a while. Then she pulled her face towards her. "Look at me." She said gently. "Tomas loves you with a fierce passion but he would never hurt you intentionally. It is hard for men. They are driven to have sex. Tomas would believe that you would allow it. Did you refuse him?"

"No. I tried to accept his body but then I was afraid and............" She stopped and dropping her head began to sob once more.

Scribonia let her cry and then when the sobs had eased off, she pulled away. "We will say no more now but remember you can talk to me any time. But you should talk to Tomas. He will be confused. He needs to understand. As I said before he would never do anything to hurt you."

Cleolia thanked her and went back to the vegetables. She knew only too well that she should talk to Tomas but it was so hard. She pushed any thoughts of it away just as Arria entered the kitchen. She danced across and took a carrot from the dish and bit into it.

"Cleolia," she said happily. "What is it like to be Tomas's wife? Will you have a baby soon?"

Scribonia spoke severely. "Now my child. Leave Cleolia to her work and don't eat all the food before it is cooked. Tomas will not be happy if there are no carrots for our meal."

Arria laughed. "I shall only eat one. Mother, what shall I do until our meal? "Go and study. Or you can go down to the barn and see if you can help Tomas. Tell him the meal will be ready in half an hour. Just leave us in peace." And she shooed the girl from the room.

"Sorry about Arria. She is just a child."

Cleolia put down her carrots and came over to Scribonia. "Well," she said slowly "Actually. I think I may be with child already. I have not seen my bloods since we were married."

Scribonia dropped her knife and turned to look at Cleolia with a broad grin on her face. "How exciting!! Does Tomas know? I thought you were putting on a little weight, but you were so thin when you came here I never imagined.....

"I have not told Tomas. I wanted to be sure."

"So you have had sex with Tomas then. I will take you to see the physician tomorrow. But there can be little doubt."

"Doubt of what?" said Tomas as he entered the kitchen.

"Cleolia has something to tell you, my son."

Tomas went over and put an arm round Cleolia's shoulders. "So," he said gently, "What is there no doubt about my love."

Cleolia looked up at him. She smiled. "That I am going to have a baby."

Tomas let out a squeal of joy! "A baby!!" For a moment his face became puzzled. "But........."

"It was on our wedding night."

"You mean something good has come of that terrible........."he paused.

Scribonia walked to the door. "I will leave you to talk." And she went quickly from the room.

"Yes, my lord," Cleolia said to him. "Something very special has come of that night."

"The Gods have indeed blessed us." Tomas stood back and stared at her stomach. "There was me thinking my wife was getting fat! So when is this baby due? It is nine months I believe and we have been married for over three. So it will be in the Spring." He stopped and pulled up a chair. "Now sit down. There are going to be some changes round here. No more work for you."

Cleolia laughed. "Now Tomas," she chided, "I am not ill or weak. I feel well, in fact very well. So stop fussing." She paused for a moment. "We need to talk about that night Tomas."

"None of it matters now, Cleolia. You are to be a mother and I will have a son!"

"It might be a girl, you know." said Cleolia laughing.

"If it is she will be as beautiful as her mother." And Tomas kissed her softly on the lips. His body ached with passion. All he wanted at that moment was to gather her to him and make love to her, but he let her go. He pulled himself away from her and took a deep breath. After a moment he said."Pybus was here a while ago. I must tell him. What a shame my father did not live to see his grandchild."

"Perhaps the gods will tell him." Cleolia dropped her voice. "Tomas, I am so sorry I have not been the wife you need in bed. But now I am pregnant you can go to another woman's bed and no one will ask questions and I shall not stop you."

"Cleolia, my love. I do not want another woman. I want only you and if I have to wait, I will bear it well. When our child is born, we will talk of it again but now let us celebrate. I will go and fetch a good strong wine to have with our meal and then I shall wash as I don't think I am fit company for you at the table unless I do." And kissing her lightly on the cheek he strode out of the room and Cleolia heard him whistling happily as he went.

Cleolia sat back on the chair, a worried look on her face. Why could she not express her love for Tomas like every other woman did? Why did the demons from her past rush into her brain whenever he came near her. She did not want to be the person she had become. Even the thought of Tomas's naked body filled her with horror. Yet when he kissed her she felt warm and loved and inside she desired him but then............ How could she overcome this terrible disaster which she knew her marriage to be? Now she was pregnant she had thought he would accept it and go elsewhere. In her heart she did not want that but it was an accepted thing and she knew many men did just that. It would assuage her guilt at least for the next months until the baby arrived. She shuddered to think what the soothsayer had told Tomas. Was she right? Would her body never accept him? Was this a total disaster, this marriage? Yet she knew they loved each other deeply. Surely one day things would sort themselves out. If she wanted more children, she had to accept him. Would time heal her? She was not sure. Was there not anything she could do? Perhaps she had to let him make love to her without getting distressed and panicking as she had done that one time. But what would happen? Would she be able to bear it? Married three months and only once had he taken her. And what had she done? Screamed at him. It was all her fault. She had thought it would be all right. Had encouraged him and then.......... Maybe she should go away. Leave him. But how could she do that when she knew how much he longed for a child.

Cleolia got to her feet and went out of the room to change for the meal, pushing her thoughts away to the back of her mind. "You are a silly woman," she told herself. "All you have wanted in the last ten or so years was to be with Tomas and now the whole thing is a mess of your own making."

Chapter 23

It was a wet winter. Day after day, Tomas came in dripping and muddy from the farm. He brought another bed into their room, saying he felt she would be more comfortable but actually he knew and so did she that it was because he was afraid to repeat the wedding night. He felt easier that way. But still he refused to talk about it and a certain coldness was developing between them as her belly grew. Nothing was said but each hid their grief at the state of things between them. Tomas was bad tempered at times and spent more time away in the nearby town of Glanum with Pybus, drinking and gambling with the other men.

Cleolia went to Scribonia on a clear winter morning when at last the sun was sending shadows across the fields and the hedgerows were springing into life.

"May I talk with you Scribonia?" she asked sitting next to her mother-in-law who was sewing by the window.

Scribonia patted the seat beside her. "Of course, my child. Are you well? Your time must be fast approaching."

"I am very well, do not fear that. My baby is strong. I can feel him kicking inside me. Sometimes he keeps me awake with all his wriggling about."

Scribonia smiled. "No child could be more active than Tomas was. I had no peace at night then but Marius and Julia were good to me and let me rest. I was a slave then of course but they were wonderful people and treated us all very well.

But you do not want to talk about them. What is troubling you?"

"I am afraid."

"Of course you are afraid. Every woman is afraid of child birth."

"No. I am of course a little apprehensive about bearing a child but it is not that which is worrying me."

"What then?"

"This is hard for me but I need your advice. I want to be honest with you and I know I can trust you not to say anything to anyone, but I am afraid of what will happen after my child is born. You see Tomas and I do not have sex. It was only the once when we were married and that proved a disaster. Scribonia, I fear sex. I wanted Tomas but when he came to me on my wedding night I was so afraid that I panicked and screamed at him. That is why he went walking that night. It is my fault that he was caught in the forest." Her eyes filled with tears and Scribonia reached for her hand. "I am no wife to him. And when the child is born he will again expect me to accept him and........and I am not sure that I can."

Scribonia leaned closer. "You have had a terrible experience when you were a child and I suspect also after we left Rome it was hard for you.. It is no surprise and you must not blame yourself. You must make Tomas listen to you. I told you before."

"He will not listen. And we are drifting apart. You know how much time he spends with his friends now. He drinks too much and gambles away so much money. I cannot believe that I have done this to him. He will be happy to have a child I know that, but his joy will not last long and then we shall be back at the beginning again. How can I learn to be the wife he needs and deserves?"

Scribonia sighed. "I understand, Cleolia. This special time when your child is born must not be spoilt by your fears. Do you want me to speak to him? I can perhaps help him to realise what is wrong. If he can understand, maybe things can be worked out."

Cleolia nodded. "I was hoping you would make him listen. Make him talk to me. If things go on as they are, there will be no happy family for us."

"I will do my best, my child, but we all know how he has changed recently. Even his work is suffering. Only this morning Ovilium came to tell me that the vines have not been completely pruned. He seems to have lost interest in anything except drinking the wine, not growing it." Scribonia got to her feet. "I will talk to him after the evening meal. And thank you for your trust."

That night as they sat at the table, Scribonia leaned towards Tomas;

"My son. I need time to talk to you. When we are finished our meal come with me to my room."

Tomas grunted."I am going to meet Pybus, mother. I don't want to waste good drinking time discussing domestic issues."

"You will do as I ask, Tomas. It is a matter of great importance. You can meet Pybus later. Be there!" She rose from her chair and left the room.

"What does she want now? Do you know?" he asked Cleolia.

She shook her head. "She just wants to talk to you, Tomas. You are hardly ever here now."

"Are you going to be a nagging wife and am I to be nagged by my mother as well?"

"Just go and see her. Then you will find out."

Tomas took a long drink of wine and went round the table towards her. He patted her belly and grinned. "Time you got rid of that and gave me a son, isn't it?" He patted her again and left the room. She sighed. Would Scribonia get him to understand? He was a strange man now. He was not the man she had married. She shuddered to think what he would do when the baby came. Go drinking, no doubt.

Scribonia was sitting by the window when Tomas entered the room.

"Well, mother. What have I done wrong now."

"Tomas what is happening to you? You seem only interested in drinking. I am worried about you."

"Don't be, Mother. I am just enjoying myself until the baby comes. I will be a good father."

"I have no doubt of that but Cleolia needs you."

"Would that were true!" he grunted sitting down on the floor and crossing his legs.

"Tomas, Cleolia has asked me to speak to you. She is very worried about your marriage. She feels guilty because things have not been easy between you. She even blames herself for your getting hurt in the fire. She wants to talk to you but she says you will not listen."

"That's great. She talks to you about what is our business."

"Tomas. She did not want to talk to me but she is desperate. We have all witnessed a change in you. We are all worried about you."

"So I suppose she has told you what I did to her on our wedding night?"

"What did you do?"

Tomas rose and began to walk the floor. At last he stopped and turned to his mother. "I raped her." He said through tight lips. "I spoilt everything. I don't know how to put things right. She offered herself to me and then when I went to her she screamed and I took no notice. I forced myself on her and when it was over she told me to go away and never come to her again. I went to the forest to sort out my head. I do not understand. I tried to say sorry but she would not listen. I have stayed away from her since then. But I am desperate. All I want is to put things right but I don't know what to do or say. I love her. I want her. I want her to forgive me. I want to start again." Tomas dropped to the floor and began to rock. Tears ran down his cheeks. He brushed them away with his sleeve.

Scribonia dropped to her knees beside him. She gathered him to her as if he were still a child.

"My poor boy. This must be sorted out. You are both in turmoil. You <u>must</u> talk to each other."

"But I don't know what to say. Where to begin. It is easier to push it away back into my head."

"And the drink makes it easier?"

"I thought it did. She even said that I should find another woman for sex when she was pregnant. I don't know why she can't understand that I only want her..........it is terrible to be in the same bedroom and not be able even to hold her."

"Do you want me to try and get the two of you together to talk? I wouldn't stay just sort of get you started. You know this must be sorted out."

"Maybe that is a good idea."

"What you two need is to have your heads knocked together." Scribonia smiled and rose from the floor. "Stay home tonight, Tomas. Don't go to your drinking friends. Wait here. I will go and find her."

Tomas rose also. "Thanks, mother. I will wait for you both. We will get everything worked out. We do love each other so much."

Scribonia turned. "I know you do. By tomorrow everything will be right again."

A few minutes later Cleolia and Scribonia came into the room. Tomas rose and went to them and kissed Cleolia gently.

"My love," he said sounding like his old self again. "I asked my mother to bring you here. I am so sorry I have not been myself these few weeks and that I have not listened to you. She has made me see that I have been a fool and that I have made you sad. We must talk and I will listen to all that you say."

"Oh Tomas," Cleolia said quietly," I know that I have failed you as a wife but I cannot bear to see you so changed. I am afraid you no longer love me."

"Of course I love you, Cleolia. You have been the only girl in my life since we were children. Now you are my wife and things are not right between us." He paused and turned to Scribonia.

"Mother you may leave us. I will listen and we will talk. Fear not that things will be open between us and thank you for your concern. I have been a poor son to you and a worse husband. It will be resolved and I swear that anything I must do I will do for the sake of those I love." And he kissed his mother on the cheek.

"Be sure that you do, Tomas," Scribonia patted his shoulder. "I want you two to be happy and welcome this child into a loving home. He or she deserves loving parents who are strong in their love." She smiled at Cleolia and left the room.

Tomas took Cleolia's hand and led her to a couch where he sat beside her. He wanted to take her hand and draw her to him but he sat with his hands on his knees as he turned to her

"Now my love. Talk to me. I am ready to listen."

For a moment Cleolia looked down at the floor but then she raised her eyes to his and he saw tears in them but still he waited saying nothing.

" I always wanted to be a good wife to you. But........" she dropped her eyes again to the floor.

"But I spoilt everything when I took you on our wedding night, didn't I? I have hated myself for that but I cannot undo what I did."

"Tomas, I know that and it is I who should hate myself. I offered myself to you and then I became so afraid."

"I frightened you?" Tomas murmured . "I just wanted you so much my body took over. I had wanted you ever since I was grown and there at last you were, looking so beautiful, naked in front of me, that my mind was overcome by the sight of you. I was possessed by you and that is no excuse I know. I could not turn away. I had to have you. There was never anyone else for me. I have lain with girls before but never been satisfied. Ever since I found you again my body has ached for yours. You were all I wanted and \I thought because we were married that it would be all right. You stood there and told me to take you so I did and when you cried out, I could not stop. I know that I should have but I did not seem to be able to."

"No Tomas, You are not to blame. It is I. I offered myself and then it was too late and I did want you. Believe me I did. But as you came to me, all I could see was that terrible man's face."

Tomas went to speak but she silenced him with her hand. "Listen, Tomas. I want to tell you. Try and be patient...." She tried to smile at him through her tears which were running unheeded down her cheeks." Tomas put his arm round her shoulders and pulled her head down to rest against him. She did not pull away but began to speak as though to herself quietly and in a weak voice which Tomas didn't recognise.

"I told you how I was taken as a slave by that man in Rome. I told you also that he was not a bad master and I was well cared for with food and lodgings. I was very thin but gradually I filled out as I have done here. I knew from the other girls that they were often asked to share his bed and were even offered to his friends for their sexual pleasure." She was quiet for a moment but Tomas waited without interrupting. After a moment she went on;

"For some reason because I was not asked to go to him, I thought I was going to be safe. One evening he did call for me but I was stupid and did not realise what was happening. I went to his room and he offered me wine and sat across from me and talked to me about my life in his household........if I was happy there and well fed. I told him I was very grateful for all he had done. He then said that a very important man had come to visit him that evening and he wanted to be sure I would be willing to serve this man. I was a fool. I really thought he meant that I would serve him food and wait on him as I had done before with visitors. So, of course I said that I would. He told me to go into the next room where I would find some new clothes to wear. I did. I found some beautiful clothes lying on a couch. I had never seen any clothes so fine and |I was excited to wear them. I dressed and sat waiting.

The door opened and I looked at the floor not wishing to appear bold in front of a man of importance. He came over to me and asked me to stand so that he could see me properly. I did but still had not looked into his eyes. Then he put his hands on my breasts and I suddenly realised what was about to happen. I raised my eyes and looked at the stranger. .... For a moment I did not recognise him but as his eyes met mine I knew who it was." Cleolia began to shake and Tomas squeezed her to him.

"And who was it?" Tomas promoted gently.

"It was him, Tomas." Cleolia's voice was almost a whisper.

"You mean Flavius?" Tomas rose to his feet, rage gripping him.

"The man who hurt me when we were children." Cleolia was now standing also, her eyes wide with fear. "And it was him who we met on our way back here. He is out to kill you Tomas. I fear for us all."

"Not if I kill his first." Tomas stamped with rage. He stamped around the room but when he saw her tears he calmed down and turned to Cleolia once more. "And did he rape you again, my love?"

" He tried. He came for me with his clothes undone. I screamed and bit and scratched him and he called my master. He complained that I was cursed. He did not recognise me, I think. But........."she paused as Tomas came and sat back with her his arm round her shoulders.

"Tell me," Tomas asked gently.

"When I saw you aroused, that night, It......" Again she stopped and clung tightly to Thomas.. Tomas waited, kissing her hair where it tumbled over his shoulder.

"Tell me," he said again. "I love you. Nothing you say or feel will change that."

"It brought it all back to me. I did not see you. I saw him. I saw him as a young man with his friends and again as an evil man in that place. It brought terror to me. My mind told me it was you whom I love, but the shadows came in great leaps to swallow me in the past. An uncontrollable fear gripped me and threatened to envelope me and I could not bear it. I cannot bear that he is alive out there somewhere."

"Well that I can change. If he were dead would you feel better my love?"

"I suppose so." She looked up into his eyes. Despite his gentle voice she saw rage and anger in his eyes. "but Tomas he seeks to kill you. That I could never bear. We have been here now for several months and there has been no sign that he knows where you are. I want that to stay the same. If you seek to kill him he may kill you first."

"I cannot let him kill our love, for that is what he is doing."

"Perhaps I will feel better when our child is born. Do not be rash, my Tomas. My child needs a father as I need a husband."

"A husband who frightens you. That is no good."

"You do not frighten me. It is only the shadow of that man who threatens me."

"So he must be killed...........you must see that."

"But supposing it doesn't work. Supposing I still feel that fear, what then? You could have put yourself in danger. Even if he does not kill you, you will be a wanted man if you kill him. You already have the merchant's blood on your hands."

Suddenly there was a crash outside the door and a voice screamed out. Tomas rushed to the door and opened it. Outside Ovilium stood pinned by Pybus against the wall. Pybus held a knife to the man's throat.

"What the hell is going on here?" Shouted Tomas. "Take that knife away Pybus."

Pybus dropped his hand.

"I found him listening at your door." Pybus turned fierce eyes at Tomas.

"Be calm, Pybus" he spoke to Ovilium who now stood quietly. "What were you doing here?"

"Master, I came to tell you that Scribonia needs your help. I was about to knock when this man........" he spat towards Pybus "this creature grabbed me."

"You were listening." Pybus cried. "I saw you bending down to listen."

Tomas stepped between them. "Now stop this you two. I will go to my mother and what brought you here Pybus?"

"I came to find you. It is time we went to the tavern as we always do."

"I am not coming Pybus. I am staying here with my wife" and he put an arm round Cleolia who had joined them in the passageway.

"But who shall I drink with?" Pybus looked cross.

"Perhaps you should take Ovilium." Tomas grinned as the other man began to move away.

"I'd rather drink alone and anyway he is but a slave. Have you forgotten that I am a Freedman Tomas."

"You never let me forget that." laughed Tomas. "Now off you go. I must go to Scribonia. Come, my love." And he walked off leaving Pybus looking angrily after them.

"

Chapter 24

When they found Scribonia she had returned to her sewing. She looked up and smiled. "Nice to see you smiling Tomas." She said."Are things better between you?"

"He's not going drinking tonight," said Cleolia, still holding Tomas's hand. "And at least we have had a long chat, which is a good start, isn't it?"

"A great start" Scribonia said gently, "The next thing will be moving on, but these things take time." She held up her hand "Now I want you to know that I don't want to know anything about what you have discussed. Now you are talking honestly, which I hope you are, I have done all I can for now. However, remember I am always here should you need an old lady's advice."

"You are not an old lady, mother. Look at you working all day keeping this house working smoothly."

"Well be that as it may, you know how much I love you both and I want this special time, with a little one on the way, to be a happy one."

"It will be. I have been selfish and horrible. I realise that now and will not let that happen again, I promise. Now what did want me to do for you?"

"Just be my Tomas who is kind and thoughtful."

"I will be that but what did you send Ovilium to fetch me for?"

"I did not send Ovilium for you. You know that man gives me the creeps. He is so like that Monster whom you father killed in the arena."

"Well as you said yourself he is not that man. He is a good slave and works well. His strength has been really valuable to me. He can do the work of two men with ease."

Cleolia spoke."Well Tomas why was he at the door if your mother did not send him?"

"I am sure there was some mistake. Pybus is such a fiery individual. He is always looking for a fight."

"Well whatever you say I can't like the man. Now you two. How about a cup of wine?"

She walked from the room and they followed.

That night when Tomas and Cleolia went to their room, Tomas sat on the edge of the bed and motioned Cleolia to sit beside him.

"Ever since we married I have not shared your bed, as you know. Do you feel able to trust me to sleep beside you tonight? I will control myself and not try anything. But until the baby is born, I should so like to lie close to you."

Cleolia looked a little anxious. "I would like to try that Tomas because I want to be close to you as well. But I am still rather worried that I may be afraid again. I do not want to be but I am still afraid."

"Shall I wear my loin cloth? Would that help?"

"Tomas I do not know."

"Come here, my love." said Tomas as he gathered her into his arms. He gently tilted her face up towards his and placed a light kiss on her lips. "I will never abuse you again. I suggest that we take things very slowly. May I kiss you again?"

"Of course you may. I love the feel of your lips on mine." And she moved her face closer and kissed his lips. Tomas drew back.

"Well. Let us take that as a start. I will sleep on the other bed a bit longer. I want to spend more time with you but I need to get on with the vines. So I shall be up early tomorrow. But after our evening meal, there will be no going to the tavern. We will spend time together with perhaps a cuddle?" He smiles at her.

"You are so good to me Tomas. I am so sorry things are the way they are."

"It is not your fault, my love. If anything it is mine. I did not protect you when we ran away together all those years ago.

"You were only a child then, so it is not your fault either. Good night my love. Sleep well" and she climbed into the bed and fell instantly asleep.

*

Cleolia continued to be well during her pregnancy but grew every large and found moving about increasingly difficult. Tomas did as he had said and each evening they sat close together, arms round each other and talked of the days happenings.

All seemed quiet and happy as the days past but one evening Pybus came to the house. He called for Tomas and Tomas went outside with him.

"Well, What news?" Tomas asked the Greek.

"I have heard from my friend in Rome. It seems that Flavius does not seem to be seeking you.. He goes daily to the Senate and home again. He grows richer as the day pass. But he is to travel to Gaul in a few days time to visit his mother who lives near Forum Julia.. This could be our chance to deal with him."

Excited Tomas slapped him on the back. "Good we will go to where his mother lives and wait for him. But we must be quick and go tonight. Do not tell anyone where we are going or for what reason. When Flavius is dead we will return and tell Cleolia. She will be delighted. Go and get Chilo. He can tell Cleolia and Scribonia in the morning where we have gone.. By then it will be too late to stop us." Pybus went off and Tomas went to saddle the horses. Half an hour later they had gone.

*

The next day, Cleolia woke to find herself alone. She suspected that Tomas had got up early to go into the fields. But after she had breakfasted she asked Scribonia if she knew where Tomas was.

"I have no idea." Said Scribonia. "I assume he is out working."

Arria came dancing into the room. She sat down at the table and began to eat.

Chilo came in with some fruit and Scribonia asked him

"Have you seen your master today?"

Chilo bowed his head. "No." He said "I expect he is in the fields."

"His horse is gone." Said Arria.

"He has probably gone for supplies" Chilo bowed and left the room.

But as the day went on there was no sign of Tomas and by the evening Cleolia was beginning to worry. She ate her meal with Scribonia and when they had finished she asked again if Scribonia had seen Tomas.

Scribonia called the slave and in came one of the old slave who had been with them since they arrived at the house.

"Do you know where Tomas is?" asked Scribonia.

"I saw him ride off with Pybus early this morning but I have not seen him return." The man said.

"Where can he have gone and with Pybus.?" Cleolia looked worriedly at her mother in law.

"It is strange that he didn't tell us where he was going." Scribonia also seemed concerned. "Maybe he has gone off with Pybus for a drinking session."

"I am sure he has not done that." Cleolia was adamant. "He has been good for a long time now." She turned to the slave. "Send someone to the town and see if anyone has seen him." The slave bowed and left the room..

But the man returned to say that Tomas was not in the town.

Cleolia was very worried but the next day a messenger came to the door. He dismounted and knocked loudly. A slave answered and came quickly to the kitchen where Cleolia and Scribonia were sitting drinking cool water.

"There is a man at the door who asks for Cleolia." He said bowing.

Cleolia struggled to her feet. She was now heavy with chid and found moving was getting more and more uncomfortable. She made her way to the door where the man stood.

"I am Cleolia" she said "have you news of my husband?"

"Indeed" the man said. "He wishes you to know that he will be returning tomorrow and will explain his absence."

"Where is he?"

"He told me not to say." The man made to move away but Cleolia put her arm on his shoulder. "Please tell me." She pleaded.

"He will come back tomorrow,". And shaking free of Cleolia's hand he jumped on his horse and rode away.

Later that afternoon, Cleolia sought out Scribonia.

"Scribonia," she said sitting down beside the older woman. "I am a little concerned. My baby does not seem to move this last day or two. Do you think he is all right/"

"Prepare yourself, my daughter. Babies often stop kicking when they are near to being born."

"I am so glad you are here to guide me," Cleolia said "I should be so much more fearful if you were not here."

Scribonia smiled. "It is nothing. All girls need a mother at times like this and I am so glad to have you." She paused. "Tomas too seems a lot more relaxed. And he doesn't go drinking any more. That is so good. I am glad things are better. I understand it is hard for you both but time is on your side. Are things better between you?"

"Oh Yes. We talk and spend the evenings together. I love him so much and I feel sure things will work out in the end. I miss him and I wonder where he has gone."

Suddenly Cleolia gasped and gripped the arm of the chair. For a moment her face turned white and she looked up at Scribonia.

"Was that a pain?" asked the older lady.

"It has passed now. I am not sure." "Well lie down on the couch over there and relax. If it is the birth pains it will happen again soon. Then we will be sure."

Cleolia struggled to her feet and moved towards the couch but as she moved a cascade of water fell from her onto the floor. She gasped in horror.

"Don't worry" said Scribonia rising to help her to the couch. "That is a sure sign that my grandchild is going to make an appearance.. . You lie quietly. There is plenty of time. Why Tomas took a whole day and a half to arrive."

Scribonia went to the door and called for a slave. Ovilium appeared at the end of the corridor. Scribonia took a deep breath and called to him.

"Go and see if you can find get your master "she said hastily. "Tell him to come here at once." Then as Ovilium turned to go, she stepped back into the room.

"I feel very angry at myself that I dislike that man so much. I suppose it is because he has the same name as the man Argoutus killed in the arena. And he looks much the same too."

"He is too young to be that Ovilium and anyway that man is dead."

"It could be his son."

"That is not possible also. His father is here with him." Oh.........." she grabbed her stomach once again. "It must be the child coming. Where is Tomas I want him here."

"He will come. Now lie back and be content. Think how exciting it will be when the baby comes. Ovilium will find him. And the messenger said he would be here soon."

"He said tomorrow."

.

.

Chapter 25

"So how do we lure him away and where shall we take him?" Pybus spoke as the two sat beside the road watching the horses and carts driving past, while they ate the last of the cold meat and bread they had brought with them. "We cannot just approach him in the street and kill him!!"

Thomas nodded. "Yes. You are right. Maybe we should find out if he is in the town and if not travel out the way he will come and ambush him.?"

Pybus put down his leather water bottle and stood up. "Well In that case we must hurry." He watched as a long group of horses passed by. He turned back to Tomas. "there are too many people on this road and I expect it will be the same the other side of Forum Julii. We need to lure him off the main road."

"How can we do that?" Tomas asked rising to stand beside his friend. "We need to find someone to help by getting him to say there is a sick man in the woods or something like that. He knows us both now."

"That could be difficult. But we can think about it on the way. Come on" and Pybus mounted his horse and Tomas doing the same followed.

It was a clear sunny day with not a sign of a cloud in the sky as they came to where the road was lined with tall forest. Glad of the shade they made, they pushed the horses along the road. At a fork in the road they reined in and Tomas called "Which way?"

"I have no idea but most people are going left so I expect that is the way to the town. We must be nearing it now."

Just them he saw an old man leaning on a stick near the side of the road and he moved his horse towards him;

"Sir." He called down at the man. "which is the way to Forum Julii?"

The man looked up at him. "My friends," he said in a weak voice. "Most people go that way." He pointed to the left. "But the other way is better if you don't have a cart. On horseback that road leads through the woods and is a lot quicker. Just too narrow for a cart."

Pybus signalled to Tomas and they went off along the road to the right. The road was indeed narrow and they had to slow the horses while they negotiated the twists and turns of the road as it led through the forest. Suddenly they came upon a fallen tree trunk which spanned the road. It wide branches prevented them from jumping the horses over it. They pulled up.

"Do you think we can move it?" called Tomas to Pybus who has halted beside him. Pybus dropped from his horse and surveyed the trunk.

"Yes, It may be possible to get some of the branches out of the way so that we can jump it." called Pybus. He began pulling at the branches and they began to break off.

Tomas dismounted, casually, hooked the horses' reins to a nearby tree and went to help Pybus.

Suddenly there was a loud crash beside them. The trees cleared and a group of men appeared with swords drawn. Pybus was the first to react. He had put his sword down beside Tomas's on the ground beside him but before he could reach it, he found himself pulled to the ground and his hands roughly tied behind his back. In a moment Tomas too suffered the same fate and the two were thrown against another tree and bound to it with strong rope. One of the men came close and thrust his face near to Tomas.

"Well, my friends! he chuckled. "Here we are with you at our mercy. Flavius will be pleased." The other men gathered round. The man turned and ordered one to unleash the two horses. Being hit hard on the rear, they galloped off into the distance.

Tomas watched them go. He swore to himself. What fools they had been to be ambushed by the man who they had come to kill as clearly these were Flavius' men. He could not see Flavius amongst them.

"Where is Flavius?" he said through clenched teeth.

One of the men slapped Tomas across the face. "Shut up!" Another approached him. "There is bounty out for your capture and we mean to get it. Flavius will pay well."

"What must we pay for you to release us?" asked Pybus. "We have money."

The man laughed. "Not enough. My friend." He turned to the other men. "OK. Gallus, you stay here while we go and find Flavius. Guard them well. They are a slippery pair." He spat at Pybus and the group mounted their horses and set off along the path, leaving the guard behind. He sat down and took out a bottle of water and drank hard.

For a while there was silence.. Then Pybus spoke quietly to Tomas.

"How well are you tied up?"

"Too well." Tomas tried to wriggle but his bounds were too well fixed. All he could do was move his head. "What about you?"

"No chance. I feel like a chicken trussed for the pot."

"Bloody idiots, we are. We came to catch Flavius and he ambushed us."

Gallus, the guard rose. "Shut up, there."

"Any chance of a drink?" Pybus asked.

The man crossed to him and put his face next to Pybus. "None whatsoever." He grinned.

Just as he spoke there was a sound of someone coming along the path. Gallus swung round, his hand on his sword.

Into view came a woman and child. She stopped in horror as she saw the scene before her and gathering the child to her she made to run back the way she had come. Gallus gave chase.

Tomas and Pybus listened as there came the sound of a scream and it was clear that Gallus had caught up with her. Tomas swore. The screams continued.

"What is he doing to her/"

Suddenly, the small child who had been with her broke through the bushes. He ran towards them, then hesitated.

Tomas spoke gently to him. "Come here boy. We will not hurt you." The boy looked at them with a frightened expression. "That man is hurting my mother."

Tomas spoke in a stage whisper. "If you will untie me I will help your mother."

The boy looked uncertain but another screech from the woman and he came nearer. "Go behind the tree, my son and see if you can untie my hands. The rest I can do myself." As the boy hesitated he smiled at him. "I will not hurt you but I promise I will save your mother."

The boy did as he was asked and after a few vain attempts Tomas felt the bonds loosen. He pulled himself free and leant to untie his feet. Then he went to Pybus and undid his bonds also.

Pybus spoke. "Tomas. We have no weapons and the man has a sword. Maybe we should just get out of here."

Tomas sneered at him. "We promised and that man will not be expecting us. We can do this."

Together they moved towards the noises leaving the boy following behind.

They rounded the corner and there they came upon the man and the woman. The man had removed his trousers and was in the act of raping the woman. In an instant Tomas fell upon them and grabbing the man around the waist, threw him away across the clearing. He gave a muffled cry and lay there hugging his private parts and groaning. Pybus picked up the sword. He moved towards the man and placed the tip into his throat. "Great guard you are." He said. He turned to where Tomas was helping the woman to her feet. "Shall I kill him?"

"First see if you can find out who betrayed us to Flavius. They knew we were coming. Someone must have told them our plans. Then let's get out of here."

He looked at the lady who was standing a little shakily in front of him with the child clinging to her skirt. He beckoned her to follow him and he moved away along the path. "Are you all right, lady?" he asked. "Is there a man at home to protect you?"

"Thank you Sir" she replied. "I was foolish to wander out here with the child but it is usually so quiet here. I am not hurt."

"Get along home then," he said patting the boy on the head. He paused. "Did you know that man. Is he from around here?"

The lady shook her head. "No. I have not seen him before. You are a stranger here as well. Why were you tied up?"

"It is a long story," replied Tomas. "and your little boy has saved our lives. He is a hero!" He put his hand in his pocket and brought out a coin. He passed it to the woman.

The boy peeped at him from behind his mother's skirt. She accepted the money and said "What did he do?"

"He untied us so that we could come to your aid and deliver us from a group of men that are after us. I fear we must be on our way before the rest of them come back to finish us off." He smiled at her. "Are you OK to get home?"

"Yes I am fine mow and thank you again."

There was a scream from behind them and Pybus came back grinning. He went over and picked up the ropes and walked off saying over his shoulder. "I think I'll tie him up and leave him to wait for his friends."

The lady and child moved off and Tomas went to see what Pybus had done.

He entered the clearing to see Pybus dragging an unconscious figure towards a tree. Tomas went to help and they managed to tie the man up and leave him trussed against the tree. His face was blooded and there was a tell tale damp area on his trousers, which were still gaping open.

"Will he live?" asked Tomas.

"I hope so for a bit anyway. Now let's get out of here. The horses are gone so we must walk" and they set off back towards the main road.

Within an hour they were again at the cross roads. The old man had gone but there were lots of carts and people on horseback travelling along the road.

"I don't suppose we have any money?" asked Pybus searching his pockets.

"No. They took all I had and there is nothing to barter with."

Pybus pulled a gold pendent from his shirt. "I have this but I would rather not part with it."

"I will give you another if you let us use it. I really feel that I should get home. I don't want to miss my child being born and it will take days to walk."

Pybus unhooked the pendent and passed it to Tomas. They approached the next cart and stood waving for it to stop. It was old and rickety. The driver stopped and glanced at them.

"What are you stopping me for, Tomas!!?"

"Well. If it isn't Gaius!" Tomas went close. "you look strange in that hat. Are you going home?"

"Yes, indeed. I expect to be there by night fall. Want a lift?"

"We do indeed." Tomas smiled. "You are a gift from the Gods. We were set upon by thieves and left with nothing. I need to get back and we lost our horses as well as all our money but I will pay you later."

"No problem, Tomas. It will be company."

So Tomas and Pybus clambered onto the cart and they set off for home.

**

Scribonia had taken Cleolia to her room. She sent a slave to fetch the midwife and sat holding her hand. When the pain came again, Scribonia was counting. "It is a long time yet my child so relax. Tomas will come."

"I wonder where he went!" Aria sighed.

"Perhaps he has gone to find a present for the baby."

"Maybe. But what if he has gone to fight? He could be killed!"

"Now, you are worrying far too much. Why should he go to fight? Pybus is with him. He will come to no harm."

It was a couple of hours later when the physician arrived with the midwife. He examined Cleolia and was happy that all was well and that the baby although on its way would be some time yet before it arrived.

The midwife settled down to wait. She had brought with her an array of potions and ointments which she laid out on a table beside the birthing chair. This was a strange stool with a hole through which to deliver the baby and high sides for the mother to grip onto. She put this to one side and taking some of the ointments which smelled strongly of herbs, she rubbed it into her hands. She instructed Cleolia to lie down and put her hands into her smearing the ointment as far up as she could.

Scribonia watched in silence. She knew the risks of childbirth for both mother and child and remembered her first birthing when the baby had died after only a few minutes but she kept a smile on her face and tried to reassure Cleolia that all was well.

The midwife was an oldish lady with grey wispy hair but she had a kind face and seemed confident in what she was about.

"This has been my job for over twenty years," she said smiling at Cleolia "so you need not fear I will see that you are cared for." Just relax when you can and I will tell you what to do."

As she spoke another pain wracked through Cleolia's body and she screamed.

"Now, Now" said the midwife. "There is no need to make such a noise. Remember it will be for only a few hours and you will have a great prize at the end."

"A few hours!!" gasped Cleolia as the pain subsided.

The midwife laughed. "It will pass quickly. Tell me when the pains change and you want to push. Perhaps a glass of wine would be good." She turned to Scribonia. "For me not her," she chuckled, "She can drink water."

"Where is Tomas?" moaned Cleolia. "Has Ovilium returned?"

Scribonia shook her head. "I have not seen him but I am sure Tomas will come, if the Gods wish it" Again Cleolia screamed in pain and the midwife brought more herbal drinks to her. As the pain left her and she had spat out the horrid liquid, they heard the door open and in rushed Arria.

"He is coming!!" she shouted, "I have seen the dust the horses make on the horizon/"

Scribonia heaved a sigh of relief. "Thanks to the Gods!" she said as she hurried to the door.

She ran through the house and was standing on the terrace as the horses came to a halt. "Come My son," she called "Your child is being born. Hurry, Hurry."

Tomas sprang from the saddle throwing the reins to a waiting slave. He ran through the house and into the room. The midwife had helped Cleolia into the birthing chair and she was gripping the arms as she pushed the child out. Tomas grabbed her shoulder and leaned to kiss the sweating forehead. Cleolia managed a wan smile as the next contraction raked her body.

Tomas turned to his mother who had entered the room. "Why is the child so early? I thought it was not for days yet."

"Babies come when they are ready. Where have you been? I sent Ovilium to find you. Did he do so?"

Tomas took Cleolia's hand from the chair and held it tightly. "We saw no one. Pybus and I had some business to deal with." Again Cleolia strained down and screamed as with a rush of fluid the baby slithered out into the waiting hands of the midwife.

"A son!" She called holding the little bundle up high. As she did so a lusty cry filled the room. She smiled. "He is well." She wrapped the child in a piece of cloth and handed him to Tomas.. The tiny baby gulped and opened his blue eyes and let them rest on his father. A tear ran down Tomas's cheek as he passed the child to Cleolia. "We are indeed blessed. My beautiful wife now has a beautiful son and I am the proudest of fathers." He kissed Cleolia again and together they looked at their new son with unabashed adoration.

Chapter 27

They called him Tomas and as the days sped by the baby grew healthy and strong. Cleolia recovered from the birth with ease and refused the services of a wet nurse. She delighted in feeding 'baby Tomas' as he was soon known, and late at night Tomas would sit by the bed as Cleolia suckled the child, his eyes alight with joy.

"I had no idea that having a child was so special" he said happily taking the baby from Cleolia and putting him over his shoulder to wind him.

Cleolia laughed. "You make a great slave to him Tomas. Most fathers have little interest in babies."

"I can't imagine why. He is a perfect child and the love I bear him surpasses everything I have ever known."

"Even me?" Cleolia smiled.

For a moment Tomas was silent. He turned to her and passed the baby back. "You know." He said seriously. "I have never loved anyone as I love you but with a child the love is so different. I want to protect him and watch him grow and give him everything I can to make his life perfect."

"I don't think we can ever do that but we will try. That is the best any parent can do."

"Do you think we will love our next child as much?"

Instantly Cleolia's eyes seemed shadowed. "Our next child?" she asked with a low voice.

But Tomas had not heard the shake in her voice or seen the change in her face. He rose and walked to the window. "I want lots of children. Boys and girls to love the land as I do and feel the warm earth beneath their feet. I want to grow old with a big family around me and you, of course, my lovely girl. with grandchildren on your knee."

Cleolia was silent dropping her eyes to the floor. Tomas swung round.

"Don't you want that too?" he asked moving towards her.

When she raised her eyes there were tears in them. Tomas dropped down beside her. He looked into her eyes.

"Cleolia." He spoke softly laying a hand on her knee. "We have to sort this out. We love each other and I desire you. I know that I was unforgivably cruel on our wedding night......."

"It was not your fault." Cleolia interrupted him. "I offered myself. I thought it would be all right and then......"

"We have talked about that time and we need to put it behind us. We now need to start afresh. I believe I can make you happy and unafraid now because I understand better what happened to you. I can control my passion and teach you to enjoy our coupling too. Last time we talked you said that you would feel happier if Flavius was dead. Well that was the reason I went off with Pybus. We heard that Flavius was near visiting his mother and we went to fine him."

"What happened?"

"Somehow he knew we were coming and set a trap for us. Of course we got away but it was close. I cannot see how he could have known as I only told Pybus. He would never let me down. I trust him implicitly. I'm afraid there must be someone who heard us talking. It must have been here or on the journey but somehow Flavius found out. There was an old man at the cross roads who gave us directions which we followed and his men were waiting for us. They captured us and took our horses but a child came and set us free. We left the guard tied to a tree and had to beg a lift back.

Anyway now we have a son and all will be well."

"Does Flavius know where we live?"

"If he did then he would have been here by now. Let's forget him and concentrate on being a family." But although Tomas said the words he was all too aware that he had not got rid of his enemy yet.

***

Tomas had become used to going to bed half dressed. Many nights he had lain awake desiring his lovely wife but he had restrained himself. He was always tired after his long days in the fields but often he would toss and turn longing to love her and sometimes he got out of bed and went out into the night alone.

One night when the child had begun to crawl about the floor and would talk in strange noises to his mother and father, Tomas took Cleolia to one side.

"Now little Tomas is growing older. We could leave him with his grandmother in the afternoon and I could take you to bed and teach you how to love me. I will be very gentle and not do anything which may distress you. That I promise. But now that Tomas is six months old we should be thinking of another child."

Cleolia was silent a moment. Then she said "You are right and I would love another child but I am still afraid Tomas. I will lie still and you can take me."

"Never." Tomas rose from the chair and stamped across the room. "How can you suggest that? You want me to rape you again!? "

"It was not rape Tomas. I am your wife.."

"What difference is that.? To take a woman unwilling is rape."

"But I am willing."

"No you are not. Willing means loving and caring and with passion."

"But I do love you and care about you."

Tomas returned to sit beside her. "Cleolia my love. You have to desire me. When I see you I am aroused with passion. My body and my soul long for you. I want to touch you and kiss your body. What I did on our wedding night was ugly. But it should have been beautiful and gentle and all encompassing. Your body should sing for mine as mine does for yours. You have started because you lie beside me and my body does not frighten you. I kiss you gently and you do not draw away. But you do not open your mouth to me.

Cleolia made to speak but Tomas stopped her with a wave of his hand.

"Let me finish." He spoke kindly. "Do you not feel anything for me? Does not your body make feeling in you? Are you never aroused? Do you never want to touch my body? Let me try and bring you to desire. I know you have it in you. I will be gentle and not penetrate you until you ask me. Is that not a fair deal, my love? I have needs and you have too. Can you not forget the past? You are safe here with me and I swear I will never take you against your will and against what your body says to you. It can be slow and you may take as long as you wish. I will always love you whatever happens. If it takes a lifetime I will wait for you."

Cleolia was silent. "I get so afraid. The past looms over me. I want things to be right between us and I feel so guilty that I do not give you what a wife should give."

"I know .Cleolia I see in your eyes the love you give our child. I see in your daily life the love you have for me. But duty is not enough for me. I could not bear to have sex with you when you fear it. That time will always stay in my heart as a betrayal of love. I will never repeat it. I would rather stay all my life celibate then cause you the pain and distress that I did then. It still haunts my dreams. I am determined that you should heal from your past and become a true wife by choice not by duty."

"But I do not know how to do that. I do want that too, of course, but I do not know how it can happen. The sight of you aroused fills me with dread and fear. How can that change?"

"Leave that to me. I will help you. All I need from you is a promise to let us try. If it fails I will still love you. I can never love anyone else or, for that matter, do I want to. You have been mine since the first day we met as children. We have a strong son. We are a family. And I promise I will never leave you and also I will never take you sexually against you will."

"I can but try and for you I will do anything."

"And will you trust me?"

"Yes, I will trust you."

"Well, tomorrow we will leave Baby Tomas with his grandmother and we will spend the afternoon together. I will come home from the fields for my meal and then we will take a walk in the woods and I will teach you to kiss me."

He leaned over and gave her a peck on the check. Then he cupped her face in his hands . "All will be well. my love. For you will overcome your fears and we will be lovers one day when things are right for you and not before."

Cleolia rose and watched Tomas walk from the room. A moment later Scribonia entered, carrying the baby in her arms. She smiled at Cleolia and passed the baby over.

"Tomas looks happy" she said. "What have you done to make him so jolly? He was whistling as he went and I have not heard him do that for ages."

"Nothing special," Cleolia replied lightly. "He is so happy to have a son. I believe him to be a real father. He cares so much for his little one."

"So he should." Scribonia commented. "but his little one needs a feed. I will leave you in peace." And she went out the door.

Murmuring quietly to her son Cleolia put him to her breast. She sighed. "Will everything be all right from now on and will I be able to be a good wife? She shuddered. "But I will try. Tomorrow Tomas will guide me and one day all wlI be well."

But tomorrow things were about to change.

Chapter 28

The next morning Tomas rose early and slipped out of the room. He paused only to look at his sleeping wife and their little son lying quietly in his cot. It had been a long night. Little Tomas had cried a lot and he was happy to see that now he looked peaceful and quiet. There was a spring in his step as he walked through the kitchen, grabbing a warm loaf of bread plastered with soft cheese. He bit into it as he made his way across the grass and over the gate towards the fields. In the clear blue sky several birds floated above him. The air was cool and clear. He shouted to Olivium to come and help with the vines and strode off whistling to himself. He really believed that he was going to make things right with Cleolia. "All she needs is time and gentleness." He said to himself.

Back in the house, Cleolia stirred and rose from the bed. The baby had slept fitfully and as she dressed and lifted him from the cot he struggled and began to cry again. She carried him into the kitchen where Scribonia was sitting eating her breakfast.

"I do not know what is the matter with him." She told her mother in law. "He has been crying most of the night. Do you think he is hungry? Shall I give him some solid food?"

Scribonia nodded. "You could try. Just a little at first and see if he seems more content. I will mix him a little milk and bread. That is the best way to try."

She took a bowl and poured a little milk into it, then added some crumbled bread. When it was soft she pushed the bowl towards Cleolia.

"Try that. Put a little on your finger and let him suck it off."

The baby made a face and burst into tears. Cleolia rose and began to walk round the room to comfort him but he just cried louder.

"Give him to me." Scribonia said rising and holding out her hands." I expect he can smell your milk."

Cleolia passed him over but to no avail. Little Tomas screamed and struggled. Scribonia put a hand on his head. "Cleolia," she exclaimed. "he is hot. Feel his head. I think he is ill."

Cleolia took the baby back and cradled him to her breast. She offered him the nipple but he just screamed the more and pulled his head away.. "What shall we do?"

"Let's cool him down and then if he is still ill we will call the physician." She rose and dampened a cloth and held it to his head. After a moment the screaming dies down and the baby fell asleep.

"Thank goodness for that," said Cleolia. She gently cradled the baby in her arms looking down at his calm face.

Suddenly the chid began to shake and the calm left his face.

"Help" screamed Cleolia. "Fetch the physician."

Scribonia rushed from the room. A few moments later she reappeared with Chilo. "How is he now?" she asked. The child lay still now with little beads of perspiration across his brow.

Scribonia turned to Chilo. "Go send word to the physician. Then go and find your master. Tell him the baby is sick. Hurry"

Chilo left the room.. Within a moment the baby began to shake again. Scribonia took him from Cleolia and laid him on the table. "Bring cold water." She shouted at Cleolia. She began to remove his clothes. "He must be cooled down." she said ripping the clothes from him. "See he has a red rash on his chest. I will bathe him. Bring more water."

There was a noise behind them and a slave stood at the door.

"There is an old woman at the door . I told her to go but she insists on seeing the baby. She says he is ill and she can help."

Scribonia answered. "What old lady? How does she know the baby is sick?"

Just then a weird figure pushed past into the room. She wore a long black cape and from it wisps of grey tangled hair protruded over her wrinkled face. She brought with her the stink of damp leaves and rotten fruit and the slave retreated quickly. Scribonia moved from the table where the child was lying suddenly quiet again.

"Who are you and what do you mean by pushing your way in here?"

"Where is his father?" the old lady croaked, coming towards the table and looking down at the baby.

Cleolia rushed towards her and pushed her away..

"Go away! She screamed "Don't touch him." She gathered him up and clasped him to her.

The old lady laughed a laugh which sounded more like a creaking door than a laugh. "You need me." She croaked. "Without me the child will die. I can see the future and I am a wise woman. I came here before on your wedding day. I warned your husband but he denied me. Now you will suffer unless you do as I say."

"We have sent for the physician. He will help us."

"He will be too late. See how the child breathes. He is very ill."

Cleolia took a step towards her, suddenly subdued, all her anxieties coming to the surface. "What can we do?"

"Get his father. He has the power to save the child."

Scribonia hurried from the room. "I will find him." She called over her shoulder. The old lady held out her arms to Cleolia.

"Give me the child. I will keep him safe until Tomas arrives."

"How do you know my husband's name?" Cleolia said still hugging the baby to her.

"Never mind that." The old lady made to grab the child. "You must give him to me."

Reluctantly Cleolia let her take the baby. He was quiet but deadly pale and he struggled for each breath. The old lady put her hand out and touched Cleolia's arm in a strange way which made Cleolia relax a little.

"I cannot lose him," she said tears running down her checks. "He is a part of me."

"As the Gods wish, my child." The old lady began to rock the child in her arms.

"You must save him! He is my world." cried Cleolia.

"Only his father can do that." The old lady said.

"How can Tomas save him?"

"He must make sacrifice for him"

"But...."Cleolia began as the door flung open and Tomas strode into the room.

"What are you doing here?" he shouted seeing the old lady with the child. He tried to wrench the child from her arms. She pulled away grasping the child closer to her. She looked up at him and their eyes met. He stopped in his tracks, glaring at her.

"It is you." He shouted. "What mischief do you do here today?. Give me my child."

"You remember me Tomas?" the old woman replied. "I came on your wedding day. I tried to warn you but you didn't listen. Now your child is dying in my arms. A child cursed by your passion."

Tomas stood transfixed, his eyes caught by hers. "What can I do?" he stammered.

"You must choose. Do you love this child?"

"More than my life!"

"Well said. because that is your choice. Him or you. Would you die for him truly? Give up your life that he may live and grow old.?"

"I would." Tomas dropped him glance. The room went cold and Cleolia tried to speak but could not. She went to Tomas and took hold of his arm.

"Don't listen to her." She cried. "The physician will come."

"He will not". The old woman cried. "You sent the wrong man for him. It is now up to Tomas. The Gods want a sacrifice and Tomas is that sacrifice. He can pass his life to his son."

Tomas suddenly jumped towards her and grabbed the baby.

"Go away you wicked woman. My child will live and so will I. Get out of my house." And passing the baby to Cleolia, he grabbed the woman by the hair and pulled her to the doorway. He threw her out into the bright sunshine.

"Never come here again." He called after her. They all stood silent as her cackling laugh echoed into the distance.

For a moment they stayed quiet. Tomas was the first to speak. He looked down at the child;

"He is breathing better" he said. "and look his colour is back. I believe he is asleep now."

Cleolia and Scribonia crowded round. Cleolia took the child. "I do believe you are right. He seems all right now." She took him and sat with him sleeping peacefully on her knee. "We should still see the physician."

"I will go and get him." Tomas moved to the door. "I will ride fast and come back soon." And he went from the room.

**

When he returned with the physician, it was to find Cleolia with the baby on her breast suckling happily.

The man followed Tomas into the room. He was gaunt and old but his eyes were kind. He put a bag on the floor and walked towards the mother and child. He held out his arms for the child and Cleolia passed him over. The man took him to the window and looked him over. Cleolia explained how the child had shaken and had been gasping for breath. "It sounds like he had a high fever but it has gone." He passed the child back to Cleolia. "I see nothing wrong. But watch him closely and come for me should it happen again."

Tomas gave the man money and ordered a slave to accompany him back to the town.

Scribonia asked "Did you see Chilo. I sent him for the physician earlier?

Tomas shook his head. "No! That is strange. I am rather concerned about him and his son. They work hard but seem unsettled. You remember when Pybus found Ovilium eves dropping by the door. He said that he had come to ask me to go to my mother but when I went you said you had not asked for me. I did not think much of it at the time. Could it be that they are spying on us?"

"But they helped you escape from Ubis. You asked them to come here. Why should they spy on us? What reason could there be?"

"I have no idea but I will watch them." He leant over Cleolia and kissed her forehead. "Do not fear. Everything will be fine."

"That awful woman said you would die!"

Tomas laughed. "Well. I feel fine, so stop worrying. Do I look as if I am dying?" and he kissed her again. He put his hand on the sleeping child's head. "And my son is calm and well again. Forget that old hag. She is just a trouble maker."

"She is a soothsayer. She is a wise woman. She knew the baby was ill but no one had told her. How did she know?"

Tomas crouched down on his knees and took her face in his hands. "My love, remember little Tomas is well now and that is what matters. Maybe he was just cutting a tooth."

"I am afraid of her, Tomas. Who is she and where did she come from? And suppose Little Tomas is ill once more and you are out in the fields. We live so far from the town. He could die before anyone comes."

Tomas rose and looked at his mother.

"Make her see sense, Mother. I must go back to the fields. I will come back as soon as I can. If you need me send for me but send another slave not Chilo or Ovilium/ They worry me."

Scribonia smiled "Go to your work. We will be fine here." But as she turned away, her face became anxious.

Chapter 29

For the next few days Cleolia stayed close to her baby anxiously watching his every move but he seemed fine and returned to his happy chuckling self. He was learning to crawl and would gurgle and babble to himself as he rolled about on the floor. Cleolia took him outside while she picked flowers and held them to his little nose trying to get him to smell them. She kept him in the shade and let him play on the ground beside her while she stitched small garments for him.

She was doing this when Tomas strode into the yard. He knelt down and lifted the child high into the air and the baby squealed with delight and clapped his hands.

"I have come to care for my little Tomas" he said to Cleolia. "You should go and rest. I know you do not sleep well, .always afraid for him but he is well. Whatever happened is over. He is thriving. There is no sign of any illness. Nor has there been since that day. You must think of yourself and rest for his sake as well as your own."

"I fear to leave him. Should he be ill again I would not know what to do. If that dreadful woman had not come he might have died."

Tomas sat down on the ground beside her and put little \Tomas next to her.

"You must forget all that. It is passed and little Tomas is well."

"If only we were nearer to the town so that the physician is at hand. I would feel better then."

"Do you want us to move?"

"Is it possible?"

Tomas was quiet for a while. "Well since Argoutus is dead, there is nothing to keep us here."

"But you have worked hard in the fields. Should we move to the town, what work could you do?"

"There could be many things I could do. I must admit that I have thought of a change ever since the fire. Although my back is well healed, heavy work does give me pain now."

"And Scribonia is getting older and she often just sits alone. She could make friends in the town and there is much to do there. The best thing in Glanum is the sacred spring. You can go there and get help for your back. It would be good for Scribonia too. There are baths and entertainment there and when Tomas is old enough he can go to school there."

"I had thought to teach him myself."

"Well" Cleolia shouted "There is the answer. You could be a teacher. There is no heavy work in that. You can read and write and work with numbers."

Tomas laughed at her with her shining eyes full of excitement.

"Wait a minute." He said "Not so fast. Let me think about it and tomorrow we will go to Glanum and take a look. I know the town well but I had not thought about going there to live and what about my mother? She must be consulted."

"But you will consider it?" Cleolia put her hands up to his face.

"How can I refuse you anything?" He dropped a kiss on her forehead. "And I think there is some sense in it. We will rise early and go in the morning. However, a good teacher speaks Greek and that I never learnt. I really cannot see ,myself stuck indoors all day. There are other jobs" and he kissed her again and walked from the room.

The next day they set out as the sun climbed over the hills and sent little ripples of shade before it. Tomas sat on the cart driving the horses while Scribonia, Arria and Cleolia with the baby on her knee, sat behind him. Scribonia had greeted the news of a possible move with some trepidation but smiled at her daughter in law and waited to see what might transpire. It was true she was lonely since Argoutus had died but she would be sad to move from her home with all the memories of their last years together. But as ever she would accept what the gods had planned for her and she knew that Arria would be pleased to be with other young people. It was time to marry her off and living so far from other homes she had met hardly any suitable men. She had seen her eyeing one of the slaves and that would never do!!

Arria was thrilled at the news. She hardly knew any people of her own age since like most young girls she had never attended school and had been taught by her mother. She could read and write but all else she learnt was to be a good wife to someone one day. At her age of eleven years she would soon be old enough to marry. Now her father was dead it would fall to Tomas to select a husband for her and she knew he would let her help find the right man. But at the moment she was more interested in meeting other girls. So far her companions had been slave children, which was all right but not really the people she wanted to meet.

It took only an half an hour to reach the outskirts of the town passing through little settlements until they came to the great mausoleum standing to the left of the road dominating the cemetery which stretched a long way under the trees. Just passed that was the curving lines of the ramparts There was a new arch being built over the road here to form a grand entrance to the town but as yet it was unfinished and they had to pass through the construction site. Groups of slaves carried stones up wooden scaffolding and on the ground stone masons sat carving figures and decorations into slabs of stone. Passing through, Tomas drew the cart up to the side of the road where there was a large flat aria for parking the carts and a slave came forward to take hold of the horses. From there they made their way into the town on foot along the curved main street. First on the right, they passed the grand houses of the high ranking citizens and opposite that the Baths. It was a busy road with people of all sorts crowded along its length. It was noisy and bustling and a complete contrast to the calm fields which surrounded their home. There were merchants and sellers of all sorts mingling with the crowds and the sights and sounds of the town. It was hard to move along the narrow road but soon they came to the large forum and the road widened out in front of the twin temples. Here the market was in full swing and small children ran about under the feet of the merchants picking up fruit and vegetables dropped by the stall holders.

"It is so noisy here" complained Scribonia but her voice was lost as Arria and Cleolia ran from one place to another wide eyed at the multi coloured fabrics and gold and silver jewellery set out before then. Tomas carried his little son and talked to him as he gazed about him, his little eyes shining and a smile on his lips.

"Would you like to live here, my son?" he laughed and carried his son up high on his shoulders. Then he called to the family and directed them to a tavern outside which were a row of benches. He and Scribonia sat down and soon the others joined them.

"This place is magic." cried Arria.

"You have been here before." Tomas replied. "Many times I have bought you here to sell the goods from the farm."

"I know but to live here would be so special. When can we move?"

"Have patience." Tomas smiled. "First we would have to find a house to live in."

Arria's eyes blazed. "What about that grand house we passed as we entered the town?"

"Don't be silly." said Cleolia "Someone already lives there and anyway we could not afford such a grand place." She turned to Tomas. "How do we find an empty house, Tomas?"

"First we must talk to the owner of this Tavern. He will know."

As he spoke and red nosed man in a great while apron came out and crossed towards them

"Hi Tomas!" he said. "What brings you here today? What can I get you to drink? "

"Wine for us all." replied Tomas. "But Vitus." He continued." We are considering moving into the town. Do you know if there are any empty houses here?

"I do not know of any at present. Tomas. Go to the Basilica." He said pointing back the way they had come. "Someone there will help you It would be good to have you here."

"Because he thinks you will be drinking here even more." whispered Cleolia, as the man moved off to get their drinks.

Tomas took the baby back onto his knee. "Well Little Tomas seems happy. What do you think, Mother?."

"It all seems a bit strange to me, but it reminds me of Rome. A lot smaller of course, but I think I am a city person at heart. We will soon settle."

Tomas smiled at her. "I love the countryside. I do not think I am a town person." He paused; "maybe it is because of my early life. But here we have the best of both worlds" He turned to Cleolia. " And you, my love? What do you feel?"

"I think we could be happy here. I should feel a lot happier being near other people so that if little Tomas was ever sick again, there would be help near at hand."

After they had drunk their wine and the cold water brought with it, they continued their exploration of the town. Past the Forum it was not so busy and they moved easily along until they came to the sacred spring. Here they stopped and watched as people queued to walk down the steps and sample the health giving water.

Passing on they came to the humble houses of the lesser citizens and Tomas went and knocked on a door.

"Who lives here Tomas?" asked Cleolia. "Do you know them?"

As she spoke the door opened and an old lady with unkempt hair and a grey lined face opened the door.

"Why Tomas!"She said smiling at him. "this must be your family."

Tomas went forward and embraced her. He turned to the others and said.

"This is Julia. She is Pybus 's mother."

Turning back to her he asked. "and I suppose Pybus is out?"

"Well. He is out but where I do not know. He is his own master as you well know. But come in. Tell me what brings you here."

They entered the cool vestibule and through into a small Atrium around which was a series of doors. They sat around the central column and told Julia about their plans and what they thought of the town..

"Well, Tomas," the old lady said when she had listened to their story, "I think you may be in luck. The old man who lived next door has died and he has no family.. The apartment is owned by a Roman senator who visits Glanum rarely and if you go to the Basilica they can probably tell you if it has been rented out yet. I do not know of the name of the Senator but the old man's man was Galo. He was here before the Romans came. His house may need to be updated but it could be a good home. I believe It has several rooms and he had a courtyard built recently with a small fountain."

Just as she finished speaking the door burst open and in strode Pybus.

He threw up his arms and hurried to embrace Tomas. "My friend." He cried. "What bring you and the family here?"

After Tomas had explained once again, Pybus laughed happily.

"My drinking partner on the doorstep," He cried.

Tomas put a hand on his shoulder. "I shall not move here to drink." He said. "So you can forget that. I am taking my duty as a father and husband very seriously now."

Pybus slapped him on the back. "I know Tomas. I know. I am joking. But I will enjoy having you around. But where will you live? And what will happen to your farm?"

"All these details are yet to be sorted out. We came today to see how the place felt. That was all."

"And how does it feel?" Pybus replied.

"I love it!" Arria called out getting up and moving towards Pybus. "I really want to live here."

Pybus put a warm hand on Arria's shoulder. "Well. That is one certain anyway" and he ruffled her hair. He put his hands on her shoulders and stood looking at her.

"The little lady is growing up." He said smiling at her. "Do you suppose you will find a husband here?"

Arria laughed at him. "I might. At least there is more chance for me here than stuck on that farm."

After a little while they gathered themselves together and left. They went on and looked at the outside of the apartment block next door. "I am not sure about living in an apartment." Scribonia complained.

"Well," said Tomas. "I will make enquiries and then we can arrange to see inside. There is plenty of time to decide. I have to find someone to buy the farm first of all."

They retraced their steps along the road passing the Forum and stopped beside the Basilica. Tomas went in but a few minutes later came out again.

"The place is not open at the moment. I shall return tomorrow. Come now I think we should be making our way home."

**

That night after their meal, the family sat discussing their trip to Glanum. It seemed that generally they all felt happy about the idea and Tomas promised to visit again in the morning.

As darkness fell Scribonia and Arria went off to bed and Tomas and Cleolia remained. They sat beside the central fountain and Cleolia fed the baby who then drifted off to sleep in her arms.

Tomas rose and took Cleolia by the hand.

"Come." He said "It is time we went to bed." And he led her to their room. She laid the baby in his cot in the corner of the room and turned to Tomas. She went to him as was their custom and bade him goodnight with a kiss on the check. But as she turned to go to her bed, Tomas held on to her.

"Cleolia. Wait a moment." He said turning her to face him. "Do not go off to bed yet." And he pulled her to him and buried his head in her hair. For a moment she seemed to be resisting him but gradually she relaxed against him.

"My beautiful girl," he murmured into her hair. "I love you so much. I want only for you to be happy and if moving will make you feel safer then that is what we will do." He lifted her face towards his and cupped it so that she could only look straight into his eyes. "Do you see the love in my eyes?"

"Yes, my husband. I see it" Her voice trembled a little but she did not pull away.

"Do you believe I would never hurt you again?"

Her eyes dropped from his and he felt her body stiffen, but she whispered "Yes."

"And I never will. But I want to teach you about true physical love. It is not a thing to fear. What happened when you were a child and what has happened since we must put behind us."

"I cannot forget."

He pulled her against his chest again and put his arms tight around her.

"Listen to me. What we will do together is nothing to do with what happened in the past. First I need you to feel confident in me. So many times I have told you that I will not take you unless you want it. How can I make you believe me?"

"I do believe you Tomas. It is not you, it is me. I am the cursed one."

"Of course you are not. That is nonsense. If anyone is at fault it is me. But I do not want to go over it all again.. We are making a new start. The past is gone and we cannot undo it. So now we will look only to the future and in that future you and I will learn to show our love in the special way that lovers do. Not sex but love. Not for physical release but for love of each other. The two are not the same. If I went and had sex with a slave girl do you think I would love her? Of course I would not. I want you to want me. To want the feel of me inside you. To feel the ecstasy which comes from an act made out of love. And I promise as I have a million times that until _you_ tell me you want that, I will not do anything for my own pleasure. We are in this together, Cleolia. It is not about your fears or my needs, it is about us. Put you face up to mine, Cleolia." She did so and he put his lips on hers and kissed her gently like a passing whisper and then pulled away.

Then he pushed her away and turned from her to his bed.

"Well," he said loudly. "We should get some sleep." He went over and looked at the sleeping child. "Goodnight my little one. Sleep and dream of conquest and honour and grow to be a good man."

Cleolia stood for a moment feeling in some way bereft but unsure why and she then turned herself and went to her own bed.

Chapter 30

The following day, Tomas rose early and went off to the fields to see that the slaves were busy at their work. Scribonia and Arria were in the kitchen where Scribonia was showing Arria how to bake bread.

Suddenly there was a commotion at the door and Pybus strode into the rom. He bid them good day .

"Whatever you are cooking smells good," he remarked ruffling Arria's hair. "Are you learning to be a good cook, Arria?"

"I am anxious to learn all I can now so that when we live in the town I can be out with my new friends most of the time."

"What brings you here Pybus?" asked Scribonia.

"I have news for Tomas. Is he here?"

"He is out in the fields. But he should be back soon. He is intending to go into Glanum again today."

"Good because I came to see him before he goes"

Just then Cleolia entered the room carrying her child. "Why Pybus" she said. "Tomas was coming to the town later and was hoping to meet you."

"I am glad, because I have a plan to talk to him with regard to your moving to Glanum"

Arria ran over and took the baby. "Cleolia" she said excitedly "It seems we may be going to Glanum. Pybus has a plan."

"Does he indeed!" Tomas said coming into the room. He embraced Pybus. "Tell us more."

"I met Emil who works at the basilica and he told me that Galo has two sons to take over the apartment so it may not be available."

"Well, that seems a pity but anyway first I have to find someone to take over here. I don't know where to look and was going to ask at the Basilica and see how I do about finding someone."

"This land was given to Argoutus, was it not?" said Pybus. "so it is yours and you could let it out and use the money to fund a home in Glanum."

"Do you know anyone who might want it?" asked Tomas.

"I am sure there must be a young Roman who wants to have land and grow crops as you have done. In fact I know one particularly who would be interested!"

"Who is that?" asked Tomas/

"Well, this man is reliable and honest/ A great worker and in fact more or less perfect in every way........handsome too!!!"

"You Pybus!" Tomas laughed.

"You see, you recognised me from that description. Yes Tomas. I do feel that this could be a chance for me to settle down and make real money. My mother and I could run the farm as it is and if I have problems you would be near to help me. What do you think?"

"Well, what about your town house. Is it yours or rented?"

"It is rented and I thought we could do a straight swop. I will rent the farm from you and you can take over my lease on the town house. That way if things don't work out for either of us then we have options to move out without bothering with buying and selling. What do you think?"

"Oh Tomas," said Scribonia, "That would mean we could be in a house and not an apartment. I liked your home, Pybus. Not too large but self contained. It seems a great plan to me".

For a while the family discussed the plan and then Tomas went off with Pybus to make arrangements at the Basilica and see if they could take over Pybus's lease.

Three hours later Tomas returned. Arria was waiting for him at the gate.

"Well!" she cried running to meet him "What news?"

Tomas dropped from his horse. "I think the plan will work. The house Pybus lives in is owned by a Senator in Rome who does not really care who lives there as long as he gets his rent."

Arria clapped her hands and jumped for joy. She turned and ran to the house to deliver the news to the rest of the family.

Tomas stabled his horse and followed her into the house.

Scribonia came up to him. "Well. We hear that things are good for the move. When will we move Tomas? We need time to get sorted out even though Arria would like to move tomorrow!" She added smiling at the girl's happy face/.

"I fear it will take time. First I need to instruct Pybus as to how to run the farm. And then I need to find myself work in the town as long as all are happy with the idea. I thought I would take you down to the town again to look more carefully at Pybus's house. I want to be sure it is going to be right for us all."

During the next few days the family visited Glanum and spent time exploring the house and Tomas and Pybus put their heads together and worked on a plan that would end in the move. Pybus spent each day with Tomas in the fields and each night he came home tired and hungry. The only problem which remained was what work Tomas would do in the town.

**

It was just after mid day when a lone horseman came up the hill towards the farm. He dismounted and tied his horse to the fence which surrounded the house. He came up the steps to the front door and banged loudly. A slave opened the door asked the man his business.

"I come to see Tomas Argoutus" the man replied.

The slave bowed and asked the man to enter.

"My master is in the stables. I will tell him you are here." He led the man into the Atrium and went off to find Tomas.

Cleolia entered the room and stopped on seeing the man there.

The man bowed. "I have come to see Freedman Tomas Argoutus" said the man formally. "One of the slaves has gone to find him."

Cleolia smiled. "I am Tomas's wife" she said. She clapped her hands and Chilo appeared.

"Fetch wine for our visitor, Chilo." She said. Then turning to the man she asked "Have you come far?"

"I have ridden from Glanum today." The man replied.

Just then Tomas entered the room. He was dirty and unkempt from working with the horses and he brushed down his tunic as he spoke.

"Please excuse me." He began. "I was working in the stables and that is not a very clean job." He held out his hand.

"I am Tomas Argoutus and I see you have met my wife Cleolia. What is your business here?"

The man smiled. "I can see just by looking that you are the son of Argoutus the gladiator."

"You knew my father?" Tomas asked.

"Indeed. I lived then in Rome and have recently discovered that you are living here. I am sorry that your father has died." He paused. "He never fully recovered from his accident?"

Tomas shook his head. "It was a great blow to him that he could no longer fight. Here he found some peace at least in his final days."

"Tomas" The man said as they sat down on the wall around the central seat "I work for Vitruvius the architect. You may have heard of him. He has designed the dam which supplies water to Glanum. Over the last few years you may be aware that Glanum has developed a good supply of water from this dam and now we need to find engineers with the knowledge to maintain and in many cases to improve the system. I met a young Greek, Pybus by name, when I was in Glanum yesterday and he told me that you are looking for a change of career. Is that true?"

Tomas nodded. "Yes. I have had some difficulty farming since I hurt my back in a fire and my family are keen to move into the town, so it seems a good idea to move to Glanum. However, without a job I cannot support them."

"Would you be interested in such a project?"

"I would but I know very little about the movement of water. Here all is taken from the river in the valley and we use slaves to carry water to the house. We have a pit out the back where we put all used water and sewage."

"Pybus tells me that you have had a good education, that you can read and write Latin and some Greek also?"

"Yes, my father had a tutor for me as a child and my Greek comes from spending time with Pybus. I do not read Greek but understand much of it. Also I was lucky enough to have a tutor for mathematics also when I first came here. My father was determined that I should be well educated when we became Freedmen of Rome."

"Your father was a great forward thinker. I feel that you could well do the work required so if you could come with me to Glanum we could discuss it further. The man who is now controlling the work wants to retire but he will stay on and teach a successor. His name is Felix and he is Greek but now speaks Latin well and I think he would be a good teacher."

"When would you like me to come?"

"Would it be possible tomorrow as I have to return to Rome as soon as possible."

"I can arrange that." Tomas replied. "And now may we offer you food and wine and if you want you can stay here tonight."

"Thank you, Tomas, but I will return to Glanum now and make arrangements for you to meet Felix in the morning."

That night Tomas and Cleolia went to their room and discussed their future. Tomas sat beside her and keep an affectionate arm round her shoulder. She leaned against him delighting in his warmth and closeness. She was beginning to feel safer with him and she knew that he would not force himself on her again. She wanted so much to be a real wife to him but she could not seem to banish her fears of intercourse.

He dropped a kiss on her check. "Oh Cleolia," he muttered. "I feel so much love for you. You are so beautiful and kind and have given me such a fins son that sometimes I think my heart will break.

What else can I do to make you able to love me truly?"

A tear ran down her check. "I do want so much to be a real wife to you. I fear you will leave me and find someone who can love you properly."

He let his hand drop slowly to her full breasts.

"Do you never feel a need for me? Are you never aroused?"

"If I feel that, I throw it away. I do not understand it. I believe I could not love you more. You are as you were from childhood, my only love. I want so much to give you more sons and daughters too. There seems to be a curse on me. I pray to the gods every day that they will cleanse me and take away the fear which haunts me. I do not know what to do."

He lifted her face to his. "My love, be sure I will never leave you. I am totally yours and the fault if there is one is mine. I did not save you from that man and then I left you to be sorely abused." He paused kissing her lips gently.

"I suggest that after we move to Glanum if all is well, which I feel it will be, then we will go to the scared spring every day. Maybe the answer lies there. Now dry those tears and let us sleep." And he rose and lifted her in his arms and placed her gently into her bed. Then he crossed the room to his own bed and lay down.

He could not sleep. He tossed and turned thinking of any way he could teach her to love him. Then he remembered what she had said that day before little Tomas was born. He had not killed Flavius. He should have done it all that time ago when he had visited Rome and had him at his mercy. Why had he not done it and why had Pybus not killed him. What had stopped them. He had failed his love once more. He swore that as soon as they had settled in Glanum then he would go once more and find Flavius and kill him. Nothing would stop him this time. Flavius must die. Perhaps then Cleolia would be able to accept his body.

Chapter 31

A month later the family moved to Glanum. Tomas began his work with Felix and Pybus and his mother moved into the farm house. They had agreed to leave the slaves and so Tomas and Cleolia had now new slaves. Ovilium had begged to go with them but Tomas decided not to take him because of Scribonia's unrest but did agree to Chilo accompanying them. He was old and frail now and not much use on the farm.

The house was not as large as the farm but it was light and airy and had all the modern conveniences like water and heating for the winter. It was also attached to the drains which helped to make the place smell fresh and cut down on the work in the house. Scribonia was delighted by all this and also that she could go out and buy anything she wanted at the shops in the town. She and Aria and Cleolia took the baby out into the town daily and they explored everything with fascination. Their house lay at the southern end of the town past the forum and twin temples in the residential part of the town under the hills which served as a boundary to the East. Behind the house was an open area which contained some shelters for the slaves and behind that the ground rose up to the ramparts which defended the town from wandering tribes. Cleolia immediately felt safer there. Anyone coming to their home was bound to have walked along the main road where the door was situated, so no one could enter uninvited. The only drawback was that they could not see who was approaching the door. But with slaves to answer the door that seemed safe enough.

Tomas went daily with Felix to inspect and learn about the flow of water to the town. The dam had been built high in the hills to the North West of the town and from that a great aqueduct stretched to the town and supplied the fountain, baths and general water supplies. Also near the home of Tomas and Cleolia was the sacred spring which it was believed could heal the sick and support those in trouble. It was Tomas's job to watch these constructions and see that they were kept in good order. The aqueduct was covered to stop debris entering the water supply but despite this sometimes it had to be cleaned out. Inspection stones were distributed along the route so that he could lift them and check the water flowed smoothly.

Tomas, who at first had had reservations about this work, soon found that he enjoyed it. He never had to do any heavy work, there were slaves for that and it kept him fit walking the aqueduct in all weathers. In fact by the time the family had been in Glanum for a year it felt as if they had never lived anywhere else. By that time little Tomas was walking on his little wobbly legs and they had good friends in the town. Arria was now at an age to be married and Tomas and Cleolia were discussing who would be the best suitor for her. There were a number of young men in the town but Tomas wanted her to be with someone she could love and not just marry for the convenience of the families. Soon after their arrival in the town a young man had come to work in the Basilica. He was well educated and came from a rich family in Rome.

Cato was tall and slim with a crop of black hair. He spoke both Latin and Greek and went hunting in the forest whenever he was free. He was 25yrs old and had not yet found a wife but seemed to prefer taking turns with his friends with the slave girls. He had met Tomas several times at the baths and they had developed a casual friendship. Recently he had told Tomas that he felt now he should settle down and find a wife. Tomas had gone home and spoken to Scribonia about the young Roman and she seemed happy to allow Arria to meet him and see if they would be happy together.

Therefore one afternoon Arria was taken by Scribonia and dressed in her best tunic as Cato was coming to the house to meet her. She was allowed to put up her long blond hair and Scribonia lent her gold jewellery to wear. She was excited as she had seen Cato with her brother and liked what she saw. He was older than her but that was only thought to be a good thing as by his age most young Romans had established themselves and could offer a wife a good home and had the money to buy slaves to serve her. Later that afternoon Cato arrived at the door and was ushered into the Atrium by Chilo.

Scribonia was waiting for him and rose to greet him.

"Welcome," She said holding out her hand in greeting and Cato bowed his head and smiled at her. "I believe that you are seeking a wife?" she continued "and that you have met my son. My husband is dead so I rely on Tomas to select a suitor for my daughter."

Again Cato smiled. "Yes, indeed. I am anxious to meet her. Her brother speaks highly of her."

"We are, of course, biased, but Arria is a good girl. I have taught her well and she is fit and healthy." She paused. "You work at the Basilica, I hear?"

"Yes I do. I have been in Glanum for three years now and love the place so I shall find a wife from the young ladies here. My father has agreed to buy me a house so that my wife will have a good home."

Scribonia directed Cato to sit and ordered Chilo to bring wine and fruit. . A few minutes later Tomas entered the room. He had washed and put on a clean tunic after his long walk along the aqueduct. He smiled and held out a hand to greet Cato;

"Well, my friend. You are welcome in my house. You have met my mother so there seems only one more person for you to meet." He turned to his mother. "Is Arria coming?"

Scribonia nodded. "She is coming but she is a little shy I think."

"Shy! That I do not believe. Not Arria."

As he spoke there was a sound of footsteps and into the Atrium came Arria. Her hair was braided and although she still wore the tunic of a child she seemed in that moment to be more of a young woman than Tomas had realised. She seemed to have gained a presence and walked with her head held high and a slight smile hovered about her lips.

Cato rose and bowed slightly towards her. "Good day Arria," he said.

She in turn dropped her head towards him. "I am pleased to see you Cato."

She walked across and sat beside her mother while Cato still stood watching her. Tomas rose and said to his mother. "Shall we go and leave these too young people to talk?"

Scribonia rose too and walked out of the room with Tomas following.

They let the two people together for half an hour and then returned to the Atrium. When they entered, Arria was sitting beside Cato and laughing, her head thrown back and her eyes sparkling. Cato rose as Scribonia entered.

"Well," he said "We have had a good chat and if you are willing I will take Aria for a walk tomorrow so we can talk more."

So it was agreed and as they spent more and more time together it seemed clear that both of them were happy with the match.

∗∗

A few weeks later Tomas met Cato in the baths and asked how things were going between him and Arria.

"Well, Tomas, I think it is time for us to talk seriously about marriage. Your sister is a beautiful girl and she brings light to all she meets. I should be honoured to make her my wife, if you agree."

"Cato," said Tomas patting him on the back. "It is not me who should agree. What does Arria say?"

"I am sure she will agree too." said Cato laughing. He nudged Tomas in the ribs. "I have found her very happy to agree to most things I have suggested. But do not fear her virginity is intact and will stay so until we are man and wife."

That night Tomas took Cleolia in his arms and buried his face in her hair. "I cannot believe my little sister is to be married." he said.

Cleolia leaned against him. "They will be happy. I know it." She had taken off her tunic and Tomas could feel the swell of her breasts under her cotton slip. He was bare chested, his loin cloth tight between them. He knew Cleolia could feel his erection but she no longer moved away. Over days and weeks after little Tomas was born, he had gradually come closer to her sexually. He had sometimes been amazed at his patience. But each night whether they were tired, whether the baby was crying, whether they were late to bed, Tomas never let his wife go to bed without his cuddles and gentle sexual advances. At last he felt her relax in his arms and knew his patience was paying off. Yet he was still so careful. He wanted her to want him as he wanted her, had wanted her it seemed to him, all his life. And this night he felt her nipples harder. He felt his heart was thumping in his chest with delight. He muttered into her hair.

"Oh Gods! You are so beautiful. You will never know how much I love you. You are my day and night, my moon and sun. Nothing matters to me but you."

"I love you too Tomas." She replied, her soft breath against his hands as they encircled her breasts. Was he imagining it or did her voice falter?. Was there passion rising in her? Be careful he warned himself. The moment will come.

**

Two months later Arria and Cato were married. It was a noisy affair with much drinking and celebrations which lasted for two days. They moved into a fine house at the other end of the town and the family's life went back to normal although Scribonia missed Arria and felt herself getting older by the day. Little Tomas was growing tall and strong nearing his third birthday. Scribonia loved him dearly but found she spent more time resting and did very little in the house.

One day some months later, as she sat outside the back of the house gazing at the hills and breathing in the gentle scents of the forest a young slave came running out of the house and called to her.

"Mistress," she said, approaching Scribonia, "Please come. Chilo is ill and asks for you."

Scribonia went with the slave into the shelter where the slaves slept and found Chilo, pale and drawn lying on his bed. His breathing was laboured and his eyes dull. Scribonia went to him and took his hand.

"Tell me, Chilo. What is the matter?" she said gently.

Chilo turned his grey limpid eyes to hers and spoke slowly. "I have to tell you something. You have been a good Mistress to me. I feel that I am dying" He stopped and coughed, catching his breath.

Scribonia leaned closer to him. "Would you like me to send for your son?"

Chilo was silent for a moment. "I do not have a son," he said.

"But Ovilium is your son." Scribonia told him thinking perhaps his illness was affecting his memory. "You came here with him and Ovilium works up at the farm with Pybus now. But I can have him fetched for you."

"You do not understand," Chilo said sadly, "This is what I need to tell you. Ovilium is not my son. We had an arrangement that we would pretend that was the case."

"But why?" asked Scribonia.

Chilo moved nearer her. "He is a wicked man who wanted to get near to your family. He does not wish you good. He is the son of the Ovilium who was killed by your husband, Argoutus. He is after revenge. I am ashamed to say he offered me money so that I could pretend to be his father and then Tomas would accept him"

Scribonia rose. She wrung her hands in distress. "I knew it but I thought it was my fancy." She turned back to Chilo. "If this is so, why has he not taken his revenge already?"

"He is determined in little ways to make Tomas's life difficult and in danger. He wants Tomas to suffer. He feels death is not sufficient punishment for him. He is an evil man. He met Flavius and heard of the feud between him and Tomas and agreed to help Flavius capture Tomas. He was the one who told him Flavius was nearby and set the trap for him" He paused. "I too have been wicked. When Little Tomas was born I did not go and fetch him as you asked. I regret that. I beg your forgiveness. I cannot die without telling the truth. Tomas is a good man who does not deserve hatred. While I lived with Ovilium I was too much of a coward to explain but now I am dying I wanted you to know."

Chilo fell back and closed his eyes. He shuddered and then whispered so Scribonia could hear "Forgive me Mistress?"

Scribonia took his hand again. "I do forgive you." She said. And at those words Chilo let out a great sigh and breathed out his last breath.

Scribonia rose quietly from the bed and turned to the young slave at her side. "Go and get help. Chilo has died." And she walked from the room deep in thought.

So many things went round in her head. She had known there was something wrong with Ovilium. She had never trusted him right from the moment she first set eyes on him. She wondered why he had not taken a chance to kill Tomas. She thought back to the fire. Had he started that? And what was she to do now. Was he a danger to Pybus? After all, Pybus had been with Tomas when they went to fetch Cleolia. It was all very confusing. And if she told Tomas he would just go and kill Ovilium. More bloodshed. She shuddered. She decided to wait and give herself time to think. She walked down the passage and out into the street. The sun was shining on the cobbles and the air was full of the sound of cicadas in the trees. There were few people about. She went down the road and into the temple. The air in there was heavy with the scent of burnt candles but the light of the sun spread itself over the marble floor and the wooden seats. She went to the front and stood before the statue of the goddess who looked down at her. The face was gentle and Scribonia felt a warmth coming from it. She felt comforted by it and falling on her knees she let all that Chilo had told her pass through her mind.

After several minutes she rose and walked back from the temple crossing the street to where the steps led down to the sacred spring. There was an old man waiting on the steps and the attendant came to speak to him leading him down to put his feet in the cool clean water at its base. Scribonia waited until the man came up again and then she too went down the steps. The attendant asked her why she had come. Was there a special reason? Was she ill? Scribonia told her that she was confused in her head about what she should do about some news she had heard and the girl took her hand and led her down to the edge of the pool. From the wall gushed the spring splashing almost silently deep in the ground. The girl told Scribonia to kneel and she took a bowl of water and poured it onto her head. The water was ice cold and as it cascaded down her face she breathed in the metallic scent of it. Afterwards the girl gave her a cloth and she wiped her face and head. Then Scribonia rose and went up the steps into the brightness of the summer afternoon. She was still unsure of what to do but she felt that the right moment would come when she could tell Tomas. The Goddess and the sacred spring would help her find that moment. She continued up the road and turned into the house.

"

Chapter 31

Tomas was walking the aqueduct. The clear air around him was tinged with a cold breeze. It was winter and the ground felt hard under his feet. But there was a spring in his step as he thought back to the night before.

He knew he was almost there. He had spent hours cradling his beautiful girl before he went to his bed. Now he was sure the time was coming and one day not so far away, she would be his in every way and a true wife. A small shiver went through him as he remembered the soothsayer on their wedding day. He brushed the though away. He saw only his beloved, sitting beside him and seeing his erection and not turning away. Next he would let her touch it and then……. He knew she was not frigid. He had heard her sighs and heard her voice falter. She wanted him but she needed to learn how. For a moment the face of Flavius flashed into his head. He swallowed the ball of hatred which seemed to rise in his throat. Why had he not killed him years ago when he had the chance? Should he go and do it now? Would Cleolia be more relaxed if the man was dead? She had said so. He would consult with Pybus again.

He stopped to lift the inspection stone. Usually he took a slave with him for that but he had wanted to be alone. He had wanted to feel his heart beating and let his thoughts drift into the clear blue sky above him. Everything was going well. Arria was happily married. His mother seemed content and his son was growing. Soon he would be able to bring him as he walked the aqueduct. He imagined his son walking along beside him, his hand in his. What a great gift the gods had sent out of such a terrible act. He still could not believe that such a beautiful child had come from a moment of such wickedness. He shrugged his shoulders. "The past cannot be changed." He told himself as he moved on..

When he reached the dam, the sun was high in the sky and was sending shadows flitting across the water. A bird rose shrieking from the surface of the lake and for a moment he felt startled. He looked about him. Was it his imagination or had he seen the shape of a person near one of the arches. He screwed up his eyes against the glare of the sun but there was nothing there. He felt unnerved. What reason could there be for that? He felt his excitement and good humour vanish. Pushing the negative thoughts into the back of his head, he climbed onto the dam wall and looked along it. All was quiet except for the rush of the water. Satisfied he turned back for home.

That evening he met Pybus at the baths. As usual Pybus was chatting about his latest conquest. Tomas laughed at him. "Pybus" he said smiling. "Do you not think you should be thinking about taking a wife?" Pybus put on a serious look, but his eyes were still glistening with humour. "Me! With a wife? Can you really see me settling down with one woman?"

"If you found the right one it would be easy."

"I think you are very lucky, Tomas. You have a beautiful wife and child. When will you have the next one?"

"That is difficult to say. Cleolia is still very anxious about Flavius. She still fears him and thinks he will try and destroy our family."

"But we haven't seen or heard of him for ages. He may have died or just decided to forget you."

"I don't believe that. But I think it is our turn to set a trap."

"What had you in mind?"

" I went to the Basilica this afternoon. I found out that there are to be gatherings in Arelate of Senators.. The Emperor Augustus must at some time visit and they will come to make sure the preparations are complete. Flavius will be amongst them. They will come by sea to Fossae and then move onto the main route to Arelate. They have a caravan of soldiers to protect them, of course but there must be somewhere they can be intercepted, maybe when they are camped for the night. After all we are true Romans and the guard will not challenge us and if they do, we can talk ourselves out of any trouble on the way in."

"Excuse me Tomas for interrupting you but you seem to be saying 'we'?"

Tomas clapped Pybus on the back. "I know you will come with me, Pybus. You love a fight and I know you will be at my side, will you not?"

Pybus laughed. "How well you know me Tomas. OK. I will come but tell me more about this plan. Do you intend that we just walk in and kill Flavius? I think that would be a good way of getting ourselves killed by his guard. We would need to get the man alone."

"Yes. We might be able to get in with his retinue. Befriend them. Let them learn to trust us."

"The trouble is that not only Flavius but also some of his followers may well recognise us."

"Well my friend. We will have to disguise ourselves."

"How? Will you dye that shock of blond hair? Pybus ruffled Tomas's hair with his hand. "Hair like yours would be more natural on a woman!."

Tomas rose. "You are a genius! Of course. That is the answer. We will dress as women. That way no one will suspect us."

"Not unless they want to lie with us!"

Tomas did not hear him. "Well. First I will need to get someone to oversee my work with the water. Then we will be free to go when the time comes. May I ask Olivium because he is a good strong man who will keep undesirables away? Can you spare him?"

Pybus rose also. "I will get him to meet with you at the tavern some time soon. In the meantime I will be sure my other slaves can care for the farm. I am a farmer now, you know. I have responsibilities too."

" Good. Don't forget we must not let my family know what we are planning. Cleolia and Scribonia would try and stop us. I want to just walk in one day and tell them Flavius is dead."

∗∗

When Tomas got home, he found Arria and Cato sitting in the Atrium with Scribonia. Arria came running towards Tomas. "Tomas we have great news. I am to have a child." She jumped up and down. "I am so excited. Can you believe I am to be a mother?"

Tomas smiled at her and walked towards her to give her a hug. "No I cannot imagine that. My little sister a mother! Unbelievable.! You will have to calm down a bit. The poor little thing will not want to be bumped about. You will have to learn to walk and not bounce everywhere."

He turned to Cato and went to embrace him. "Congratulations brother, I am so happy for you. I only hope the child has not as much energy as its mother or you are in for a wild time!"

Scribonia smiled. "How true. Arria has always had such a love of life that everything excites her. I think she has a special gift for life and if her child has that it will not be a bad thing at all."

Into the room came Little Tomas. He looked around at the happy faces.

"What have I missed, my father?" he said bowing slightly towards Tomas.

Tomas put an arm round the young boy's shoulder. "You are to have a cousin, my son. Arria is to have a child."

The boy eyes widened. "When?"

"Not for some time. A baby takes a while to grow in a ladies' stomach."

Little Tomas went over to Arria. "Is he in there now/" he asked.

"Yes. But I cannot feel him or her yet. When I can I will let you feel him or her move."

He looked puzzled. "Don't you know if it is a boy or a girl?"

"No. But that is the lovely surprise when a baby is born."

"I hope it is a boy. Then I will have someone to play with all the time."

"Not all the time, my son. Soon you will be old enough to start lessons. You must begin to learn to read and write and use number."

"Who will teach me?"

"I will." said Tomas. "I think we should start very soon. I was thinking today when I was walking the aqueduct that I should take you with me soon and you can learn much as we walk. Then when I am home at night we will begin the real work with slates and books." He leaned down and looked the boy in the eye. "You will be a well educated man one day. I will pass on all I know and perhaps I will ask Pybus to teach you Greek."

"Why must I learn Greek?"

"Because many great books are written in Greek and they hold such knowledge as you should have." He turned to Cleolia. "Is this a good plan?"

Cleolia replied happily. "It is a good plan. He is a lucky boy to have a father like you."

And so it happened. Tomas took his son out and showed him how the water came to the town and taught him to count the inspection hatches and the arches by the dam. He told him about the trees and flowers which grew on the way. He made a small bow and arrow for him to learn to kill small animals and birds for food and found the child an astute pupil. Every evening after they returned from the baths, he sat him down with books and taught him to read and write letters on his slate with chalk.

Chapter 32

Tomas was leaning over the boy as he drew the shaky letters which formed his name, when the door flew open and Pybus hurried into the room.

"I have news Tomas," he cried.

"What news Pybus that makes you enter this place when I am teaching my son to write?" He scowled at Pybus. "It must be important for you to disturb us so."

"It is very important," Pybus was breathless from his hurrying, "You remember we wanted to know when the Senators were coming to Arelate? Well it is to be soon. I heard today that they have left Rome and are expected to land in Gaul soon."

Tomas turned to the boy. "Go now, my son. I must talk to Pybus."

The child's eyes sparkled. "Am I done for today, father? Can I go and play."

"Yes. Yes. Go" Tomas pushed him towards the door. "and tell everyone that Pybus and I are discussing business and must not be disturbed."

When the door closed behind the boy, Tomas turned back to Pybus.

"Now. Tell me all."

"As we expected, A group of senators are travelling to Arelate. They will disembark at Fossae. Then they will make their way across to Arelate. It may take two days to get there and they are due to land in Gaul in three days time. That does not give us long. We need to travel on the Via Domitia until it meets the Via Agrippa. When we get to Arelate we can go to meet them as they travel up from the coast."

"Can't we just go across the hills?"

"Difficult! The way is treacherous and we would need to travel on foot. The horses could not manage such a hilly journey. And would we find the way? There are only rough tracks, not to mention the wild tribes."

"OK. So we will go via the main road. If we go early in the morning, we should reach Arelate by nightfall. That will give us plenty of time to hide up and make contact."

"As far as disguise is concerned. I don't think either of us will make a good woman! I think you should dye your hair with walnut oil and I will try and make mine lighter with lemon juice."

"Good. I think we are best to be just travellers. They should have to stop for the night along the route but ambush may not work when they have so many soldiers with them."

"True. So let us go and prepare. At first light I will join you on the road. Bring provisions and your best horse." He thumped Pybus on the back and they embraced. "We will succeed, Pybus my friend. This time we must."

**.

This time Tomas did not go without telling Cleolia. But he could not tell her the truth as he knew she would not let him go. He had no fear. Not only was he confident but he knew that it was going to be the most important thing he would do. He was sure that killing Flavius would set Cleolia free and let her come to him completely.

Last night he had sat beside Cleolia as he did every night. He played with her body and she with his and now she was able to satisfy him with her hands and in return she would let him excite her. They were so close and only the final coming together still eluded her and the tension in her body would rise and she would finally pull away. He was so close. He knew one day very soon he would win the battle with her demons and .he would feel his body inside hers and his happiness would be complete.

He spoke casually to her when they lay down to sleep.

"I have to go away for a few days."

"Where are you going?"

Pybus and I are going to Arelate on business. Pybus needs to find new merchants to take his produce and he needs me to introduce him to the right people." He hated lying to her but when he came back he would be able to tell her the truth. "Ovilium is going to take care of the water systems. I have explained to him what he needs to do. Nothing is likely to go wrong in such a short time. I will be home before you know it."

"I do not like you going away Tomas. It makes me nervous."

Tomas smiled at her and kissed her gently. "Do not worry. All will be well."

In the morning he got up early and went into the room where his son lay asleep. He went to the bed where the child lay with arms spread and his curly blond hair decorating the pillow. Tomas stood looking at him. The pride he felt in his heart for the child was overwhelming. He leant over and dropped a gently kiss on the boy's cheek. "Be good my son, and when I return I will make you brothers and sisters." The child stirred but did not wake. Tomas crept from the room and hurried into the kitchen where his provisions were ready. Scribonia was drinking goat's milk and had a crust of bread in her hand. She smiled at her son.

"You are early today, Tomas. Sit with me and tell me what you will be doing today." She patted the seat beside her.

"I am in a hurry Mother. I have business in Arelate and want to get on the road."

"I need to talk to you Tomas. It is important. It has been hard to get you alone and there is something I must tell you. It has been on my mind since Chilo died."

Toms went over and kissed her. "I am sure it can wait a few more days then!" He said making for the door. "Farewell mother. I will be back soon." And he went from the room. Scribonia sighed. She knew she must tell him about Ovilium. Perhaps she would talk to Pybus. But Tomas was right. A few more days would make little difference. But she was to be proved wrong.

Tomas went out and found his favourite horse prepared and being held by a slave. He mounted and set off to meet Pybus. He stopped a little way from the town and took the phial of walnut oil from his saddle.. He rubbed it into his hair and splashed water over it. He could not have done this before as he had no excuses for Cleolia on this score. He put some on his eyebrows as well. He had not shaved but there was little he could do with the dusting of light stubble on his chin

When he reached the main road Pybus was already there. His hair appeared to be a dark red. Pybus had a full dark beard which seemed to have caught the red tinge also.

"What do you think, Tomas?" he said, greeting his friend. "One of my slaves gave me something called Senna. She said it would make my hair red."

"Discussing hair colour is part of your sexual encounters now is it Pybus?" He joked.

"Well it looks good to me and I have some old clothes for us when we get to our meeting with the senators."

They set off in high spirits and had reached the Via Agrippa by night fall. From there they went on to Arelate and found a place to stay the night.

"I expect the Senators will have disembarked by now." Tomas said crashing down on the bed. "In the morning we will set off to meet them."

"We haven't really any plans as to how we will do this." Pybus stated. "Are we going to tag on behind? We really should get to Flavius before he gets to Arelate. "We are not in a position to ambush them. Just the two of us."

"The trouble is getting close to Flavius." Tomas mused. "He will be well guarded."

"The trouble will be getting away afterwards. I suppose they have tents for the nights. And night time will be best for a speedy getaway. We will need to find which tent he is in."

"I am afraid we are going to have to see what the gods have in store.. Let's get some sleep and then make an early start."

Tomas did not sleep well. He tossed and turned going over what he was going to do and what could go wrong. Killing Flavius was his aim and that he was not prepared to give up this time. But getting himself killed would ruin everything. He wanted revenge but not if it made Cleolia a widow and rendered his son fatherless. He heard Pybus snoring beside him and envied him his slumber. But at last it was dawn and he was able to wake his friend and set off along the road to the coast. They had changed their usual clothes for old ones and there seemed to be lots of people travelling along the road in both directions. Tomas stopped one and asked if they had seen the caravan of Senators on their way. The man glared at him and made a rude comment.

"Well at least he mistook us for poor travellers." Tomas remarked, dismounting from his horse. "I think we should wait here. At least there is a wood to hide in. The other side seems to be only marsh land." They took the horses into the wood and tethered them to a fallen tree. From here they could see the road but were almost hidden by the trees.

Pybus went out and stopped another man on foot who looked equally dishevelled. The man looked behind him.

"They are camped not far back there." He said pointing. "Loads of them. Soldiers and guards and smart men. Mean men at that. I asked for a drink from one of the soldiers and he just pushed me away."

Pybus told the man to follow him and took him back to where Tomas was waiting with the horses.

"This man has seen them." he said offering the man a drink from his water carrier. The man drunk thirstily. When he had finished he sat down on the tree trunk.

"What is your business?" he asked.

"We want to meet the Senators group. They are on their way to Arelate and we have business with one of them." Tomas said grinning.

The man spat on the ground. "Not good business I guess. They and all their soldiers. Do they expect someone to murder them?!"

"We hope they don't expect that." Said Pybus sarcastically.

"Can you tell us about the party? How many soldiers are there? Are they well guarded?" asked Tomas.

"Lots," the man replied. "Nigh on fifty, I should think. They were just settling down to camp for the night when I passed. They are beside the road in a field. They took little notice of me except when I asked for water." He swore loudly.

Tomas offered the man some bread which he took greedily. Then he asked."So do you think it would be hard to get among them?"

"Well, there seemed to be plenty of people just milling about, not doing anything. The soldiers seemed bored. After all no one would want to hurt the senators, would they? It would be easy to do but an act of suicide. They would never get away. The guards would be on them in a moment."

He stood up suddenly and stared at a clump of wild flowers. "The gods be praised. I nearly sat on that."

"What is it?" asked Tomas following the man's glare.

The man pointed to the flowers and looked at Tomas. "That is Coris my friend. If you get that on your skin, it will make you ill. Someone I know ate it and died a horrible death. Nasty stuff. You keep away from it. I will be off and thanks for the hospitality. You take care now." And he stamped off towards the city.

"Well that seems fair enough," said Pybus "We can get in and murder Flavius but then we will get killed for our trouble.! He sighed. "Not a happy prospect."

Tomas was still staring at the Coris plant. "I have a better idea." he said clapping his hands. "We poison him. That way we have a chance of getting away safely. He deserves a horrible death," he added," after all the pain he has caused me."

Pybus was on his knees looking at the plant with its innocuous looking white flowers. "This can <u>kill!</u>" he said with disbelief.

"Yes. My father warned me about it when we first came here to the country. If you eat it it causes horrible symptoms and in an hour or two you can be dead. All we have to do is get it into Flavius' food. It tastes bitter but can be disguised by plenty of garlic."

"Let us go over to the camp and make friends with the cook or the guard. Before we go we need to pick some leaves and tie them in a bundle." He tore a piece off the hem of his tunic and carefully picked a bunch of flowers and leaves and laid them on the log which was now in the sun. He took a log and smashed into them until they were reduced to a messy pulp. "There. That should do the trick." He stood up and carefully scooped the mess into a piece of fabric and tied it round his waist. . He went down to the stream and washed his hands.

"Well, done." Tomas was thinking hard. "How will we know Flavius is dead? He might recover."

"I am quite sure the news will travel to Glanum when he does die. It will be great news. And" he added. "It will be more difficult to find the murderers......us I mean. Finding Flavius alone and sticking a dagger in him has got to be a risky option as we said before. If that old man is right then our chances of getting away are pretty poor. "

"OK. Now we have a new plan to make. I suggest we go and see what is going on at the camp. See if we can find a slave to bribe, perhaps, or someone who dislikes Flavius enough to help us kill him."

They left the horses tied up near a stream and having given them a drink They left them tied to a tree in the shade.

They set off along the road and in only a short time came upon the camp. There were several large tents and smaller ones housing the soldiers who milled about looking bored. There were also slaves working, carrying water and logs for a fire which burned in the middle of the camp. Two slaves were turning a spit. They saw a couple of senators in their bright togas but no one stopped them. They were soon mingling with the crowd.

"First we need to find out where he is." hissed Tomas in Pybus' ear.

Pybus went up to a young girl and said in her ear.

"Hi! beautiful. Do you know which tent belongs to Flavius, the senator." The girl spoke quietly. "What is it worth?"

Pybus put his hand is his bag slung over his shoulder and took out a handful of coins. He passed them to her. Her eyes brightened. She pointed to a tent in the far corner. "That's his. You don't want to go near him, he's mean. He takes us girls when he feels like it. He's a violent man.. He likes hurting girls." She shuddered. "I just hope he doesn't take me!!"

Tomas moved close. "Is he liked by men too?"

"You mean does he go with men?"

"No. I just wonder if he is popular in general."

"Well the other Senators seem happy to drink with him but they are the only ones. The rest of us hate him."

"What about the soldiers?"

She shrugged her shoulders. "I don't know. They seem OK. Some of them are kind to us."

"No," said Tomas. "I meant do the soldiers like Flavius?"

"Who knows. I can't tell you of anyone who likes him really" She backed off. "You aren't friends of his are you?"

Pybus touched her arm gently. "No No" he said. "My friend here has reason to hate him."

The girl relaxed. "Well. That's all right then. If you want to know more about him the best person to ask is Spiro. He's his head slave and he hates him. He promised him wealth and freedom and treats him like a bit of dirt. The trouble is we are all afraid of the senators because they can have us whipped or sent to the arena. No one is really safe."

"Where can we find Spiro?" asked Tomas.

"He's outside the tent. He guards him most of the time when the soldiers are off duty. They just protect us from wandering tribes when we are on the move."

Pybus gave the girl a quick peck on the cheek. "Thanks." He said.

The girl blushed. "Are you staying around?" she asked winking at him.

"I would love to but I don't think that would be wise." And he patted her bottom and followed Tomas who had walked on.

They arrived outside the large tent where a guard stood leaning on a large piece of wood. When he saw them approach he picked up the wood and brandished it at them.

"We are friends." Tomas said quietly. "You are Spiro?"

The man dropped the piece of wood. "Who wants to know?" he asked grumpily.

"You are a slave I assume?" asked Tomas.

The man nodded. "What of it!"

"Is your master in?"

"You want to speak to him? You'd better come back later. He didn't want to be disturbed."

Tomas beckoned to the man, who moved a few feet away from the tent.

"My friend and I need a bit of help. We hear that Flavius is not nice to the girls" The man moved closer.

"You are right about that. Evil he is. If they don't do what he wants he whips them. He's got some nasty habits in bed. He nearly killed one of them the other day."

Suddenly an idea crossed Tomas' mind. He winked at Pybus hoping he would not interrupt.

"You see we have found this plant which affects the phallus. Thought it would serve him right if he can't perform!!" .He turned to Pybus. "You got the stuff there, my friend?"

Pybus pulled the bag from his waist. He passed it over. Tomas held it out to Spiro.

"Can you get this into his food?"

Spiro grinned. "You bet I can. But if he finds out I am for it."

"He won't. He'll think it is just him losing his powers with the girls. He is not likely to admit it to anyone is he?"

Spiro took the bundle. "Will he taste it?"

"Not if you put garlic with it. You can get that I am sure."

Spiro was still grinning. He nodded. "I will tell the cook. He hates Flavius as much as all of us. It will be a great joke." He looked at the bundle. "How much do we need to put in?"

"The more you put in the longer he will be impotent."

Spiro laughed. "I'll put the lot in then."

Tomas shook the man's hand. "Thanks. We thought it would be a popular move."

"You bet it will. Be the talk of the camp." And he waved to Tomas and Pybus as they hurried from the camp.

In ten minutes they were galloping along the road to Arelate. They were there by the time darkness had fallen and went to the same tavern for the night.

Early the next day they were on the road again. The sun was high in the sky as they drew near the town. They stopped to let the horses drink at a stream beside the road. As they dismounted they became aware of the sound of water rushing. Both men stopped in their tracks.

"What is that?" Tomas exclaimed rushing forward to where the stream had been and where he now found a wide river.

They stood astounded as they took in the scene. Before them cascaded a boiling, gushing river carrying trees and debris in its wake. The noise was tremendous as it roared on its way.

"God help us" screamed Tomas "the dam is burst. The town will be flooded!"

He threw himself onto his horse and turned back towards the road shouting at Pybus to do the same.

As they galloped along the road they found the water stretched across it in front of them. They reined in the horses.

"It is too dangerous to ride through." Tomas shouted at Pybus. "Follow me." And he swerved sideways following the river through the forest. The going was rough and the horses shied up at the branches of the trees as they snatched at them. The two men lay low across their backs clinging onto their saddles as they tried to keep their seats. Suddenly the trees ended and they found themselves in open country. The swathe of water powered across the open fields pulling not only bushes but on the water floated the carcasses of animals and even birds.

They galloped along beside it. Tomas's heart was racing not only because of the exertion but with a terror at what they might find in the town. Had the water reached it? Had it gone straight through?

There was no doubt that it would easily destroy everything in its path. He did not know where the original river had flowed before the dam was built. Hopefully the town would not have been built near to it. But this was no gentle flowing river. This was a torrent tearing all before it. He silently prayed that his family were safe. Before them they saw a building and knew it was the farm. The water was full of the bodies of dead cattle and many had been thrown out of the water and lay bleached in the sun. For one desperate moment Tomas remembered the carcasses in the arena all those years ago and his heart stopped in fear. Then they saw the farm house. The water had passed so close to it that the side walls had fallen in to ruins. A group of people stood silently beside it and they stopped beside them.

Tomas and Pybus dismounted and went towards the group. There were the slaves huddled together weeping openly.

"What happened?" Tomas asked breathlessly.

"Oh Master." said one."We were sleeping and suddenly we heard this terrible noise. I rose and went outside and saw this wall of water moving towards us. I shouted to everyone to get out. Some did not and got caught in the flood. At least five of us are dead and we have put the injured in the barn. It was so sudden. We had no chance to help anyone."

"Have you heard anything of the town?" Tomas asked.

"We do not know." The man replied. "May the Gods have pity on us all."

Tomas remounted. "I must go on Pybus. You stay and see what you can to help the injured." And he galloped off towards the town.

Beside him the water rushed downwards and as he galloped along his heart was like a drum beating in his chest. How had the dam burst? He was sure there had been no sign of a breach when he lad last seen it only two days before. Supposing he was responsible for the disaster? It was his job to keep the water flowing to the town and check for leaks in the dam's structure. He knew deep down that all had been safe when he left. He had told Ovilium what to look out for. He had explained all to him. Round and round in his head the thoughts ran as he neared the town.

He passed familiar landmarks and saw in the distance the top of the Mausoleum. At least that was still standing. Soon the city ramparts came in sight winding their way around the town. But between him and the city walls was the rumbling crashing river. He reined in as he came parallel to where the first of the houses would be behind the wall. Dismounting he stepped near the edge and stood straining his eyes to see if the river had missed the town. With a cry of relief he saw all seemed as normal. The ramparts were standing solid. But how was he to get across? The river here seemed a little less turbulent. There was still a lot of debris floating along but Tomas could see that the river had established its path to the west of the town. All he now had to do was get to the other side. He was afraid if he tried to swim across the current might take him. Then on the far bank he saw a figure. He called out and the man turned and waved to him shouting something Tomas could not hear.

Then he saw that the man was pointing further down and was walking along the ramparts beckoning for him to follow on his side of the river. He began to walk southwards until the man stopped. He was pointing ahead down the river. Tomas saw a huge tree which had been uprooted was spanning the river where it had fallen.. Tomas ran to it. Carefully he sat astride the trunk and inched his way across the river. Just as he reached the far bank the trunk swayed and rolled him into the water. He struggled against the current which was pulling at his feet as he tried to make for the bank. As he surfaced he saw a long pole sticking out into the water in front of him. The man was trying to move it towards him. He managed to catch it and he clambered to the bank holding tight to the pole. Wet and exhausted he got to his feet.

"Thank you." He said to the man. "Tell me is the town safe?"

"Yes," the man replied. "There is a breach in the ramparts at the end of the town but the water has not gone close to the houses, thank the gods."

Tomas shook himself. "I must away to see my family." And he trudged off towards his home.

When he arrived he found the family together and as he entered the room Cleolia ran to him. "Oh Tomas, You are safe! We feared for you."

Tomas embraced her."All is well with me but I left Pybus at the farm. It is destroyed and some killed."

"It was so terrible. We heard the most enormous roar coming towards the town. I was outside with Little Tomas and I ran in and shut the door. I thought the world was ending. The noise got louder and we huddled together with fear. Then as we thought the end was coming, we heard the noise pass by. We knew then that it was water. It has destroyed the ramparts on the south side and there were people swept away who were out in the fields. It was so quick they had no time to flee. Do you know if Pybus's mother is safe?"

"No. I came on as fast as I could. I was so afraid you had been drowned. I just do not understand how this happened. All was secure when I left".

Scribonia asked "Tomas, Did you leave someone to watch the dam?"

Tomas nodded. "Yes. I left Ovilium to watch the whole water course."

Scribonia cried out. "Oh. Tomas you did not tell us you were going to do that. I would have stopped you.. He was the son of Ovilium the gladiator who was killed by your father. Chilo told me on his death bed."

Tomas swung round to face her. "Why did you not tell me?" he shouted.

"I did try and find a moment but you were so busy and I never got the chance. I am so sorry." She wrung her hands in distress.

Tomas swallowed hard. "Well, what's done is done. I must go and find some men to help me put things right. The dam must be repaired. I assume there is no water coming into the town?"

Cleolia went to him. "We have arranged for slaves to carry water from the new river."

Tomas turned to her. "When did this happen?" he asked.

"The day before yesterday. After you had gone. Do you think Ovilium is to blame?.

"There is little doubt of that. Has anyone seen him?"

"No. He has disappeared."

"If I find him I'll kill him" shouted Tomas.

"Tomas! Tomas! Calm down.! There has been enough killing." said Cleolia moving towards him and taking his arm. "Just go and sort out the problem. You need to mend the dam and quickly or your job may be in jeopardy."

"I suppose that is true." He kissed her gently. I will change into dry clothes and go and see what we need to do." And he hurried form the room.

It was midnight when Tomas returned dishevelled and dirty. He found Cleolia waiting for him. She had managed to get enough water for him to wash and was anxious to hear what he had found out.

"We were right about Ovilium." Tomas said "I went to the dam and found it had been deliberately breached. I found a group of slaves who had been with him and he had whipped them until they followed his instructions. The best bit was that when the water was thrown out, Ovilium was standing on the wall and they pushed him in. So at least he is dead. But a lot of them were swept away too. I have spoken with the council and they have accepted that it was no fault of mine. But there is a lot of work to do and so many dead or injured." He passed his hand over his eyes. "Now I must sleep for I must be up at dawn to continue the work."

Chapter 33

Tomas was out all the next day but arrived home for his meal. He had been to the farm and found the devastation there. There was a chance that the house could be saved but the fields were all awash with mud as the water had returned to a channel it had made near the house. Pybus was busy helping to clear the mess and bury the dead animals.. That night Tomas found it hard to restrain himself from telling Cleolia that with luck Flavius was dead. He could not risk telling her in case for some reason things had not gone to plan. He must wait for news.

But as he held her and caressed her he felt a new excitement running through his veins. Soon everything would be good at last. The shadow which had blighted his life would be gone and surely then Cleolia's body would accept his. He caressed her breasts and let her touch his erection as she had learnt to do over so long. There coupling was so near that now she would let him excite her by running his fingers along the folds of her sex and bring her to orgasm. That night he knelt before her and let his head rest on her thighs. Fingering her swollen clitoris he changed from fingers to tongue and for the first time tasted her sweet scent and felt the rivers of delight pass through her body at his touch. He wanted so much to offer himself to her mouth but held back as he had done for so long, but now feeling that soon everything would be possible. He could not stop himself asking.

"If Flavius were to die, my love." He whispered. "Would you let me into your beautiful body so that we can make a child.?"

Cleolia did not reply for a moment. "I don't know Tomas but we cannot talk of that. He may live a long time more. I want you so much and yet when the moment arrives I feel such fear.

Tomas kissed her along her thigh and ran his tongue over the soft skin between her legs. "That day will come and I know it will be soon if the gods allow it."

It was three days later that the news Tomas was waiting for arrived. A merchant travelling through the town had stopped at the tavern and told the crowd that a senator had died on the road to Arelate.

Pybus was there drinking and he went across to the man.

"Which Senator is that?" he asked nonchalantly sitting down beside the man.

"Chap called Flavius" the man replied.

Pybus leant closer. "What happened? Was he stabbed and if so were there no guards to protect him?"

"Oh. He had guards all right but they could not help. You see he was poisoned!!"

"Who poisoned him?" Pybus asked.

"No one knows for sure. He was fine until he had his meal a couple of nights ago and then he became very sick. Screaming in pain and rolling in agony. They got the physician but he could do nothing." He rubbed his hands as if in glee. "He had a horrible death by all accounts. Bleeding from the mouth and ears and his stomach swelling up like a melon. At one point they thought he would be torn apart" he spread his hands "Boom!!...bits of him all over the place."

"So he is really dead?" Pybus spoke almost to himself.

"He is dead all right. There will be trouble when the Emperor comes to Arelate. Flavius was one of his favourites. "

"What will be done? Can they not find the murderer?"

"It could be almost any one of the people who travelled with him. There were slaves and soldiers as well as the other Senators. It is thought it could be one of them because they are jealous of Flavius. I guess we will never know."

Pybus walked towards Tomas's house but met him on the way. He gave Tomas the news. Tomas was delighted.

"Well. Things are going well. Ovilium is dead as well as Flavius. No more threats for us. I feel sure we are safe now. We expect to get the water flowing back into the town in a few days. Thank you, my friend". And he turned back towards his home.

. He went into the Atrium and there sat Cleolia, Arria and Scribonia playing with his son who was pushing a little wooden cart around the floor chattering away happily. Tomas ran to him and picked him up.

He spoke to him. "Today I have heard great news which will make my family complete."

Cleolia asked. "What news is that, Tomas?"

Tomas spun the child round and hooped for joy.

"Flavius is dead.! " he shouted. "Flavius is dead!"

Cleolia rose and move towards him. "Is this true?" Her voice shook.

"It is really true. And I know for sure because I killed him. Well Pybus was there too but now he is dead and we have nothing to fear anymore."

"How.....When....?" Scribonia interrupted.

Tomas let the child down on the floor and he ran to his grandmother.

Cleolia stared at Tomas her mouth dropping open.

Tomas knelt in front of her. He took her hands in his. "My beautiful girl. All is well now. Flavius can no longer hurt us. Pybus and I went to meet the caravan approaching Arelete. We got talking to a guard and he agreed to put Coris in his meal. He was dead in hours after horrible suffering. I wanted to run him through with my sword but then we should surely have been killed. It was the only safe way. Now we are free of him but be discrete." He added," no one outside the family must hear of it."

He rose from the floor and gathered Cleolia to him in a big hug. "Care for my child, mother. I must talk with Cleolia."

He took her by the hand and went to the bedchamber. He gathered her up in his arms. She looked up at him with shining eyes.

"It is the morning Tomas," she said. "There is lots of time."

Ignoring her he began to remove her tunic. "I want you my lovely. I promise I shall not hurt you and you still can tell me to stop and I will. But Flavius is dead. He can never hurt us again. Nor can anyone. We are as one now. No shadows to blight our life."

Cleolia shuddered. "I don't know Tomas." But she helped him remove her clothes and when she was naked she took his hand and laid it on her breast. He sighed and pulled off his clothes too and when she saw his arousal she laid a hand on it.

"I love you Tomas and my heart swells with love and now even my body seeks yours."

Tomas laid her on the bed and knelt over her. He continued to play with her nipples until they were hard in his hands. Then he ran his fingers down her front until he felt the hot wetness there. He moved gently until his penis brushed her moisture. Then he felt her move nearer and whisper in his ear.

"Yes Tomas." She breathed. "take me." And he slipped into her so gently that she did not even notice for a moment. "Are you in" she whispered.

Tomas began to move softly inside her and she moaned and called out. "Flavius is dead!" and with a rush of desire the world around them disappeared in a cascade of love and they both lay satisfied and content.

For a while neither spoke. Cleolia stroked his hair as it lay on her shoulder. "My dearest." She muttered. "Thank you."

"Thank you for what?" he asked against the soft flesh of her shoulder.

"For making me complete again. For undoing all that that wicked man started. I know now I am free of him and my world is complete."

Suddenly there was a gentle knock at the door.

"Wait a minute" he called out.

"It is me papa." shouted Little Tomas. It is time for my lesson."

"I am coming." Tomas replied

He laughed and they began to dress but before they left the room, Tomas took her to him again. "Cleolia. You have made me the happiest man in the world. I have everything now. A good wife, a lovely child and soon the dam will be mended and life will be so good as we fill the house with children."

"It is all I want, Tomas," Cleolia replied hugging him.

They went down to the family

."Now ",said Tomas taking a slice of bread. "I have work to do" He turned to the child.

"My son," he said. "I think with your mother's permission it is time you came with me. Would you like that/"

"What of my lessons?" Little Tomas asked.

"Today is a holiday!" Tomas said taking the boy's hand. "Can I take him out?" he asked Cleolia.

She nodded. "Are you sure it is safe?"

"I will just take him up to the high rock so that he can see the view of the town and the water. I will take him to my favourite spot .He will love that as I think he loves our country as well as I do. I want a rest from all this work. But first he needs stronger shoes. Can you find him some and we will need a flagon of water."

Cleolia went to the door and made for the child's room.

Tomas took the child by the hand and followed.

"And" said Arria getting to her feet and kissing Scribonia. "I must go home and see to a meal for my husband." She rose and left the room.

**

When she arrived home Cato was waiting for her.

"What kept you wife," he said angrily. "Is my meal not ready?"

"I am sorry, Cato. I was delayed by Tomas who came home with exciting news."

"What was so important as to delay you?" Cato asked.

"Tomas has heard that one of the senators is dead."

Cato swung round and caught her by the shoulders "Which one is dead and who killed him? Tell me."

Arria was a little frightened by Cato's hard face and his hands gripping her. "It is a secret but as you are in the family I can tell you. But you must promise to tell no one." She stammered.

"Tell me," Cato roared. "You know my father is a senator."

"Do not worry, Cato. Tomas would not harm your father. This man was a wicked man who has done the family wrong"

"Tomas killed him?"

"Yes. He was a man called Flavius. Have you heard of him?"

Cato grabbed her by the throat and shook her.

"Where is Tomas now?" he screamed at her. "Is he at home.?"

"No. He has gone to walk the aqueduct with Little Tomas. What is the matter? Why are you so angry?"

Cato yelled in her ear; "You stupid bitch. Flavius was my father. I married you to get near Tomas and keep an eye on him. Now he has killed my father. I will have revenge!"And he threw her across the room and made for the door grabbing his bow and arrows from the table as he went.

Arria struggled to her feet. Her toga was torn and bruises were appearing on her arms and neck. Her hair had fallen from its pins but she had only one thought. She must warn Tomas.

She dashed out and down the street ignoring passersby who stopped to stare at her. If only Tomas had not left yet. She prayed to the gods as she ran. Her heart beat fast as she ran not only with the exertion but with the fear which thundered in her chest.

She burst in on the room where she had been before and saw Scribonia and Cleolia sitting sewing by the fountain. Cleolia got to her feet at the sight of the dishevelled girl.

"What on earth is the matter Arria? Who has hurt you?"

Arria struggled to speak. "Has Tomas gone?" she spluttered.

"Yes. He has gone to the aqueduct with little Tomas."

"We must stop him. He is in great danger. Cato has gone to kill him."

Cleolia tried to make Arria sit down. "What are you talking about? Why should Cato want to kill him?"

Tears were shining on Arria's cheeks but she shook them off.

"Flavius is Cato's father. I did not know. I told him what Tomas had done and he has rushed off to find him and kill him. We must warn him."

Cleolia had turned white with fear as the realisation dawned on her.

Letting go of the girl she ran from the room and out of the town and into the forest. "Tomas" she called as she ran until her breath died in her throat. She felt no pain from her legs as she ran. Only one thought pounded in her head and drove her on. She must get to Tomas first. She must prevent Cato from his aim. She must save her man.

**

Tomas stood on the rock high above the forest, his son beside him as he held the child's hand.

Through the silence came a whistling, rushing blast and Tomas opened his mouth to scream as a clear feathered arrow dived into his broad chest. He clutched at it, a look of sheer astonishment and disbelief as a roll of weakness began to creep up his body. A searing pain grabbed at him as he tried to breathe. Then, like a felled tree, he began to tilt forward. In a slow, graceful motion he fell – down, down, towards the velvet green below.

The child hesitated, bewildered, unsure, then he dropped to his knees and watched the perfect figure of his father as it met, and was swallowed by the green swathe below. He stayed still, unaware as the trees closed over the figure and his little hands sought to cover the image from his eyes and he wept.

Tomas lay crumpled and destroyed on the forest floor. He now felt no pain – no agony – his breath came no more and his eyes, open, drank in the moist heather and moss on which he lay. A cry came to him, a wild, unearthly cry of despair and hopelessness. Through the undergrowth came the young, beautiful Cloelia– her hair torn by the brambles and her skin blood scratched by twigs. She dropped to her knees beside him, taking the broken body to her breast.

"Tomas, my Lord" she cried, tears of fear splashing unfelt into the silent face. "Tomas, my love! …."

A faint wisp of lavender reached his dying heart. A dried crackling bloom fell from her breast on to his. He stirred and forced his sightless eyes towards her. His lips moved but no sound came. She leaned over and placed her lips on his. And as her soft breath whispered into his mouth his soul slipped from his broken body and flew like a rising bird up, up into the blue sky that was his heaven.

THE END

Printed in Great Britain
by Amazon